A Black Saturday Afternoon

By

R.D. Valentine

This book is for you, because life with its stampede of trouble only inspired you to overcome and change the world

Acknowledgements

I would like to give thanks to God, for granting me the physical and spiritual strength to persevere and complete this novel and because he's the orchestrator of justice.

The wicked man may smile, but his day of judgement will come. No crime shall go unavenged, particularly against those who rise in bigoted hatred against another person.

I would like to thank my partner who's been a person that's listened to the detail and content of this story and I'm grateful for the advice and support.

I give acknowledgment to my literary mentor who consistently helps me to improve, provides critical feedback and has been relentless in ensuring I produced the most creative and imaginative story possible.

Thank you to all of those who've endured racial abuse, repeatedly told that they're inferior and have been murdered, because of the colour of their skin. Their strength and commitment is the motivation to all men to strive for harmony, create a world of one colour and bring down the strongholds of prejudice.

The readers are the main reason why I've written this novel. Thank you for purchasing this book and I hope that it moves your emotions and gives you significant reading pleasure.

Chapter One

David glared. The chanting increased on the main road of the seaside town Skegness, in the late hours of the July summer Saturday morning that pounded his eardrums and created a riveting fear.

The pink candyfloss was no longer a sugary attraction. Toffee Apples coated with a deep red glacier covering, had no appeal for his lips to lick the candy and bite until his teeth sunk into a juicy green apple.

Deckchairs on the beach with the blue and green salty sea water that had his imagination focused on walking in the sand, with the rays of the sun shining through the deep blue sky and the breeze blowing in his face, now made him look in the opposite direction, rather than join the droves of sun worshippers lapping up the ambience of a sunny, but a chilly atmospheric day.

He watched the police bracing themselves and advancing towards the crowd, who donned green plastic jackets, three quarter length jeans and red Doc Marten boots.

"Niggers, you fucking black bastards, you fucking niggers!"

The screams of the mob made his body shake and he smelt the stench of hatred towards him, as they saluted to Hitler and called out for white supremacy.

"Get back, get back now!" shouted a special squad officer.

Intimidation ransacked David's mind, as he watched the marauding skinheads on a march of hate. He looked behind him and grabbed a grey signpost.

I'll walk through the skinheads. God is with me and I won't be scared.

Twists of terror were in his head at the crazy thoughts and one thing was on his mind, run before he, Angela, Elaine and Ray ended up in hospital beds with wounds of racist revulsion.

Gulps lodged in David's throat and the aggressive scratching leapt through his veins. He wanted to be the big man of war, but their shrills of detest for the colour of black skin, flat noses and broad lips sent an uncontrollable rattle of his bones through his knees.

Queasiness undressed his assurance of Godly protection, and he momentarily blacked out before he felt Ray's hand of support on his arm.

They thumped their chests, fuelling adrenalin of aversion and seething with contempt that confirmed to David, the skinheads reviled him for contaminating the purity of white by his very presence.

"Niggers, you fucking black bastards. Niggers," screamed the skinheads.

David's body trembled at their fearlessness under the eye of the law. Their security in numbers made him cower and regret his idea to visit the seaside town for the day, to continue planning the next good cause and how to change the lives of the under-privileged.

The chants, said with venomous delight of smashing skulls and stripping flesh made him forget fleetingly, that he should love his enemies and pray for them that persecuted him. Instead he wished for the law in the old testament of the bible to be enforced. He wanted God driven destruction upon those who despised because of their hatred for differences in race, colour and creed.

"Niggers, black bastards, fucking monkeys, get back to your monkey land."

They charged at the police, separating them from David, Angela, Ray and Elaine. David clutched Angela's hand. The shivering in her fingertips fuelled his quivering nerves. Desiring to protect her, he wondered, *where's my guardian angel to keep us safe from danger.*

One of the skinheads threw a fifty pence coin that hit David on his forehead. He immediately grabbed his head and wiped away a smear of blood. The police formed a barricade and shouted at the skinheads to shut up. David looked at the mob, searching for the perpetrator who threw the first stone. He knew that he was there, but unrecognisable in the array of venom that spewed from the mouths of the racists and covered him with scornful abuse.

He picked up the coin, threatening to throw it back at the crowd. He remembered, *according to the bible I'm supposed to love those that persecute me, rather than treating them with the same level of hate.*

"Niggers, fucking black bastards, get out of our country and go back to Africa."

A policeman signalled to David, Ray, Angela and Elaine to follow him.

David watched the crowd who were at a standstill, shouting and perpetually performing Nazi salutes. His imagination revealed pictures of being ripped from limb to limb if he became cornered. He was a fighter of the faith and not of the sword. He recalled the three Hebrew boys who were delivered from the burning furnace, but struggled to ignite confidence by reflecting on the outcome of their deliverance. All he could hear and see was a mass of green that struck his heart with horror that his young life could be over.

"Will you take us to somewhere safe?" he asked, trying to quell the fear and holding his stomach that constantly brought a regurgitation of vomit in his mouth.

He recalled the lesson from his father when he kneeled down to pray for protection and safety from the devil. He needed stronger words than "Yellow belly" which didn't provide an advantage over the racists who he knew given the chance would annihilate him.

David gazed at the policeman who didn't smile.

"Get out of here, you should have known it was a National Front day, just leave now."

"Black fucking bastards, you rubber lipped monkeys, niggers, niggers, niggers!"

The skinheads charged at the police and David shivered under his skin. Gladness and relief intervened into his pulsations as the police held their stance and shouted at the skinheads to stop the verbal abuse.

"Let's go. Why did we come here? We should have stayed in London."

He grabbed Angela's hand and squeezed her knuckles, pursing his lips to stop them from twittering. Everything he'd been taught about God being with him in his time of trouble disappeared from his mind, and his emotions bubbled up the fright that he couldn't prevent his body from responding with bouts of shudders.

"Don't be afraid. Remember, God isn't fear, but love."

David mused on the words Ray uttered that he'd heard many times, but Sunday school verses were easy for him to repeat in the church full of God-fearing people. He prayed silently, seeking to find the inner strength to stand tall in the face of adversity. He reminded himself of the vision he saw to change the world and make it safer for the abused and the unloved.

"Why are you waiting, niggers? Look at your black skin, its filth, it's a disease. You need to be purified, nigger," screamed one of the skinheads.

"Follow me, now," commanded a policeman.

David, Ray, Angela and Elaine followed him away from the horde.

David wiped the sweat from his forehead. The racist jibes dwindled and no longer blasted his head with insults, that conflicted with who he'd been told he was in the church and by his parents.

He looked behind and his whirring pulse began to slow as he beckoned to the others to take refuge in a candy shop.

"The white bloody pigs, they're only strong in a crowd."

"If it was only four of them, I could have taken them on. I would have beaten their faces until they became unrecognisable," Ray said.

David had similar thoughts to Ray as he followed Angela to the counter, ordered two cups of tea and walked back to the table where Elaine and Ray were seated.

Angela sat down and David gave her a fleeting gaze, shaking his head and contending with the images of payback, that clashed with his spiritual lessons of loving every man as Jesus loved him.

The rage bubbled in David's chest and he squeezed the paper cup that burned his hand with the hot cup of tea. He tapped slowly underneath his seat, wallowing in his thoughts of, *why do the racists hate me because of my black skin.*

"Father Theo says love those that hate you, love those that despitefully abuse you."

His mind searched for understanding of judgement based on the colour of skin. He chewed on the word nigger and monkey and replayed the meaning over and over until his brain fell into a freefall of anger. As he gripped the chair and pressed his feet into the ground he hated every white person, even those who attended his church.

"Remember, we're not like them, we're here to make a difference to the world and God will protect us," Elaine said.

He shook his head and for the first time he lacked conviction in her belief.

Where was God when the racists launched their attack? Why didn't God burn them with fire and brimstone?

David reflected on Father Theo's words of comfort that seemed like he'd been lied to. They were words that were masqueraded as truth to persuade him to accept a false doctrine. When he heard them from the pulpit, they sounded compelling, but in the face of trouble they lacked the impact to carry out the promise.

The sunny day in Skegness with the blue sky, golden beach and theme park where children screamed, was supposed to be a day where his mind was free to see the goodness of God in the enjoyment of life. Instead, the emotion of peace to all men had been changed to repulsion and ponders of, *God, why have you allowed me to suffer abuse when I didn't deserve it.*

He ordered another cup of tea and looked out of the window at the flurry of people, wondering, *who hates me because I'm black.*

His hand brushed through his black hair with pride at his curls that glistened when gelled with coconut palm oil. He looked at his reflection in the glass and touched his broad nostrils. He remembered the taunts and wished he had a straight nose like his dad whose father was a white Scottish man who'd come to Jamaica and married his grandmother.

He pondered on the word, *nigger,* and detested the inference that a black person was inferior to white. Despise for a word used with such malicious intent to keep people of his race firmly in their place as second-class citizens and trained only to answer, yes Bwana incensed his mind with a flare-up of fume.

I know that not every white person is racist, but I've never been confronted by skinheads and had this type of racial abuse thrown at me before.

"Hey, what are you thinking? Forget the bigoted thugs, they can't harm us. What can man do unto us if God is for us?" Angela said.

David looked over and nudged her shoulder. He liked her naturally long hair, hazel eyes and voluptuous curves. He smiled at the sound of her giggles and a warm glow radiated from his face when he flicked her hand and touched her multi-coloured nails. It was the worst kept secret that she fancied him and desired more than friendship, but for now he was happy to revel in her attraction. He was aware that a lot of girls were attracted to him, but liked to keep them all hanging on a string, deliberately remaining aloof and not committing to anyone.

His mind wandered on his ambition and it didn't include having a girlfriend, at least for now. He focused on his dream of running a major business empire from a New York law office, where he was the boss with subordinates reporting into him, and using the funds of his wealth to spread the love of God and bring hope to a lost world.

Maybe, Angela, maybe.

"Ok, you two love birds, the flirting is over. Hurry up with your drinks and let's get out of here," Ray said.

David quickly moved Angela's hand from his arm, suspecting that she already had ideas that she was the chosen one. He had to keep her in her place and ensure that all options remained open for that beautiful black girl, who would one day become Mrs David Morgan and wear his diamond ring.

David followed Ray to the counter and smiled as Ray stretched out his palm towards him. David placed the two pound notes in his hand. It was his contribution for the teas and the cakes and he laughed at Ray's insistence of fifty – fifty all the way.

"You're all beautiful people, especially created for a great purpose, don't let the views of a few change your course of destiny," said the shopkeeper.

If only it was that simple. All men standing as one without any prejudice, thought David.

"C'mon, let's go, we need to get home. Thank you for the tea and cakes, they were lovely," Elaine said.

She opened the café door and David followed Ray and Angela into the empty street.

David brooded on the skinheads and their chanting still played havoc with his mind.

"Everyone wants to belong to a cause and they want to find an identity from their disillusion. The National Front provides that, and black people are an easy target for them."

The anger began to well up inside of him. He thought about the great speeches of equality.

All *things are possible and you can arise.*

He shook his head, disbelieving the bullshit statement. The black people that he knew were bottom of the pile, without power and influence. Yet, as his mind churned he saw the unfairness of blame and black skin being publicized as the root cause for problems in the world which weren't their fault.

"C'mon, David, stop thinking about the skinheads, we're better than them," Elaine said.

David smiled as he watched Ray embrace Elaine. He knew that Ray had a soft spot for her, and he remembered their discussions that were sometimes unrighteous. David laughed as Ray scampered along the pavement like a chimpanzee. He listened to his hooting and watched him grab the tree branches and gnaw at the bark that coloured his teeth with a black residue.

"What do you think? Do I look good as a chimp? Would you fancy me more?"

Big mistake Ray, that's not the way to a black woman's heart.

"If you want to become what the racists see you as, then do it alone. Be the nigger they want you to be, but leave me out of it," Elaine said.

David put his arm around Ray's shoulder and whispered in his ear, "Elaine's right, you can't make a joke out of getting verbal abuse for being black and calling yourself a monkey like the racists do."

"Don't be so hard on him, he's only joking around. It's been a rough day for all of us. We came here to discuss the goodness of God, but met Satan and his demons."

David looked upwards to the clouds and softened his heart.

God, thank you for your protection.

Help us to see the good out of the bad, and that we can still make a difference.

Chapter Two

Charles and Mary, his parents came into his mind.

They know what's like to be condemned for being black, but they always seem to be able to forgive.

He struggled to comprehend how to show love when you received hate, preferring to love with an eye for an eye and a tooth for a tooth.

All the teachings in the bible that he'd heard about love in the church seemed easy to apply, until confronted with hatred from the enemy who'd cursed him and whose words attacked his confidence of becoming an ambassador for good and not for evil.

Elaine brushed past him and walked over to Ray and it disrupted his reflections on love and hate.

David sniggered as he watched them settling their differences. Their faith in God was aligned to his and he remembered their common passion that stirred up his fight to heal the world of strife, sickness and disease. He admired Elaine and Ray and he recommitted to their joint cause to destroy all walls of divide and set people free from their chains of bondage.

David mulled over Elaine's reprimand of Ray. *I'm on the same page as her*. He knew that she was correct to stop Ray making a mockery of prejudice and racial abuse. He thought, *many black people died in slavery* and was prepared to chastise anyone who made light of it, even in jest as he hated the disrespect it showed to their deaths.

An overpowering belief rose in his spirit that black people had to stand in pride at the colour of their skin. They had to trust in a higher power of justice that would fight their battle and take vengeance on the oppressors, and the more he reflected, his reason for existing burned with a bright flame.

Today has been a massive lesson. It was frightening seeing those skinheads chanting for blood, but I can't be afraid of them.

The cry of *nigger* rang aloud in David's mind. He reaffirmed his pledge to keep walking in the shoes of Martin Luther King and never fear those who persecuted him. His choice was absolutely clear to not become the brand that the racists tried to label him with, but to be what God had created him to be.

He crossed the road and Elaine and Angela followed him. He stopped at the bush with its prickly green leaves and thorns growing through the middle. A piece of paper lay perched with one corner blowing in the breeze, giving him the impression that it yearned to be blown wherever the wind desired. He studied the empty page, visualising an auditorium filled with one million people that applauded his message of freedom and equality for all.

***

"Last one to the neon sign."

Angela's challenge disrupted his thoughts of the crowd erupting with fervour at the rise of the black man from his position in the dirt.

Elaine and Angela responded by putting their heads down and sprinting on the uneven pavement.

David chased them, deliberately staying one metre behind to watch their backsides flutter from side to side. He reached the destination point, arriving in the midst of disdainful and mocking stares from his compatriots, with a big smile on his face at the enjoyment of sexual innuendo's that revolved around his head.

"What happened to you, slow coach?" asked Angela.

She circled David and he grinned, revelling in the flirtatious attention. He raised his hands and smiled at her flickering eyelids, but pondered on her bottom with his imagination struck by a string of romantic helices.

"You do know that I let you win. A black sister can never beat a black brother."

David moved his body to an imaginary reggae beat for he loved to showboat whether in the church or on the street. His head toss was an extension of the line with a hook that he knew was drawing her in. He continued to perform his dance moves, enjoying the attention and mentally slapping his head that began to overflow with sinful suggestions.

Angela punched his arm and flicked her hair.

"Yeah, yeah, of course you let me win. Anyway, where's Ray?"

David looked into the distance and watched the wanderer strolling along the road.

"Hey, c'mon Ray, catch up man, we need to get home, It's getting late."

David waited for the sprint that didn't happen and suspected that Ray was in his dreams, just like him.

The cause for justice had solidified his friendship with Ray and he viewed him as a birth brother, aligned to his cause to make mankind see the love of God, and for the black man to arise out of the ashes.

"Message for Ray, God calling from heaven. Get your backside up here now!"

The shrill of Elaine's voice had more impact than his. It got Ray's attention and he waved.

David chuckled, dwelling on Ray's description of Elaine that had been unholy in many ways. It made him fight with his flesh that was weak and he had to keep his sprit strong. A constant conundrum with lust played mind games and he made confessions regularly to purge his heart of the filth of sexual desire.

"Hold on a minute, I'm coming," Ray said.

David looked at Angela and smiled. She waved and he waved back. His mind mused on a double wedding in the future, a likely possibility providing it was in the plan of God. He loved that she had the qualities of a strong black woman and shared his views of a broken system that required a major change, particularly for the black man to stop being the underdog and to break his slave mentality.

"Oh shit, shit! Oops, sorry, lord. You decide on the future, not me. Where's that nappy head boy, Ray?"

***

"Ray, Ray! Run, run!" screamed Elaine.

She ran forward, only to be gripped by David. His heart thudded and his hands began to shake. He jumped on the ground, waving his arms furiously and with every fibre in his body screaming for the universe to intervene and release angels of protection immediately.

"Ray, get up now, run, run!"

He ran past Elaine towards Ray, but stopped before he reached him. He jumped on the pavement, thumping his hand and grabbing the prickly leaves that left numerous thorns in his flesh. There wasn't any pain. It had been overridden by terror and he cried out with all his might until his lungs could only jitter with one more breath.

David turned around and began to run. He grabbed Elaine's hand as he raced towards Angela.

"God, Jesus, help us, help us!"

Panic ripped through his body and caused frenzied convulsions that refused to stop. Fear shot through his brain as he urged God to match the stampede and crush the enemy before they spilt innocent blood.

"Oh God, oh God!"

David turned his head, seeing the dust blowing in the atmosphere and hearing the hammering feet of the skinheads. He was torn between protecting Angela and Elaine and going back to defend Ray.

His body shuddered. Mentally he saw their eyes fired up, visualised their necks bulging and knuckles crunching as he watched their contorted passion at the symbol of black.

"I need to go back!"

"No, don't leave us. We need to get help!" cried Angela.

David grabbed his head. His brain was under pressure from indecision and the recurring taunt of, *nigger, black bastard, you fucking black nigger, you fucking nigger.*

"No!"

The image of Doc Marten boots lighting up the road with a sea of blistering red replayed in his head. Chanting became louder and louder and filled the air with a chilling storyline that drummed against his ears. A picture of Ray, laying on the ground with blood in his throat, urged him to leave Angela and Elaine to save him.

"You fucking nigger, black bastard, redemption's here!"

David ran towards Ray and stopped. He jumped on the ground and his heart panted with repeated rushes of fear

"For God sake, Ray, run!"

David beckoned him to run faster, screaming and waving like trees brutalised by the uncompromising storm. He saw Ray fall to the ground and turned to see Angela and Elaine running along the pavement. Every nerve in his body compelled him go to Ray and stand by his side to defend him, even if it meant sacrificing his own life.

"Nigger, nigger, nigger, you fucking, nigger!"

Feet began to scamper towards David. His courage flew away and his will wilted. He turned and sprinted along the road, hearing the faint cry of, "Help, help," from Ray.

His mind returned to the replay of Ray, laying dazed on the pavement and in pain from his bleeding back. The skinhead's foot connected with his unprotected stomach and he saw him vomiting blood that christened the red Doc Marten boot.

"Ray! Ray!"

He kept seeing the blows coming with unrelenting force and Ray's nose broken and splattered. His mind wouldn't let go of the boots coming towards Ray's head and mauling it over and over until it became a bloodied pulp of red and black flesh.

The cry of, *fucking white power, every nigger must die, die nigger, die,* reverberated in his mind.

No more feet chased him and the cries from the wolves no longer rang in his brain. David dropped to the ground and shuddered at the blade that he saw being slashed across Ray's throat and his body that dropped to the floor to eat up the debris from the pavement.

Broken, powerless and helpless, the anguish dripped through his body and fear of the nightmare stamped on every corner in his mind. The promise to never leave Ray and defend him as a brother turned into guilt and shame. A tear fell into the road and mingled with the dirt. The gasps, utters of breath and the gunfire of recrimination pointed the finger of accusation in his direction, and he looked up with his heart whispering a truth that he didn't want to believe.

"No!"

Chapter Three

"Help me! Help us. Oh God, Ray!" screamed Elaine.

David ran to her side, dropped to the ground with ricochets of terror causing a stampede in his head. The horns that beeped incessantly fuelled his emotions of fear. He looked up at the queue of drivers exiting their vehicles and despised every face gazing in his direction.

A young white woman who weaved in and out of the Ford Cortinas and Morris Minor cars, crouched by Elaine's side. She touched Elaine's arm gently and put her coat over her back.

"Get away from her, don't you touch her, you white people did this," shouted David.

He slapped Angela's face to bring her out from the trance then clutched her hand and reached out to embrace Elaine. His mind whirled with a conclusion that he didn't want to imagine.

Tears ran down his face. He clasped his hands and looked up to the darkened sky. Right now, God seemed far away and David thumped his head to block the image of a stream of red running through his brain.

"Is Ray safe? God, are you listening to me?"

Why did we come to Skegness today?

He'd been ill-advised by God and contemplated why a warning from the almighty, that it was a day for Satan to demonstrate his power through the national front march, hadn't come to his mind.

Elaine stood to her feet and said, "Take me to Ray, we have to find him."

David pushed the young white woman aside, condemning her offer to help that was drowned out by the sound of hate consuming his soul.

The police car brakes screeched at David's feet and he didn't flinch or move his head. He stared at the policemen through the windscreen, wiping running sweat from his brow and piercing the law makers with emotions that were dismantled into pieces of broken dreams.

A policeman got out.

"We've found your friend."

"What's happened to him? Did he escape? Is he safe?"

The policeman didn't answer. He stared at David, Angela and Elaine and then focused his gaze on David.

"What's happened to Ray? Do you know something?"

I am my brother's keeper, whistled through his head. It reminded him of the pact that he'd made with Ray to always stay together and his gut wrenched for he knew that he'd broken the promise. He wished that it was a different day, just like yesterday where they played a game of dominoes and had a belly laugh about Sister Lewis who they likened to Mrs little black mumbo.

"Dear God, if you love me, if you love Ray, if you believe that we've tried to serve you in truth and honour, then let Ray be safe."

By instinct, David grabbed Elaine and Angela and ran towards the direction where he'd heard the trampling of Doc Marten boots and saw the dust licking up the road.

Stopping at Mercy Way, panting, he saw the police cars and the ambulances and panic rifled through his body.

"Ray, Ray, its Ray, I know it!" screamed Elaine.

Feelings of guilt, remorse and blame flooded David's brain. Ray loved her and he didn't go back to help him. Her cry for help brought a terrorising shudder that he gripped the bonnet of the blue Hillman car and nausea swilled in his throat. *What's that, he's safe.* It was his imagination and not the expected voice of God to give him confirmation that angels had been released to save Ray.

David's eyes followed the policeman as he moved Elaine calmly and empathetically to one side.

His heart began to pump and beat to the rhythm of desired justice.

"You were supposed to protect us, you were supposed to protect Ray."

David burned with anger so fierce that he didn't see the blood dripping from his wrist. Using all the strength in his seventeen year-old body he pushed the policeman to one side and ran towards the crowd.

His five senses attacked the phrase, "All things work together for good." Condemnation of God for breaking his pledge to never leave or forsake one of his children bombarded his head.

"Ray, Ray, answer me, where are you?"

Elaine and Angela ran after David.

"Ray, is it you? Oh God, don't let it be Ray, not Ray!" cried David.

David pushed through the mob and evaded the clawing hands of the police who attempted to hold him back.

"Let me through, get out of my way. Ray, is my friend!"

He looked at the cobbled street of Mercy Way that mirrored the red stream he'd visualised. His mind could see the kicks, punches and violent attack until Ray couldn't defend himself and he grabbed his mouth and tears dripped on his fingers.

His feet twisted and he stumbled into a stutter on the ground. He reached out to grab Ray's hand with his fingers twitching against each other. Fighting for every breath, his heart collapsed in sorrow and wrenching pain. His eyes were glazed as he stared at the body that lay in a pool of blood, and he couldn't believe that it was Ray, who he'd called in friendly banter to stop dawdling and catch up.

"Ray, Ray, it's me, David!"

He ran towards the onlookers who stood next to the white Morris Wandsworth ambulances and the ambulance men who sprawled on the ground with their medicine bags, resuscitators and white gloves.

David fell to his knees at Ray's side and touched his disfigured face and beaten head. His fingers were marred with the blood and he gazed at the ambulance men with eyes that pleaded for them to explain the meaning. He looked up to the clouds without a care for the rain that drenched his hair and his clothes. Anger seethed through his grimaces and he detested a God that only a few hours ago he loved.

"No, no! You were supposed to protect Ray, why did you let him die?"

He patted Ray's body, shaking and pulling him, searching for the smile, the laughter and the fun and wishing for the vigour and youth of life to return. David placed his head on Ray's chest. He listened to hear the heartbeat and his body quivered at the response of resounding silence.

An ambulance man placed his hand on David's shoulder.

"Don't touch me! Why couldn't you save him? Why?"

"Ray, I told you to run."

Love your enemies. Love those who despise and abuse you, whirred through David's mind and he couldn't see beyond his thirst for retribution.

David embraced Elaine and Angela, pleading for a miracle where the dead would arise and walk again. He waited and conceded that today wasn't that day where the supernatural superseded science and the extraordinary stole the headlines that Ray had been raised from the dead.

"Ray, I did love you, I would have been your girl," Elaine said.

The ambulance men carried Ray's body to the ambulance. One of them looked back at David, nodded his head and banged on the side of the ambulance before climbing in.

"Let's go, we've lost him, let's take him to the morgue."

David watched the ambulance with its flashing blue lights speed down the road. He stretched out his hand towards it, clenching his fingers and squeezing tightly. His lip began to quiver and his eyes watered, slowly spilling over into a gush of uncontrollable tears and emotion of unrelenting grief, from a broken heart.

"Ray, come back, you can't be dead. Come back! We promised never to leave one another!"

Angela and Elaine huddled next to him and wrapped their arms around him. He turned to face them with his bloodied skin and irrepressible grief.

David stared at the spot stained with Ray's blood. There were so many words that he wanted to say and now it was too late. He couldn't imagine that Ray would never walk by his side to fulfil the calling of being a world changer.

Looking towards heaven he remembered the biblical verses that said, "God was a loving God." All he saw was a God who'd committed an act of evilness and cruelty.

"As far as I'm concerned, God is completely evil. He hates us. He let the white fucking racists kill Ray. What type of God is that?"

David hit his chest repeatedly, swearing vengeance and infliction of the same punishment on those who killed Ray.

He fell to his knees at the spot where Ray had died. Everything he believed in about being a witness for good evaporated. His head, his mind and his soul tumbled into a well of anger and all he could see was revenge.

Where's the God of Abraham, Isaac and Jacob now. What was your purpose in allowing Ray to die?

"David, what will we tell Thelma? She loved Ray."

Elaine knelt on the street next to him and David placed his hand on hers. The smell of death and anger for revenge consumed his heart. Pain stabbed him repeatedly as the recognition that he would never see Ray again began to take root in his mind.

"Tell her the truth, God killed Ray."

Angela put her hands on his shoulders and laid her head on his back.

A policeman walked over to David.

"We'll take you home and I'm really sorry about your friend. We've been collecting statements and we need to talk to you."

Elaine and Angela followed him to the police van and climbed into the back. Angela laid on the backseat and reached over to hold Elaine's hand.

"Ray, I'm going to miss you so much, I love you," Elaine said.

David glared at the policeman waiting at the side of the police van, watching him gripping his truncheon and keeping his intent stare on his face. He wanted someone to suffer and experience the torture that was unrelenting in bringing accusations against him, that he should have gone back and defended Ray.

Vengeance is mine says The Lord, he thought, as he got into the van and a policeman shut the door.

The more he dwelled on the scripture, it became increasingly fictitious to David. The bible, Father Theo and his great sounding sermons were all lies to him.

No one cares about the life of another black man that was murdered.

David raised his head from the musing, and his heart swelled with a mission driven by images that wouldn't let him find any rest until his soul committed that whatever the sacrifice, he'd hunt for the skinheads and one by one send them to hell.

Those murderer's, I'll find them, I'll find them Ray, and I'll kill them.

Chapter Four

The policeman driving the van beeped his horn. The onlookers gazed into the darkened windows, and they couldn't see David, but he could see them.

He marvelled at the crowd so eager to gather at the death spot.

Where were they when the bigots shouted fucking nigger? Where were they when the racist skinheads killed Ray?

"I should have gone back to help Ray, I never should have left him. I broke my promise."

He thumped the side of the police van taking them home, and peered at the policeman in the passenger side of the vehicle who opened the latch and looked into the back.

"I know that you've suffered a terrible tragedy, but please be calm, please."

David gazed at Elaine and never again would he see her with Ray, frolicking and flirting and then listening to his nasty thoughts that made him go before God to apologise. He remembered her chastisement when Ray acted like a monkey and his stupidity brought merriness to his heart amidst the pain that burned a mark of sorrow into his mind.

He reflected on the church camping trips and them both getting into trouble for sneaking out of the tent at night. His smile widened at their antics that brought him joy and fond memories. Gloom covered him when he thought, *we'll never be together again being rebellious and getting into mischief.*

"David, Ray's never going to come back to us, I want him to come back!"

He looked at Elaine, turned away and glowered at the policemen muttering in the front, questioning, *do they really care that an innocent man was killed?* His fury lay the blame at their front doorstep when they knew that there was danger, but let them wander without protection. He shook his head, holding them as guilty as the skinheads who drew blood.

"Let me out of here, let me out now!"

David got up and moved to the front of the police van. He banged, kicked the side and kicked the door. He thumped the latch and the steel bar grill, attempting to push his fingers through the small holes so he could grasp the necks of the policemen and squeeze until their nattering stopped inflicting contempt in his brain.

"You fucking bastards, you let him die, you let him die!"

He banged the latch repeatedly until his hands were sore. He kicked the side of the van again until his toes were numb from the pain. Tears unleashed like a ravishing waterfall, spilling on his blue shirt and changing the shade to a light black.

"Murderers!"

The policeman opened the latch and peered directly into David's eyes. The anger, hatred and the will for revenge burned inside David. He clenched his fists until his nails cut into his skin, and he seethed with frustration that he was in the van, when he should be walking the streets and searching for Ray's killers.

"I'm telling you to calm down. We'll do our jobs, just calm down."

David bit his tongue and Angela moved to the front of the van and touched his back. He shrugged his shoulders, casting her hand away as if she had a rare disease. He moved his face to the grill and stared into the eyes of the policeman, hating him, the uniform he wore and the racist organisation that he represented.

"I won't calm down, I want justice!"

The policeman driving the van pulled over to the side of the road. His colleague jumped out and pulled out his truncheon. They both went to the back of the van, opening the door.

"No, you don't have to come in. David will calm down, don't hurt him, please don't hurt him," Angela said.

"Are you going to behave yourself and stay quiet? We know that you're grieving, but we didn't kill your friend."

David shook his head with the pain shooting through his chest and wreaking havoc with every emotional bud in his body.

"No! You should have protected him, you should have defended him."

He threw his fists into the air and thumped the window. "Ah!" he said as he hit his chest and buried his head into the seat. Streams of red electrified his brain and he charged at the policemen, kicking and throwing punches and using his head as a battering ram to hurt them as his mind screamed with a daunting panic.

"No David, stop! Stop!" Elaine said.

The policemen grappled with David, removed him from the van and wrestled him to the floor. They held him in a neck lock and pinned his shoulders to the ground.

"I can't breathe, I can't breathe."

He heard the jangling of handcuffs and squirmed on the ground. His body writhed until his lungs fought for breath that struggled to get to his mouth and bypass the neck hold of the policeman.

"Now, you're going to stay in the cuffs until we get you home."

They threw David into the van and bolted the door.

"Father Theo, everything that you taught me about loving your neighbour and God loving me is a fucking lie."

Should I love the skinhead bastards who killed Ray?

He tried to wriggle free from the handcuffs, but they were too tight around his wrists and cut into his flesh.

His vision of changing the world and making it better for the under privileged rekindled in his mind. He reminisced on the dream he shared with Ray, a dream that he saw falling into shreds, for his spiritual eyes were blurred by the rise in his spirit for revenge.

The church and its grandiose mission of spreading the gospel to the four corners of the world floated through his mind.

What's the point of religion, it didn't help Ray. Doesn't the bible say that God will never forsake us.

Is this the love of God, that he would let Ray die.

David looked at the handcuffs and the policemen with their air of power. His recognition of God changed and he realised that he hadn't made him with equality, but as an underdog to a race that his memories portrayed had the upper hand.

You'll never amount to anything. Maybe you'll get a job in a factory if you're lucky, but you'll probably end up cleaning toilets.

Those words the English teacher said were horrible, but Ray and I never believed him, we knew that we could be more than toilet cleaners.

"David, David, we're nearly home, say something," whispered Elaine.

He hung his head, fighting with the dichotomy of God will protect his own whilst he tried to reconcile the meaning of Ray's death. He saw a young man of eighteen with good intentions and only a heart of love, but still his dedication counted for nothing and for that he decided he and God could no longer be allies in the battle of truth.

"I have nothing to say except, we've been fooled and I won't be fooled anymore."

***

The van slowed down and David looked up at the familiar surroundings.

He sat quietly for a minute and watched the house where he'd revelled in joyous laughter. He dreaded going in and facing the grief that the tension in his body signalled was waiting for him once he stepped through the doorway.

"We're really sorry for the loss of your friend. We'll find the people who did this and bring them to justice," whispered the driver.

David heard the back door of the police van open and he watched the policemen brace themselves. He heard their offer to capture the criminals, but his heart disbelieved when he was unsure if they and the Skinheads were of the same kind.

Angela and Elaine exited the vehicle and one of the policemen climbed inside and took David by the arm.

Thelma, Ray's mother and his sister Lorna stood at the entrance of the doorway.

David gazed at Thelma and Lorna and his mind brooded with sadness as he pondered, *how will they survive without Ray coming home again?*

The prayer meetings that happened in this house mean nothing. What about the lovely yam, dumplings and green banana's with curried mutton?

Ray, you and I competed for the rights to wipe up the gravy with a piece of Hardo bread and now I'll never see you again.

"Thelma! Lorna! Ray's dead," David said.

Father Theo peered through the window. He had a bible in his hand and David contemplated, *what's he said to Thelma about God's will in Ray's death?* He searched for an iota of justification, but was unable to see any sin Ray had committed that deserved such a brutal ending.

He wriggled his hands violently, looking at the policemen with disdain at being treated as if he was a wild animal.

"Get me out of these handcuffs! I'm not a criminal."

Charles and Mary ran out of the house, followed by Elaine and Angela's parents. One of the policemen held David by the arm, whilst the other policeman tensed his shoulders.

"Why have you got my son in handcuffs?" Mary said.

David tried to move towards Charles and Mary. He was desperate to be in their arms of safety and he wanted to hear words that somehow would console his mind, and let him see the reason and the meaning of the evil.

"I'm asking you, please let my son go."

The policeman unlocked the handcuffs and David ran into her arms, responding to her embrace with an emotional tide that he could barely hold himself together.

Charles touched his shoulder and David tried to speak, but instead he found himself in that place of torment where his tears gushed and his heart took another wound of loss.

"He lost control in the police van. We had no other choice but to handcuff him."

"His friend has just been murdered. How do you expect him to react? May God forgive you," Mary said.

***

David walked into Ray's house after the police had left and he sensed that the mood was sombre but still joyful.

A passage of the bible came into his mind. *God will bring a garment of joy in the face of cruel adversity that surpasses all human understanding.*

"We all loved Ray. He was a young man of bright promise, but God knows the future and why his life was required now," muttered Father Theo.

David stared at Father Theo with contempt and mulled over his words that always sounded so eloquent in his ears, but mistrust fired through his head.

Maybe he's a good man. Maybe he cares about the black community he serves faithfully year after year.

But why a white priest and not a black priest to lead the church congregation?

The penny was dropping with a clear message in his mind. The Congregation of God church that he grew up in was just like any other institution. The white man was at the top and the black man was at the bottom, believing that he'd been elevated from his position of nothing.

"Is God white or black?"

Father Theo stopped reading through his bible passages and looked across the room at David. David gazed at him with eyes of anger and love turning cold.

Charles walked towards David, but Father Theo signalled to him to remain seated. David shook his head at Charles. His impression had been confirmed and now he knew that Charles was just like a slave in Africa, who jumped when the white man said jump and crawled when the white man said crawl.

"David, God is spirit and God is love, he's not about black or white. God is all encompassing and he doesn't judge based on the colour of your skin."

David gazed at Charles and Mary. He knew that Charles could crush the skull of Father Theo with one hand, yet when told to bark he barked. Now he was beginning to see the light that shone on Charles and his own subservience to the church system. He had a clear picture in his mind of a white God that had subdued Charles and put his white people in authority over black people.

It didn't seem like freedom of choice to David, to him it was slavery and a mind-set that still affected black people who were too blind to see that they were still living in chains.

"Can you explain to me why God preferred to let a good Christian black man die, and allow a white racist thug to live?"

Elaine and Angela began to cry again and their parents hugged them. Mary linked her arm with David and he brushed it aside. Charles jumped to his feet to embrace him, but he had no desire to be comforted.

"Nobody can explain this to me. Ray's life meant nothing to God and he killed him!"

David gazed at Charles, no longer fearing having loose lips to make his point about a God he'd been taught was love and cared about those who served him.

All he saw was the foolery of trusting in a higher power that when he expected it to be demonstrated in the heat of trouble, he was left questioning where he was and why he'd refrained from making an appearance.

God, I thank you for one thing, making me see that I've been a puppet, playing to the tune of the white man and believing that it was a holy calling to be living under their rule.

"David, like you we should hate Ray's killer, we should desire revenge. We should want every skinhead to be wiped off the planet, but we don't," Thelma said.

She picked up a black and white photograph of Ray. It was one that David had seen many times and he remembered his bright smile that could fill the room. He studied his face that shone with a light of the belief that he was convicted by.

Ray loved the word of God. He was always reading the bible and all he wanted to do was share his faith and hope.

"Don't you see, David? Logic can't explain why God allowed Ray to die so cruelly, but his death will serve a purpose and something good will come out of it."

David took the photograph from Thelma and peered into the eyes of Ray, remembering the dreams and the aspirations that they shared. He could feel Ray's presence in the room, even though his body was laying in the morgue. He kissed the glass and placed the photo back on the mantelpiece, reflecting on the promise that he made to Ray.

"As far as I'm concerned, God hates black people. He let Ray die instead of a white racist. That isn't a God of love, but a God of hate!"

Father Theo closed his bible and turned down the record player. He got up from the sofa and walked over to David, placing his hand on his shoulder.

"God, let the angel of kindness help this young man to see beyond his pain and know that out of this, your glory shall be magnified."

"Don't you touch me! You're a liar and I don't need your pity!"

David went to the front door, opened it and ran outside into the lashing rain that pelted his face.

"David, get back here," shouted Charles.

***

David ran down the street and collided with the grey concrete lampposts. He scuttled in the dark, slipping and sliding on the pavement with his messed- up mind that wouldn't give him respite from the gonging tension. He had no idea where he was going but he kept running, trying to escape from the guilt and the image of Ray scampering towards him with indecision pulling him one way and then the other.

His heart pounded with exertion, but adrenalin pumped through his body and he kept going, running blindly into the night. Cars skidded on the wet surfaces of the road and he fell onto the bonnets without any compulsion for whether he lived or died.

The foundation of his beliefs shook and questions emerged towards the God that he'd served since the age of eight.

Who's this God, who says he's love and then allows hate.

Rock of ages, a song that he sung with his entire might in the church bellowed in his mind. He grabbed his head to silence the raucous chorus of a song that he remembered, always sent the church congregation into spirited rejoicing.

"God, I hate you. You never loved me, you lied to me. You promised to never forsake me, but you have by killing Ray!"

He threw himself onto the bags of rubbish left outside in a dark alley way to mingle with the debris. His tears began to fall and blended with the raindrops falling on his brown skin. His chest heaved with exhaustion and his wet shirt clung to his flesh like a leech sucking blood from the host. He looked towards the dark sky, searching for the light, but blackness overpowered it and surrounded him with a shroud of bitter gloom.

"Ray, Ray, come back, I'm sorry. Why did I leave you? What will I do without my best friend?"

He bit his lip until the blood smeared his tongue. The pain shot through his mouth and he clutched one of the black bags. The rain began to fall faster. He didn't move but lay prostrated on the rubbish heap, waiting for destiny to decide.

Opening his eyes again, he was blinded by the water that struck his eyelids and hit his body with a fury that signalled to him that he and God, were no longer allies.

"I don't believe in you anymore! If you were a real God, you'd never have allowed this to happen!"

"As far as I'm concerned, you're dead."

Chapter Five

Charles pounded the pavement with the soles of his brown shoes as he ran on the uneven concrete. He slipped, clattered into the side of a Hillman Minx and kicked the tyre. Charles resumed running, falling into a hedge and gasping for breath as the strong winds blew into his face. The rain smacked into his head and he had an impression he was still under vengeance from God for past mistakes, that seemed they were unforgiven.

He panted, heaved and clasped his chest. His cries rang out into the chaotic night as he called the name, "David" and regretted that he'd listened to Father Theo and allowed him to run out into the dark and wet night.

"David! Oh for heaven sake, why did you let him go!" shouted Mary.

The rain refused to express mercy and pummelled Charles's bearded face with lashes of water. He watched Mary clinging to the lamppost, but he had to leave her in the hands of The Lord. He whispered, "God, don't let me come back with a dead son in my arms." His heart couldn't bear if he had to watch her having a heart attack, and if he lost both of them he knew he'd call for the grave to allow his soul to go to heaven.

"Mary, go back to the house, I'll find him, God dammit, I'll find him."

Charles didn't care about the rain that soaked him from head to toe or the night sky that rumbled with thunder. Fear made him withstand the torrential rain and he wasn't prepared to lose David who he'd tried to raise as a righteous man. He ran between the parked cars, waving madly at the flashing headlights and screaming at the drivers who beeped their horns.

"David! David, where are you son?" He listened intently for the corresponding reply, but only the sound of his own voice reverberated in his head.

"David, David, David, where are you? Answer me!"

He stopped running, hoping to hear David's cry or soft voice calling out to be rescued. He only heard the night answering with an outpour of rain that flooded the street and beat down on the rooftops. His search moved to the alleyways and the shop doorways and he gazed at the drunkards, losing heart that what he dreaded was about to become his nightmare.

"What have you done with my son? You must have seen him, where is he?"

The tramp opened his eyes and Charles held him by the collars of his jacket and turned his head away from the reek of drink. He wished that it was David in his hands and not a man that spiritual teaching taught him was addicted to the demon of alcohol.

Charles let him go and he slumped back into the doorway.

On another night, he would have laid hands on him and preached the glad tidings of Christianity, to help a man in need to see that there was a better way.

He couldn't distinguish between the rain and the tears falling down his face. All he knew was that his heart was being crushed with hopelessness and a resignation that David was in trouble and he couldn't help him.

"God, help me, I love my son. Please, please help me to find him!"

He waited for the still voice of reason, but it never spoke to him. Walking slowly, he was blinded by the dark and his guilt for listening to Father Theo. He banged on the glass windows, thumped on the doors and prayed for mercy and grace to fall upon his head one more time from the God who he knew as all wisdom, power and knowledge beyond that of himself.

***

Charles clung to the drainpipe at the entrance of the alleyway. Two blinks from his eyes and he turned his head to the side. He heard the rustling of paper and the sound of tin cans that seemed as if they were being kicked against the wall. Intuition compelled him to walk into the dark space and trust that Satan hadn't struck again by killing his son.

He walked quicker, stumbling into the metal dustbin and throwing the lid against the wall.

"Who's there? What do you want? Leave me alone."

Charles's heart released a spring of joy. He knew the voice that had called out and he ran towards the sound and fell onto the rubbish heap.

"David, it's me. David!"

Charles placed his muscular arms underneath David's legs and his back. He lifted him from the debris and held him tightly, kissing his face and his mind chattered to God with a lamentation of, *thank God, thank God.*

"I've got you son, I've got you."

Charles looked at David's face and his fear turned into a passionate expression of thanks. *Imagine, if I didn't find him and he was dead.* His heart shuddered at the thought and he clasped David and walked on the road. He had a deep sorrow for Thelma and Lorna, but the distress left his mind that David wasn't the one brutally murdered by the skinheads or left for dead in the alleyway.

"Thank God. Thank God that I found you before it was too late."

He kissed David's head and kept walking until he reached the front entrance and ran towards the door. He kicked it with his saturated shoes and fell through the doorway.

Mary ran into the landing and kissed David's brow. She held onto Charles whose soul leaped with gratitude that her wails and screams of anguish weren't the cries for a dead son that he carried in his arms.

"David, David. Get him into the lounge Charles!"

Charles went to the lounge and laid him on the sofa and she crouched besides David. Mary clasped his hand and kissed his face whilst Charles fell to his knees and exhaled three deep breaths that calmed his panicked pounding chest.

"For heaven sake, get towels, get some clean clothes, don't just stand there gaping!" he shouted.

Lorna ran from the room and quickly returned with an orange towel which she passed to Mary. Thelma returned from Ray's room with some of his clothes and laid them on the back of the chair.

"Show some respect, leave the room," Father Theo said.

Angela, Elaine and Lorna left the room. Angela turned around and looked at David.

"I love you, God knows I love you," she whispered.

Father Theo opened his bible and began reading from Psalms chapter 91.

"God, protect your child, it's not his time to leave. Save him from the devils that are after his soul. Rescue him and don't let Ray's death be his demise."

Charles gave him a curt glare, but he held his tongue. The voices whispered proclamations in his head of *the white man does rule in the church and the black members are oppressed because they're kept in low positions*. He accepted that Father Theo was a man of God, but David's accusations hammered the possibility of a different truth in his brain.

He watched Mary pulling off David's drenched clothes and kneeled beside the sofa, placing his head on David's chest and listening to his heartbeat.

Charles patted his body. He tried to be strong, but broke down with sorrow at the thought of gazing at David's tombstone and reading the inscription, "May you rest in peace."

"What were you thinking? Something could have happened to you."

He squeezed David's hand and patted his hair.

"I just want to take you home, now."

Charles walked into the hallway, opened the front door and then slammed it shut. He listened to the rain that showed no signs of slowing down, but perpetually fell like his tears that streamed down his face. He wrapped his coat around his body and braved the gale winds to get to the car.

"Father Theo, bring David now."

Father Theo laid his bible on the coffee table and helped David get up, walking towards the entrance and out into the rain.

Angela and Elaine ran into the living room and stood by the door.

"David," whispered Angela.

Charles revved the car engine and turned the heating up to the maximum temperature.

I just want to get him home and wrap him up in the bed.

He wanted to hold onto him and take the burden of his pain into his body so that he would be ok. That was his worry, he couldn't be sure that David would be the same and as he gulped, his mind shivered with what the after- effects might be and if he could help him to pick up the pieces of his life.

Father Theo supported David to get into the back of the car and Mary jumped in and laid his head on her lap.

"Remember, God is with you. Don't try to understand with your mind. Let the Holy Spirit show you God's will in all of this," Father Theo said.

Charles nodded, but he thought, *right now I could punch you in the head to stop you from being so righteous*. He couldn't see God's purpose in a meaningless killing or that of David, who was full of vigour for the word of God and now laying in Mary's arms.

He heard Mary's muffles and whimpering which stirred up his heart with a tremor that sang a song of confusion and sadness in his mind.

"Mary, don't cry. We need to be grateful that it isn't our son who was murdered and has to be driven from Skegness to London to be buried."

Charles drove slowly to South London and watched the wipers fighting furiously with the windscreen. His mind asked, *why God why* and it challenged the foundation of his Christian beliefs. He gripped the large two spoke Beige steering wheel, squeezed the leather rim and rocked in the car seat.

"Charles, why did this happen? Why is Ray dead?"

Charles couldn't provide an explanation of God's behaviour and his decision. He heard the words*, be strong and be courageous in the face of tribulation,* in his head. The words sounded wonderful when he was in the safety of the chapel, hearing the drummer beat the drum in sync with the preacher's words and the pianist letting the melody of "Amazing Grace," ring out in a rhapsody of worship and praise.

Charles pondered on the God that he served. *He's a loving God but he's also a God of terrible destruction.* He'd read the rich stories of God's hands moving against the wicked man, the enemies of his people and destroying those by water or fire and brimstone who opposed him. Yet, he couldn't fathom why his hand had moved against Ray and it battered his head with delusion and if anyone was safe from God's wrath.

He indicated to turn right and then left into Browning Road. His mind was still somersaulting with the indifferent actions of God.

"Mary, we're home now, let's get David upstairs and into his bed."

He pushed open the car door and ran to the front door, searching in his coat pocket for the key. As he turned the lock, he kicked the pile of newspapers and unwanted mail from the doormat to release his frustration and misapprehension with God's characteristics.

Charles sprinted back to the car and picked David up, walking along the garden pathway. He went up the stairs and straight to David's room, laying him on the ruffled quilt with a small bible on his pillow. Touching David's wet hair brought murmurs from his lips and he whispered, "I don't know what I would have done, if it was you who'd been murdered by the skinheads."

Charles switched on the table lamp and watched David. His heart released sighs of relief that he'd found him before tragedy struck twice.

"Sleep son, you need to rest now, God will take care of you."

He kneeled at David's brown wooden bedside cabinet and clasped his hands together.

Mary entered the bedroom and sat at the end of the bed. She put a cross of Jesus at David's feet and kneeled down next to Charles.

David groaned and Charles swiftly patted his chest, watching him and looking at every corner of the room for the smell of evil that had followed them home. He waited, rocking his body on the dark patterned green carpet, looking at David and muttering, "God help him, please help him." until his conscience assured him that at least for tonight he was safe.

He looked at the picture of Jesus Christ with his outstretched hands that hung on the wall above the dressing table with a broken brass handle thinking, *it's up to you now.*

"Mary, we can only leave him in the hands of God."

He walked out of David's bedroom and down the stairs. Mary followed him and shut the door.

Charles sat at the dinner table and stared at the blank black and white television screen.

I wonder if the police have found Ray's killers

Will anyone be brought to justice?

"Vengeance is mine says the Lord, vengeance is mine."

He picked up his bible, flicking aimlessly through the pages and hoping that he would land on a verse that provided him with enlightenment, on how and when God would repay evil with justice.

The phone rang. He jumped from the plastic covered sofa and ran to the hallway, grabbing the receiver in expectation that The Lord had moved swifter than he expected.

"Hello, Father Theo, any news? Have they found Ray's killers?" he said, with his heart pounding and thumping against his chest.

"No, I haven't heard anything yet, but the story is all over the television."

Mary entered the hallway where Charles stood shaking. She held onto his arm and he looked into her eyes.

"The skinheads who murdered Ray haven't been found or arrested."

He gazed at the picture of a white Jesus Christ with long curly brown hair, a perfectly trimmed beard and blue eyes that hung over the telephone stand. He touched the picture.

Why aren't you doing anything.

"Charles."

"I'm here."

"Be strong in the lord."

"Thank you, Father Theo, thank you for your prayers for David."

He placed the phone down and hugged Mary. He was the one who needed consoling and assurance to his waning faith. She touched his partly grey beard. He responded by kissing her cheek. Taking courage he remembered when he stood at the altar as a young man of twenty-three, and after their twenty-five years of marriage through good and bad, she'd been his solid rock when he found himself floundering in despair.

"We have to be strong. God will make a way," she said.

***

Charles went upstairs to the spare bedroom that was his office and switched on the lamp. He gazed at the picture of Martin Luther King, reading the narrative, "I have a dream that my four little children will one day live in a nation where they will not be judged by the colour of their skin, but by the content of their character."

"A great man, assassinated by white racists because he dared to desire equality for the black man."

He picked up a tray of pens and hurled them across the room.

"God, why did Martin Luther King die at the hands of racists and why have the racists killed Ray?"

"God! Explain yourself to me? You can't, can you? You can't tell me why the black man's life doesn't matter. Are you there? Why don't you talk to me?"

"What about the skinhead? When will you destroy him?"

He picked up the bible from the black stool and gazed at the gold lettering around the pages. It was supposed to have the answers to any situation that he had to face in this life. Yet, when he reflected, he thought, *the word of God never promised me a life free of tribulation, sorrow and doom, but I've spent more time in the valley rather than standing on the mountaintop in victory.*

"How will the church deal with this? Ray, who loved God, murdered and yet his killers are still free."

He feared that Ray's death would be marked just as another crime statistic. He had no belief that the police would apprehend those guilty of murder.

He studied the picture of Jesus hanging on the cross and said, "Despite your sacrifice, Ray's dead."

The pain in his heart for David intensified and he dropped his head on the desk. Worry and fear overflowed in his mind that David would be so wounded that all he could feel was bitterness and hate. He doubted himself as a father and as a man to find the right words that would lift David out of the pit of hopelessness.

"God, what if I can't help him? What if he turns away from the church and falls into sin?"

Mary's footsteps at the bottom of the stairs interrupted his confrontation with God.

"Charles, come downstairs please."

Charles trampled on the landing and stood at David's door. He didn't barge into his room like he normally did, but knocked gently and waited for the permission to enter.

David opened the door and Charles gawked, seeing his pained expression and saying silently to the Holy Spirit, *give me words of wisdom.*

"Son, can I come in?"

"It's your house, do what you want."

He walked into David's bedroom and stood staring at the picture of Martin Luther King and the gallant words he spoke that left a legacy of unfulfilled dreams.

"He was a great man and paved the way for black people to have equal status with the white man."

His words seemed like a delusion about the difference that Martin Luther King had made.

Yes, black people can ride on the same bus as white, but we aren't equal to the white man.

The Race Relations Act banned racial discrimination in public places, but the racists still say with their eyes, no blacks allowed.

"I don't care about Martin Luther King, or his false hopes. He was a dreamer without power and ended up as another dead black man," responded David.

Charles turned around and looked at the top of David's head, believing that he was partially right. His mind pondered on Martin Luther King, who'd created an element of freedom from the chains of white supremacy for the black man, but it didn't go far enough. When he looked at black people today, they still occupied the worst jobs and still lived in under-privileged communities, festering in a stench of mediocrity and making the headlines for all the wrong reasons.

This isn't the world I want for my son.

He'd seen on the news, stories of a black man killing another black man for a bag of Cannabis. His awareness was that some black men would rather steal from another black man than get a job to pay his way in society. He witnessed many examples of the black man running around with lots of women, producing sperm products and leaving the mothers to raise their children alone.

The black man is his own worst enemy, filled with anger at racism but lacking the motivation to escape from the pit of the lowest of the low. This couldn't have been the world that Martin Luther King wanted.

"David, Martin Luther King understood faith and I know that this is hard for you to understand. God knows it's hard for me to understand, but we have to try to hold onto the faith we have in Jesus Christ."

Who am I trying to convince, him or me.

"I don't care about God, or the church or the bible, none of its real. If God really loved me, there's no way he would have let Ray die."

Charles sat at the edge of the bed and lifted David's head. His strong customary stare of sternness tried to find a way to grab David's attention.

"Look at me. Look at me."

Holy Spirit, help me.

Fear rose that David had already begun to slip away from the safety of the church and God's protection, and he didn't know how to keep him on the straight and narrow path.

"I know you're hurting and selfishly, God forgive me, I'm deeply saddened by Ray's death, but I praise God that it's not my son who's dead."

David pushed Charles's hand away from his chin and he saw the disdain in David's eyes.

I remember a young man who loved God and now hate's him.

David got off the bed and pulled the poster of Martin Luther King from the wall. He removed the picture of Jesus Christ and threw it under the bed.

Charles watched him, got up and sat back down on the bed, unsure if he should hug him. He reached out to David with his heart, but experienced the gulf between what they both believed and struggled to find the words to say that would at least get his attention that the possibility of hope still existed.

David lay on the bed and Charles stood up.

"David, once down in the coal mines, I experienced racism for the first time."

He walked to the window, moved the blue curtains and gazed at the black sky and the rain that streamed down the windowpanes.

"A white man called me a black nigger. I didn't even hesitate. I picked up a metal pole and smashed it into his head and knocked him unconscious. I raised the pole again. I wanted to beat him to a pulp and I didn't care if he lived or died."

Charles drew on the windowpane with his fingers, reminiscing on the white man and experiencing a similar tension to what he felt when the term black nigger described who he didn't believe himself to be.

"I wanted to kill him. I was so angry, but something held me back from murdering him and spending the rest of my life in prison."

"What did you do next?"

Charles let out a deep sigh.

"I shouted for help and claimed that he'd fallen and hit his head. He was taken to hospital and I didn't care. No one called me a nigger and got away with it."

"You should have killed the fucking racist dog."

Charles's ears pricked at the cussing word and he spun around. Chastisement of David's unacceptable behaviour was imperative, but he hesitated, unable to admonish him when he understood why he expressed such contempt.

Instead he walked over to David and pulled him up towards his chest. He hugged and squeezed him to impart all his fatherly love, to kill the hatred he could see brimming through his expressions.

"David, as you know I was raised in Kingston, Jamaica, and had a violent life until I came to know Jesus. I was an angry young man, despising the world and the unfairness of it. I was wrong for hitting that man. God has forgiven me and if I knew where that man lived, I would ask him for forgiveness too."

David wriggled, but he held him. His mind was terrorised that if he let him go he would try to administer the same infliction that he had, but this time with irreversible fatal consequences.

"Son, please, please let it go. You must let the anger and the hatred you're feeling inside go, or it will destroy you."

Holy Spirit, God, help him, you've got to help him.

Chapter Six

David covered his ears to the Saturday morning church bells that rang out with a sound which penetrated his brain with a calling card, to come and be still in the presence of God. He shook his head at a bittersweet day and the murmurings of his heart were of resentment and not of peace. His brain couldn't withstand the cutting angst of not sitting next to Ray in the Church of God Congregation, and instead awaiting the moment when he was lowered in the ground and he said goodbye.

He watched the chorister walk to the front of the stage who was clothed in a long black robe and had her face covered by the net of her hat. She raised her hands to the cross of Jesus Christ, to commit the burial service into the hands of the Holy Spirit.

David reminisced on his conversation with Ray about their souls being released forever into the supernatural world. He smiled as he remembered Ray's comment on still being able to recognise Elaine's sexy bottom, when she was naked in the spirit.

His grin and wounded expression reflected the sadness that overwhelmed him, as another reminder of Ray's candle being blown out fluttered into his mind.

He stared at the chorister, who waited for the introduction of the first line of the opening hymn and sang, "Amazing grace, how sweet the sound, that saved a wretch like me. I once was lost, but now I'm found, I was blind, but now I see."

A song that moved him every time he sang the words was unable to pierce the hardness of his heart. He couldn't get pass the barrier of God failing him and Ray. There was an urge assailing his brain to reach out and trust in his faith one more time, but when he looked at the coffin and stared at the ceiling he was back to the point of utter despair.

His tears flowed unashamedly for Ray and he looked across at Lorna, experiencing guilt that she'd lost a brother and he was to blame. He watched Thelma's face and his heart ripped with anguish for never again would he and Ray sit together at her dining table, enjoying beef patties and Coco bread.

He pondered, *why did all this happen? We were just two young men messing around and loving life.*

"David, I tried to call you, are you alright?" whispered Angela.

He hadn't responded to her phone calls, but instead told his parents to tell her every time she rang that he wasn't in the mood to talk. He had no intention of listening to her voice or seeing her smile again. He wanted to blot out every dark cloud that haunted him and she was a girl that he once knew, but was now part of his past.

He looked over at Angela, seeing a girl pining for his attention and nodded his head as an acknowledgement of her existence. David sensed she didn't see that things could never return to the way they were. He despised God for severing the foursome bond of loyalty, and he couldn't envisage any way back unless he decided to raise Ray from the coffin positioned at the front of the church.

Father Theo stood up, walked to the lectern and stared at the congregation. His eyes connected with David's, who detested the ground he walked on and silently scoffed at the sham of a message which he was about to deliver in an attempt to convince him, that he needed to see God's perfect will in his agony.

"Though I walk in the valley of the shadow of death, I will fear no evil for God is with me," Father Theo said.

David's eyes rested on Father Theo's bible. He heard the Psalm, but doubted that it was true.

David didn't take his gaze off Father Theo and his eyes didn't blink. He looked at the bible full of so many promises for those who served The Lord in righteousness and truth, yet when he looked at the congregation, their lives didn't signify the blessing of The Lord, but rather the curse of The Lord.

David gazed thinking, *why do we have sick people in the church, when God is supposed to be a healer?* He mused on parents and turned is head remembering, *his son is in prison and her daughter's a prostitute and I don't know anyone who lives in a mansion or who runs a big company.*

Stories bubbled in his mind. *Some of them can't even pay their rent and need a miracle from God to just survive.* He couldn't remember any spiritual evidence that they'd escaped their trial or any demonstration of God's power to change their circumstances. His thoughts churned with the consideration, *is God wrong or are they wrong?*

"Son, it's well with Ray's soul, he's in a better place now," whispered Charles.

David couldn't cry anymore tears. They were cried out until all that remained in his heart was a surging torment for justice.

He looked at Charles, challenging him through his glare to prove that Ray was living in a mansion, mingling with the angels and enjoying the brilliance of God's glorious heaven.

The just shall live by faith. If the just live by faith, then why is there poverty even in the church. How is it possible that the many prayers for protection over Ray's life couldn't stop him from being murdered.

The questions kept pricking his mind and the more they came, the more the disillusionment increased. He couldn't understand why after all the numerous sermons that God was love that resonated with him so powerfully, now meant nothing to him. He looked for just one example of God's love being reflected on a member of the church, unable to find anyone who stood out as basking in the immeasurable riches of God's grace.

I don't believe anymore, it was all lies. I was brainwashed to think that God loved me, it's all lies.

He watched Thelma walk to the stage. She held onto the lectern and he dropped his head, overshadowed by sorrow and even though he knew that she didn't blame him, he couldn't stop thinking, *if I'd gone back, today could have been a different day.*

“Yes, I’m in great pain at the death of my son, but murderer, racist and evil man, I want you to know that God loves even you and I forgive you for killing my son.”

Thelma wiped away her tears and gazed at the congregation.

“You took my son’s life, but he’s in a better place now. Know that even in my sorrow and pain, God will bring good out of this. My wish for you murderer of my son, is that you find peace. Come forward and face your punishment, but understand that God loves you and so do I.”

David raised his head and gazed at Thelma. He wished that he had her courage and could see the world through her eyes. David watched the congregation and listened to their gentle prayers of affirmations, whilst his heart stirred with a commitment to not die until those responsible lay on the ground in their own blood.

“Thank you Jesus that the wicked will not prosper over the righteous,” Father Theo said.

David watched him walking down the steps that led from the stage to the front row of the church. He stood at Ray’s coffin and sprinkled holy water over his body. Members raised their hands and David desired to flow into the supernatural place of peace that he’d been many times before that brought joy, even in the face of tragedy and great affliction.

"Let's be still in the presence of God. Let's remember our brother and that we'll see him again."

Mary put her arm through David's and squeezed his hand. His heart moved slightly, but quickly returned to stone. He studied the congregation, wanting to be part of the unification, but he sat as an isolated enigma without any supporters for his cause.

"I'm sure that David, Ray's best friend would like to say a few words," said Father Theo.

Charles held David's arm and he clenched his fist.

David sensed the fear that if he spoke the truth from his heart, then the members would murmur with accusations of evil spirits entering him and corrupting his soul.

David pulled his arm away from the grip of Charles and went to Ray's coffin. He placed both hands on the base and moved slowly up towards his head. His soul was empty of emotion and his mind screamed with the promise of personal vengeance.

"David, sit down, this isn't the right time for you to speak," whispered Mary.

He shrugged his shoulders and kissed his teeth, cutting his eye in disrespect with a strong refusal to listen to parental advice and obey. He disliked Charles's and Mary's dishonesty and denial of their true feelings. He saw through their pretence that they were happy with God and expected him to adopt the same stance.

He walked up the steps to the lectern. He didn't have a prepared speech or feel the serene presence of the Holy Spirit. He heard the gentle encouragement and mutters of consolation from the congregation, but in his mind he was still cursing and criticising.

His eyes stared at the church members and he was in agreement with them that Ray was a treasured child and friend, but nothing could fill the empty space of loss in his heart.

The worn blue carpet caught his attention. He raised his head and gazed at the white coving that shined against the hanging fluorescent lights. A tambourine shook and he turned, gazing at the choir whose voices had ministered to his spirit through songs of worship to God.

That was then and this is now.

He gripped the lectern, staring at Father Theo who smiled and he thought, *lying dog*. He turned back towards the congregation with anger and hate boiling over in his heart.

"What's it like to be white?" he whispered, gazing at the minority of Caucasians in the church.

The congregation's expressions resonated with the challenge and debate he'd gone through over this question many times in his head.

Charles shook his head and Mary put her finger on her lips. He saw their attempt to silence his voice and it infuriated the fire that inflamed in his soul and he pounded the lectern. His body tensed. He blew the air through his nostrils furiously and touched his head that was about to implode from the pressure whistling like a boiling kettle.

"What is it like to be a nigger? What is it like to be called a black nigger? What is it like to be seen as inferior or less intelligent, because you have black skin?"

His mind was stirred up by provocation and he implored the church members to dig deeply into their memories by his continuous nods. David looked for the fire to burn and for someone to join him in remembrance of a dark place where a racist slur or a racist attack had occurred.

He had the right to challenge their faith in God. His eyes opened wider and his breaths were filled with emotion that incited anger at the pain of bigotry. It opened up his wounds that rippled with the remnants of abuse and he searched for an army that would join him, on the pursuit of revenge.

He dwelled on the word nigger and its many interpretations, seeing images of hate, black shit, offence and lowest of the low. The words, *Coon, jigaboo, slavery and despise for being born black,* flooded into his mind and he swiped at the tears that rolled down his cheeks.

The mood of the congregation changed from worship and praise to one of soul searching and David looked around the room, hoping that he'd ignited a light to awaken the sleeping minds that held onto to the belief that were loved by God.

David's head dropped and his body began to shake. He raised his head and saw Mary coming towards him and quickly raised his hand to stop her from advancing, when he still had a lot more to say.

"I miss my friend, Ray. Why did he have to die! I want him to come back and I can't believe that I'm staring at his body in the coffin."

Charles stood up and stretched his hand towards David, who shook his head, clenched his fists and thumped the lectern to release the emotions that were burning in his soul.

"Thelma and Lorna, I'm so sorry. I wish that I would have gone back to try and save Ray. I can't believe he's dead."

David's heart broke into splinters of remorse and pain. His tears fell uncontrollably down his face as he imagined waking up tomorrow and still not hearing Ray's voice. The crying of the congregation soaked his mind with greater sorrow and as he looked at Thelma and Lorna, it was as if he'd inflicted the fatal strike because of his cowardice.

David gazed at the men and women sitting in the pews. His eyes fell on Angela and Elaine and a kindred spirit reached out towards them. Part of him wished that they could still be just like they were, but without Ray he saw it as impossible to rekindle a friendship.

His heart was too entrenched in the memory of brutality and as he turned away from looking at their faces, he knew that they were two people that he would never see again.

David left the stage and sat in the seat next to Mary. She held his hand and he listened to her praying that God would soften his heart and help him to find forgiveness towards Ray's killers.

He watched Father Theo walk up the steps and take the microphone from the holder.

I don't care what you say. None of your praying or preaching can raise Ray from the dead.

***

"Brothers and sisters, this is the time to commit Ray's body to the ground. Please make your way to the Camberwell Old Cemetery," said Father Theo.

The congregation left the church and made their way to the burial site.

David left the church with Mary, following Charles to his Orange Ford Cortina thinking, *Ray, I miss you, I want you to come back.*

But you're not coming back.

They got into the car and Charles started it. After a short drive he arrived at the Camberwell Old Cemetery and parked.

"David, we'll all see Ray again in heaven," Mary said.

They got out of the car and waited for the hearse to arrive and for Ray to be taken to the burial plot.

I don't believe you mum, I don't believe you, it's not true.

As the hearse came to the entrance of the cemetery, David's body shook with rage and panic.

"No, it can't be. Ray, Ray," he whispered.

They all followed and as Ray's coffin was taken to the burial plot, David stood at the grave next to Thelma and Lorna, watching it being lowered into the ground. He wanted to believe that at the last moment, Ray would miraculously come back to life, but as the coffin was settled in the soil his mind tore with grief that he would never hear Ray's laughter or be able to share his deep secrets with him again.

"My son, how can someone so young be taken from me!" said Thelma.

Lorna held onto her arm and whispered, "I'll miss you, my brother. Save a seat for me in heaven so when I get there, we can have breakfast together again."

Elaine ran towards Ray's coffin and fell to her knees. She picked up the soil and let it run through her fingers onto the coffin.

David wiped away a tear as he stared at the dirt.

“You racist bastards, you fucking racist bastards,” he whispered.

Father Theo threw earth onto the coffin and said, “Dear God, we thank you that this is not the end. We commit Ray into the loving arms of Jesus and we know that one day when the trumpet in heaven sounds, we’ll see him again.”

David replayed his words in his head that no longer had any spiritual significance to him. He stared at the sky, almost daring to believe that maybe God would hear his voice. He remembered, *God hates black people.*

Angela walked to David and stood by his side. She linked her arm through his, but he didn’t turn his head to acknowledge her, but just stared at the soil that covered Ray’s coffin.

“David, why haven’t you returned my calls? I miss our friendship. My heart is broken too. I’m also suffering.”

He felt nothing towards her. She might as well have been a stranger who he passed in the street and didn’t give a second thought too. His heart was like bullet proof glass and impenetrable to love and the touch of a girl that once upon a time he would have considered dating. Now, she represented everything ugly that he wanted to dismiss from his life and forget ever existed.

"Don't you see that things can never be the same again? I can never accept that God let Ray die and I hate him for it. I don't believe the things I used to, they're all lies, forget about me."

He watched the crowd who began to disappear from the burial site. Angela remained with David and she gently pulled her arm away from his. He looked at her and turned his head back towards Ray's grave.

"David."

He couldn't make her understand that it wasn't just Ray who died on that horrible day, but he also died with him. The word of The Lord that had burned in his heart had evaporated and been replaced by bitterness, hatred and vengeance.

She walked away from David and he didn't move. He kept his eyes focused on Ray's grave, reminiscing on their close friendship and the evil day when God let him die.

"Ray, I promise you now, I won't rest until that white bastard who took your life dies. I don't know if you're in heaven or if you've gone back to being dust. Wherever you are, I'll never forget you. You're my brother for life, and I should have stood by your side and fought with you. I hope that you can forgive me."

He crouched by the grave watching the mist of his breath float into the air. He stretched his arms towards the soil and clenched his fist. His mind shifted into a place of numbness and a reality that his heart couldn't accept.

David stood to his feet and closed his eyes. The tears that had dried up began to fall again. His lips shivered and he hoped that it was just a dream and he would feel Ray's friendly punch on his arm. He waited for the miracle, inadvertently giving God one more chance to prove that he did have supernatural power.

Opening his eyes, he waited for the call of his name from Ray. He put his hand into his jacket pocket and pulled out a piece of paper that he always carried with him to remind him that God was never far away. He looked at the words and said, "I will never forsake you or leave you. I will not, I will not, I will not."

"Liar! You're a liar! You did leave me and you left Ray. I'll never forgive you for this!"

He ripped the piece of paper shred by shred and watched it blow across the ground in the wind, renouncing his faith in God. His mind was made up that never again would he step foot into the church to sing songs of praise, worship and lift God up with the congregation.

Standing in a maze, where he couldn't distinguish the entrance from the exit, put him at a dead end and wondering, *what should I do now?* His right foot kicked out at the debris that dared to desecrate Ray's grave and make him forget about his very existence.

He breathed heavily, no longer having the strength to fight the leaves that covered Ray's coffin. The sound of the car horn called his name to leave but he ignored it, preferring to stay and gaze and remember the good times. David placed his hand on his chest to let his boiling blood direct his next steps.

"Goodbye, Ray, goodbye. I'll keep my word and I won't come back to your grave until the killers are dead."

***

The touch on his shoulder made him jump and his shoulders tensed. He relaxed as he realised the touch was gentle and not threatening. He looked at the hand covered by a black glove and listened to the soft breaths.

"Angela, I told you that it can never be the same again. Without, Ray, we have nothing. You need to move on and forget about me."

He turned around and his arms and chest jerked in a nervous reaction.

The woman raised her head and her green eyes and white skin made him blink twice. She smiled and moved closer to him. He backed away. His defences were down. He stared at her slim face intently with his mind pondering and his eyes squinting.

"I've seen you before, where do I know you from?" he said.

She picked a flower from the ground and placed it on Ray's grave, kneeling down and bowing her head.

David watched her paying respects to someone she didn't know.

Hostility filled his mind when he reminded himself that it was her kind that had brought this dark day upon his head. Something about her wouldn't allow him to maintain his anger and he watched, infused with curiosity and amazement that a white girl who had a touch of familiarity was in front of him, and puzzling his mind with suspicion of her agenda.

Getting up and walking towards David she said, "I was there on the day with your friends when Ray was brutally murdered. I comforted your girlfriends and I'm so sorry."

Her voice and words were like a melody to his ears and soothing to his tormented mind. He'd never heard a white woman talk with such authenticity. She held out her hand in an expression of friendship and David met her halfway and clutched her hand.

"Why are you here? We don't need pity from a white woman who has no understanding of blacks!"

She wasn't fazed by his outburst, but continued smiling, influencing David to respond with a smile despite the harrowing experience she'd reminded him of. She squeezed his hand tighter and something lifted from his heart, that felt like she understood his pain and he could trust her even though he knew nothing about her.

"David, it's getting dark, we need to leave now," shouted Charles.

David let go of the woman's hand and began to walk away from the grave.

"I don't even know your name."

She took a piece of paper from her pocket and scribbled on it. She walked towards David and placed it in his hands. He was mesmerised by this white woman without trepidation, and who seemed to have a motive that he couldn't understand.

She kissed him on the cheek and he touched his face, looking at the smear of red lipstick on his fingertips.

"My name is Abbie, and now you have my telephone number. Call me, I want to help."

Chapter Seven

Father Theo walked through the front door and David immediately scampered up the stairs. It was the expected visit, because he hadn't attended the church, remaining true to his word that he would never walk through those doors again.

He sat at the top of the stairs, picking the thread of the multi-brown carpet, eavesdropping and wondering, *what type of persuasion is he going to use to influence me to come back to the church.*

"David, get downstairs immediately," shouted Charles.

David went to his room and lay on the bed. The ambience of his room was different. Once upon a time he recalled it being filled with peace that surpasses all understanding, but now the atmosphere was ice cold, just like his heart. He listened to the familiar footsteps trampling up the stairs and advancing towards his bedroom.

Charles opened his bedroom door and said, "Did you hear me call you, bwoy? Show some damn respect and get downstairs now!"

David kissed his teeth and eyeballed Charles. To him he was just another black man who was a puppet on a string, running the white man's errands and still a slave and he had no compulsion to end up the same way.

Walking down the stairs, he entered the room and stared at Father Theo's face and casual clothes. *He looks old.* His smile and friendliness didn't endear him, and he stood without emotion and with his arms by his side as Father Theo hugged him.

"How are you, David?"

David pulled away from his embrace and sat in the opposite corner of the room on the single cream sofa, covered by plastic. He was filled with resentment towards a man who he viewed as adopting the rules of imprisonment in an environment where every man should be free.

Mary brought in a pot of tea and some Jamaican ginger cake. She poured a cup for Father Theo, and he added two cubes of brown sugar and stirred the tea.

"We've missed you at the church. You need to come back to where you belong, so we can help you."

He raised the cup to his mouth, slurped the tea and placed it back on the saucer.

David’s eyes ferreted on his face. He despised the instruction to return to a place that he no longer had an affiliation with. The anger with Charles and Mary fuelled, for allowing him through the front door to work his systematic and forcible charm on his mind. David raised his head and tensed his shoulders in an act of defiance that he wasn’t going to be cajoled into taking a seat in the pews at 10.30am next Sunday morning.

“God is dead, he doesn’t exist anymore and I won’t sit in Satan’s house with hypocrites like you.”

“Don’t ever come back again to talk to me about God.”

Mary bowed her head, keeping her eyes on the floor. Charles looked across at her and turned to stare at David.

“How dare you! How dare you speak to Father Theo with such disrespect! You’re not a man, you’re still a child and this wasn’t how we raised you.”

Leaping from his chair he grabbed David by his neck. He raised his hand and slapped David across his face, knocking him to the other side of the room.

“I never raised you to be a ragamuffin! You want to be de big mon now? Apologise!”

Lifting David from the floor, he threw him onto the sofa and jumped on him, throwing cuffs at his face and his body.

David lifted his hands to shield his face from the blows and the slaps that kept coming. He tried to keep his composure, but the agony from the physical assault intensified, ripping through his shirt and battering his body with blue murder until he collapsed on the floor. He was beaten, bruised and racking with pain, but with a strong will that he wouldn't humble himself and put aside his pride and dignity.

"Charles, enough, stop! Enough! Don't hit him anymore, stop!"

Mary pulled Charles off, putting her arms around David and shielding his body from any further blows.

Charles shook his head and sat down.

"I'm sorry, Father Theo, you see what de bwoy mek me do?"

Father Theo looked at him and walked over to David, who tried to hold back his tears, but the suffering in his body was too great and he let them fall. His lips trembled and his hands shook. David drizzled in embarrassment that he wanted to run upstairs to his room and curl up under the bedcovers.

“Charles, this is not the way, this isn’t the way of God.”

“David, this is why you must come back to the church. God loves you and I love you. You’re like a son to me. Come back and God will heal your heart.”

“I know you’re hurting from Ray’s death, but you need the church.”

David wiped his face and winced, holding his side as the brutality for the wrong word, numbed his back with the sting of the assault.

The ferocity of the blows inflicted their marks on his body, but he stood up and gazed at Charles who reminded him of a child riddled with guilt after disobeying the instruction given by her mother. David hobbled over to him and Mary tried to pull him back.

Charles took his hand away from his face and looked up at David.

“I made a vow that I’ll never go into a church again. You can beat me a thousand times, but I won’t change my mind.”

Charles stood to his feet, but David remained resolute in his determination to not be intimidated. The attack and chastisement no longer had the desired effect to bring him back into line. He was like a man who had nothing else to lose and therefore feared no one, not even Charles.

"De bwoy is possessed by Satan. Ray's death has opened his heart to a legion of demons. He's not the son I used to know."

David walked out of the living room, taking his jacket from the coat stand. His back was bleeding and he opened his shirt and touched the welts on his chest. The pain made him grimace, but he kept pressing, ignoring the discomfort and using the angst to intensify his dissent at a hypocritical authority.

He stared at the front door with intent. A strong urge welled up inside of him, to go outside away from the pretenders of Christianity and find a brotherhood with which he had common ground.

"David, before you leave, I have an update from the police," said Father Theo.

David took his hand away from the front door handle and walked back into the living room. His ears were on radar alert and his stone-cold heart beat faster. He sat down next to Mary who held onto his arm and his body tensed at the potential capture of Ray's killers.

"The police have arrested fifteen skinheads. They're in custody, but I don't know if any of them have been charged with murder yet."

"Surely, they must know that it has to be one of them, they're all guilty," Charles said.

Father Theo drained the last drop of his cold cup of tea. The statement he made was like a fire burning in the forest in David's heart. It was the sign that he'd been waiting for and now he could gain recompense for the injustice.

"Which police station are they at? Tell me where they are!"

The image of the skinheads shouting nigger and black bastards reappeared in his mind. He began to convulse as the rage ignited inside of him at the perpetrators of the murder. He wanted them to endure the same pain that Ray did until they begged for their throats to be cut to escape the torture, but even then he wouldn't stop the punishment.

David didn't wait for the response and ran into the hallway. He threw the door open, ran outside and onto the pavement.

Wait, David, don't leave," shouted Mary.

He kept running without a care for his destination. He couldn't see anything else, but the colour red. Justice and vengeance screamed in his head. The killers had been apprehended and being incarcerated for life was too kind a sentence that he had to reverse.

He wanted them to bleed and die and never have the opportunity to verbally abuse another black person, or lay their hands on them again.

***

David stopped at Cavalier Street, gazing at the grey and miserable high rise flats and the broken down brown fences that were held together by pieces of green rope. He held his nose to resist the smell of the aroma of Indian spices that flowed through the front doors into the atmosphere of dusk, and always left a seasick sensation in his stomach.

He kept walking, kicking up the dust from the crooked pavements and touching the roof of a green Ford Cortina. He recalled Ray always boasting about his love for the Ford Cortina car and smiled as he imagined sitting next to Ray and honking the horn to get the attention of the black girls who couldn't resist his good looks and charm.

Familiar territory of the Indian delicatessen where the black people shopped to buy sweet potato, green bananas and yams made him stop and gaze through the shop window. He inhaled the smell that came across the road of fried chicken and curried mutton and rice that reminded him of Jamaica alive and well in South London.

If Ray was here now, he'd be telling me to go to Mrs Brown's house and see if she wanted any odd jobs doing, just so we could get a plate of her jerk chicken, rice and peas.

The image of the chicken juice running down the corners of his mouth was interrupted as he recalled that down the road was the youth centre. It was a place he'd visited before, to persuade the black youth to give their lives to Jesus and come to the church to be saved from a life destined for mediocrity and crime. He visualised the young men laughing in his face, and the black girls taunting him with their flirtatious behaviour and offer to make him speak in tongues when he experienced their lips on his body.

They never attacked him, but tolerated his spiritual philosophy which when he reflected was a fabrication of motivation and idiocy. He recalled the words that he'd spoken to give a false hope that they could inherit the riches of the kingdom rather than the depths of poverty.

Not one of them had forsaken their life of sin for the church and now the blindfold had been taken off his eyes, he understood why.

"Reggie must be there! I need to see him."

David pulled up the collars of his black leather jacket and sauntered towards the youth centre. Usually he'd walked without fear, but trepidation bubbled inside his mind. Gone was his bible and leaflets to implore the wicked to change. He felt like Adam, naked and exposed, having tasted the fruit of life and now he could no longer rely on a spiritual defence to withstand the bullets of sin.

He stood at the entrance of the youth centre and Reggae music pounded in his ears through the power of the speaker boxes. The smell of Ganja wafted in his nostrils. He pulled at the door and let it go, hearing a silent voice to turn away and run from the danger.

Run away from what. Back to the church.

David walked into the dim room, observing the group of black youths who stood in the corner playing pool. He looked through the window into another room and heard the black girls shrieking, laughing and arguing about nothing.

The youth centre leader, a Rastafarian looked at him.

“Wait a minute, is dat, David! David, de church bwoy?”

David’s left foot tremored as the volume of the music reduced to a gentle beat. The chit chatter of the girls stopped, and he looked through the broken window at the faces gazing back at him. He was in the spotlight and trying to stand with courage, whilst his fingers twittered behind his back.

A pool cue that clattered on the floor sent a nervous twinge of anxiety through his mind. The man that he never feared hit the white ball against the black ball, missing his pot.

“Raasclaat! To bumba! Look what de devil has blown in,” said the Rastafarian.

He stood to his feet and walked towards David who gazed at his dreadlocks bouncing in front of his face. His gold teeth shone against the faint lighting and David looked at his tee-shirt of Bob Marley that had the inscription, “We shall all be free from oppression,” that resonated with his mission. He knew that he was in the right place where violence was the only message to demand change.

The black youths stopped playing pool and followed Reggie.

David watched the notorious gang leader ambling towards him, donned in his black jeans, brown leather coat and grey flat cap. His stomach became more unsettled and the vomit climbed up to his throat and pressed against his lips.

Reggie stood by the Rastafarian's side and peered at David from head to toe. He removed his cap and patted his afro, moving his face closer to David's.

"Kiss mi rass! Pussyclaat! The black Jesus has arrived."

The arrogance and fearlessness in David had gone. The words of condemnation about Reggie's life of crime that used to flow from his lips were silent. Instead, he stood with his head hanging down in submission and with acceptance that he had no other option except to plead his case, and get help from a man that he'd never wished to emulate.

"I don't want any bloodclaat trouble," said the Rastafarian youth centre leader.

Reggie raised his hand and put two fingers in the air. The signal indicated silence and the Rastafarian backed away to the purple sofa. Reggie eyeballed David and encircled him. The gang members held their positions, watching David whose legs began to tremble and the terror went up a notch in his brain.

David looked into Reggie's eyes with a hard stare in an attempt to be tough when he was wilting like a dying flower.

"I want a gun."

Reggie stopped and put his hand inside his belt. He walked back to David and he turned away, experiencing a rush of fear for the first time in the youth centre.

"Raas! De church bwoy wants to become a gangsta! I know about the fifteen skinheads in custody. So, you want to kill dem?"

David's head vibrated from the Reggae music that pumped again through the speaker boxes. He watched the black girls return to the other room and draw the curtain. He was in unfamiliar territory and no longer preaching a sermon about God for he knew that was over.

Redemption of a different kind stirred in his spirit. Only a strong hand of justice administered with black power could do that, and David was ready to pull the trigger and spill blood.

Reggie lit a spliff and blew the smoke into David's face. The smoke went into his nostrils and scratched his throat, causing him to splutter like an old man with bronchitis.

"You want a bloodclaat gun to kill de white skinhead bastards and then what?"

David's thoughts hadn't gone that far. His mind could only see Ray laying on the pavement and his blood gushing from the slash across his neck. He had made a promise that his killers would meet the same end and now was the time to deliver that promise with a swift reprisal.

"Will you give me a fucking gun or not?"

Inside he was quaking and bubbling with angst. He tried to stiffen his upper lip and stared at Reggie's eyes. He twisted his head from side to side and squared up his shoulders to appear as broad as Reggie. He hadn't eaten and water swilled in his stomach and tingles ran down his legs, but he stood his ground with nowhere else to run except be in the devil's playground, and drown every ounce of truth that lived inside of him.

"Come again! Give you a bloodclaat, fucking raasclaat gun!"

Reggie put his ray ban sunglasses on, put his hand behind his back and pointed to the floor. One of the gang members walked up to David and punched him in the stomach and as he fell to the floor, Reggie put his foot on his head and pulled out a blade.

"Ah! Ah! My stomach."

David held his belly, gasping and squirming on the ground. Reggie put the cold steel on David's face and David's mind erupted into panic that the door he'd walked through wasn't the same one he would leave by.

"The only reason why you're not bumbaclaat dead right now is because I hate white people more than black Christians."

Another gang member kicked David in the back and slapped his forehead with a pool cue. Reggie raised his hand and brought David's lesson of disrespect to an end. He pulled David to his feet and shook his head.

"No more!" cried David, wiping the smear of blood from the gash in his forehead.

Looking at the door, he wanted to run, but he knew that it was too late to pull himself back into the line of truth. He regretted that he'd crossed over into the dark side where dog ate dog and the gun was more powerful than the bible, the sword of truth that he'd wielded with great effect.

Reggie held David's arm and peered into his eyes.

"Ok tough man, Jesus, we'll see what you've fucking got."

The gang led David to the Ford Econoline vans parked outside the back of the youth centre. He studied their weapons, blades and guns. His mind whispered, *it's wrong for me to be here. Maybe I can ask Reggie to let me walk out of the youth centre and go home.* He couldn't imagine that he wouldn't be scarred or maimed to remind him to never get into the fire if he wasn't prepared to get burned.

As he looked at Reggie and the gang, he saw the vermin that he believed they were. His eyes saw dumb black men, killing themselves for a ten-pound drug deal or having an altercation for a piece of ground, but he needed them, and even though he feared for his life, the passion to avenge Ray's death was stronger and pulling him to join an army of hate.

"Where are you taking me?"

His request for a response was denied. David's head thudded from the turned up volume of the gang style lyrics to stop oppression and kill the Babylon before they killed you. The weed passed from gang member to gang member. It burned David's eyes and began to anaesthetise his brain cells.

"Smoke dis, you're gonna need it," Reggie said.

David took the weed. He'd never smoked in his life. The weed brought a nauseating aroma into his nostrils and the cloud of smoke crippled his lungs. Putting the spliff into his mouth, he inhaled and couldn't swallow the smoke that settled in his throat and brought dizziness into his brain.

"I don't need this to kill those white skinhead bastards."

Reggie and his gang scoffed.

David's fear began to rise. He knew about gang culture. If he failed, he would be marked so any other member of an opposing gang would know that he was a coward, a pussy and the black man's meat. He stared out of the window of the van at the dark road, pondering, *where are they taking me and what if I can't do what Reggie tells me to do*

"Church bwoy, do it, smoke de fucking pussyclaat weed, it will make you feel irie," said one of the gang members.

David took the weed from his hand and stared at the red ash that burned and fell to the floor. He put it to his lips. *I need to be tough and hard,* he thought. He passed the weed back and his mind was still unyielding to follow any order to inflict pain on another person to earn respect and stripes. This wasn't the way that he wanted to prove that he had courage in the heat of the battle by committing the unimaginable to a person, he had no conflict with.

He wished that he'd taken the beating from Charles and ran to the safety of his room. The words, *this is wrong, I shouldn't be here,* danced inside his head. His feet tap danced on the floor and his heart pulsated with a trepid beat.

"Slow down. Kill de bloodclaat lights," Reggie said.

David gripped the seat as the driver pressed gently on the brake and switched the headlights off. He stared through the back window, watching the headlights of the other van turn from light to dark. Reggie turned the reggae music down and the chorus of murder still vibrated in David's head. He watched the lieutenant blow smoke through the open window and wish as he might to reconsider his decision, he could only imagine turning away from the entrance of the youth club and going back home.

David gripped his knees and clenched his teeth. His neck bones became rigid and the flutters in his chest created a storm of jittering underneath his skin.

He stared at the door to the club. It opened and a skinhead stepped outside. David looked at his cigarette that glowed in the dark as he walked around to the other side of the building and his right leg shuddered against the seat in front of him. Wiping his sweating hands on the van seat, he pursed his lips to stop them from trembling.

Reggie took a gun from his pocket, attached a silencer and opened the chamber that contained six bullets. He wiped his prints from the gun and gave it to David whose hands shook as he held the weapon.

"You want to kill, so kill. Put one bullet in his forehead and one in the back of his head."

David looked at the gun and gazed into Reggie's eyes, knowing that he wasn't fooling around. Now he had the opportunity to avenge Ray's death, but his mind spun in a disarray of dissonance.

I don't know if this man was involved in killing Ray, what if he's innocent.

"What are you waiting for? Those white bastards killed your friend. They kicked him, punched him and cut his throat. Take revenge. Kill de fucking bloodclaat racist!"

David's stomach churned and he swam in a wave of indigestion that pressed onto his bladder. His clammy fingers held the gun. He gazed at Reggie, seeking a way out and where the blood of another man didn't have to be on his hands.

Reggie opened the van door quietly and pointed to the street.

"Get out of de fucking car now and kill de raasclaat, bloodclaat, and pussyclaat racist. You have seconds to put the fucking bullets into his fucking head."

David stepped onto the pavement and ran to the side of the building on the toes of his trainers. He stared around the corner at the skinhead, the gun trembled in his hand and his head was mashed up in conflict with right and wrong.

David walked slowly and the hate began to rise with each grimace as he glared at the three- quarter length jeans, red Doc Marten boots and the green bomber jacket worn by the skinhead. He stepped on a twig and the man turned around to face the gun pointing at his head. David looked into his eyes and saw Ray being beaten by his kind until the exuberance of life drained from his body.

He had the power to let the man live or die and he watched the tears falling down the skinhead's face. His finger pressed slightly against the trigger of the gun. His hand twitched, and the consequences of failure to follow Reggie's order imprinted an image of permanent marring, that would make him a leper.

"Please don't kill me, I don't want to die. I'm only, seventeen, please don't kill me."

Anger, hatred and venomous revulsion for the skinhead raged inside of David. He wanted to pull the trigger and blow the man's brains out onto the pavement and watch his blood run into the dirt. Holding the gun to the man's head, his finger quivered against the trigger. Evil thoughts compelled him to press and watch the man die.

"No! I can't do this."

He ran back to the van and dived onto the back seat. The skinhead began to scream and the drivers of the vans turned the keys in the ignition and sped away along the dark roads.

David dropped the gun on the floor and kicked it towards the front of the vehicle. He opened the window and spewed down the side of the van, releasing the angst, but shaking, because in the eyes of the gang he knew that he was a coward.

"Why didn't you kill the white bastard?" Reggie said.

Chapter Eight

David quivered in the seat, making eye contact with Reggie and then gazing at the first lieutenant. He knew that he'd failed to follow the gang code and his head began to spin with an uproar of fear, that the bullet he should have put into the skinhead's head was the bullet that was going to be fired into his brain.

He looked at the door, debating in his mind, *should I try to kick the door down and run, or plead with Reggie to give me another chance to prove that I'm worthy to wear the gang colours.*

I'm fucking dead, he's going to kill me.

David wiped the vomit from his mouth and pushed his body against the leather seat. It wasn't that easy to kill when his Christian beliefs were still resonating. He could see the gun in his hand being pointed at the skinhead, but as his right forefinger twitched, he shook his head at the replay that told him again that he couldn't take another man's life without proof that he was guilty.

"Turn down dat fucking corner," said Reggie.

The driver sped around the bend and pulled into a side street, ramming on the brakes and bringing the van to a screeching halt.

David's muscles rippled with the tense mood, sensing that the gang members were ready for an all-out war. He couldn't look Reggie in the eyes, fearing the repercussion of his disobedience to a direct order, and knowing the rules that didn't include clemency for his cowardice.

Reggie removed his sunglasses and grabbed David by the throat.

"You walk into de club, asking for a bloodclaat gun and you couldn't even kill the racist skinhead whose brethren murdered your friend. What type of man would let his friend die in cold blood and not kill de fucker who did it?"

David grabbed Reggie's hand and spluttered as the choke hold forced him to gasp for a breath of air. He saw the gleaming blade being passed to the gang leader and closed his eyes. He had nowhere to run to and the fear kept his feet glued to the floor of the van.

"Cut his fucking throat, he's a pussy, a raasclaat woman with no fucking balls," said Reggie's lieutenant.

The cold blade on David's skin made him flinch. He opened his eyes, staring at the anger in Reggie's expression. *I'm dead, I'm dead.*

"Reggie, don't kill me, please don't kill me!"

His body shook nervously for the night wasn't supposed to turn out like this. A skinhead should be dead and he should have been walking on air, elated that the world was rid of at least one more bigot.

"I've a better idea. Once upon a time you believed in your God. Well, let him save you, church bwoy."

"Wait! The code says you're supposed to cut his fucking face and let him bleed," shouted the lieutenant.

Reggie leapt over the sprawled legs of a gang member, grabbed his second in command's chin and nicked his face with the blade.

"I'm in fucking control, I'm de raasclaat number one. Don't challenge my bloodclaat authority again!"

He opened the van door, pushed David out onto the street and slammed the door.

"Get us out of here now," he said.

David chased the van and tugged the door.

"No, wait! Don't leave me here, Reggie, Reggie!"

The driver of the van stopped and the window opened. Reggie threw the gun onto the pavement and David ran towards the van with terror assaulting his mind. He tripped, his body convulsed and a bolt of panic kicked into his brain that he was going to be left to fight for himself, and without the gang to stop the beating from the skinheads.

"You're either a dead man walking, or you'll live. The skinheads will be here soon. Maybe your God will save you. Live by de bible or live by de fucking gun."

David watched the van disappear and it left a trail of black smoke behind that wafted into his face. He picked up the gun, staring at the chamber and ran to a parked car, swallowing hard to keep the vomit in his stomach. Looking up at the lamppost, he watched the fading light that turned the street into a mass of blackness and put his hand to his face. He could only see the stuttered breaths blowing out from his mouth.

"What do I do now? Reggie, come back! I don't want to die!'

He ran to the end of street, hoping and praying that Reggie would have a change of heart and give him a second chance to prove that he belonged in the gang culture he once condemned. No headlights flashed and the beep of the horn bidding him to run for cover was wishful thinking in his head. He stood alone in a road that he didn't recognise, not knowing where to turn or where to run.

Left, right or stand still were his options and he stood at the crossroad in a ball of nervous jitters. "Dad, help me!" His soul perforated with escape or peril. One wrong move and the thoughts churned in his brain of a fate resembling that of Ray.

The voice in his head condemned his stupid act for believing that he could walk in the same footsteps as hardened criminals. Darkness of the night resembled the blackness of his mind with an image of a streak of red that chilled his body into a frozen stance. He looked at the gun, opened the chamber and touched one of the six bullets that brought a blasting reminder of, *live by de bible or live by de gun.*

"I won't die, I won't die, I won't die."

Fear denied the reality of his true emotions. The more he repeated the words of courage, the more his chest burned with a similar terror to the one he experienced when he ran for his life.

He remembered being enveloped by bravado and heroism when he stood under the covering of the Holy Spirit, but now he felt like Samson and completely vulnerable to the enemy desiring his blood once his hair had been shaved by Delilah.

"Dad! Where are you?"

David pined for the strong tone of Charles shouting his name. He wanted to feel his powerful arms pick him up and carry him to safety, before the skinheads caught him and peeled his flesh with their blades.

"I don't know what to do! What shall I do?"

***

He saw flashing headlights in the distance that drew nearer to him and dived into the garden of a derelict house. His body was paralyzed by the numbness of terror and he clasped the gun and shuddered at the breaking of twigs under his body.

David heard the vehicle stop and car doors slam.

"I smell niggers! I know the smell of a nigger and there's one here!" shouted the driver.

David tried to move his legs, but they wouldn't respond to the command from his brain. His body was traumatized by being discovered and stabbed or hung from a tree, dangling and choking until death took his last breath.

"We've killed niggers before. Find the niggers, find the monkeys, find the rubber lipped bastards with shit for brains, I want them fucking dead!" said a skinhead.

David cowered under the bush, peering through the gaps at the skinhead walking in his direction carrying a machete. He daren't breathe when the skinhead stopped at his hiding place and he held his hand over his mouth and nose.

The blade that was thrust through the bushes whistled by his nose. He stared at the machete as it was slowly withdrawn and closed his eyes tightly. His face was in a muscle brace as he waited for the blade to come through the bushes again, cut open his flesh and draw his blood.

"Fucking niggers! I know they're here. We'll find you, niggers, we'll find you and fucking kill you."

Footsteps moved away from his turbulent heartbeats. The kicking of cans in the distance, sent relief to his fright, but his mind still despatched warning signals that he remained in a danger zone.

David took his hand from his mouth and nose and collapsed on the ground, breathing profusely. The adrenalin ran through his body and his chest wheezed with lungs that expanded and contracted, until his pulse slowed down and returned to two beats per second.

"I'm not dead, I'm not dead."

He looked over at the car of the skinheads that was still parked on the other side of the road. The bellowing of their racial slogans in the distance made him cover his ears to block out the recurring shouts of, "Nigger."

David crouched behind the bush and parted the leaves to see the dark road. He was in a quandary of laying low or running for his life. He knew that the skinheads would be walking back in his direction and thought, *if they find me, I'll use the gun and kill them before they kill me.*

***

"Get up, nigger! Fucking get your black backside up, nigger."

Cold steel pointed at David's head. It sent a spiral of cold sweat over every inch of his skin. The strong hand on his shoulder pulled him up from the wet grass where he'd urinated and he raised his hands in the air, shaking like a flower in the blustery winds.

"This is a mistake! I shouldn't be here, it's a mistake!"

The skinhead pressed the trigger and blew his tobacco breath on David's neck. David's heartbeats pounded through his chest and his stuttered breaths mingled with the frenzied voice of panic in his head that reinforced within seconds, he would be dead.

David closed his eyes, sensing a hunger for his blood. Spit dropped on his neck and the muscles in his body felt like they were evaporating as he shook like a man having an epileptic seizure.

"Turn around, nigger, I want to see your eyes before I fucking kill you!"

David turned around slowly to face the man who panted and grabbed him and then let go.

The skinhead took a lighter from his left jacket pocket and flicked it on. The glowing flame burned against David's eyelids. His entire body trembled as the skinhead pressed the gun into his forehead and twisted it into his skin.

Help, somebody help me.

He saw himself as dead unless he could reach for the gun under his jumper and shoot the skinhead in the stomach.

“Fucking nigger! Look at me nigger. Look at me, you fucking nigger!”

The skinhead flicked his lighter on again, peering at David’s face and pulling away with the gun shaking in his hand. He took a step backwards, leaned onto the tree and thumped the bark.

“Fuck! Fuck! Fuck! Fucking nigger! You fucking nigger!”

“Why did it have to be fucking you, nigger!”

David opened his eyes to meet the angry expression of his enemy standing opposite him. His eyes met in a transfixed gaze and he recognised that they’d met before, when he held the gun and the skinhead pleaded for his life.

“You’d better get the fuck out of here. If the others see you, you’re one dead fucking nigger. Go that way and don’t stop running.”

The skinhead hit the tree again and looked at David’s face one more time.

He pointed to the area where he’d instructed David to run and walked down the road to join the other gang members standing next to the car.

They raised their heads and one of them said, “Where have you been? Did you see the black bastards or not?”

"No, there are no fucking niggers, anywhere."

David watched from the bush and tears streamed down his face. He scratched his skin without wincing, stunned that he was alive when he knew he should be dead. His heart told him that it was God who'd ensured the life he spared was the life that spared him.

The revving of the car boomed against his eardrums and the smell of carbon monoxide lingered. He inhaled the fumes and didn't care that it was filling his lungs with poison. David touched the gun under his jumper. Confusion and disenchantment mixed with tremors doused his mind in a reflection of dumb and ill calculated anger.

David waved his fist in a revolt against his emotions for revenge that had made him stupid, waltz into the former hunting ground of salvation, and cross palms with Reggie to answer evil for evil without using his brainpower to better effect.

His mind awakened to the notion that fury could be a formidable driver if he channelled it in the right manner. He considered Reggie's existence that was based on ten- pound drug deals and a dingy youth club that gave him assumed authority over a small turf.

"I don't want to be Reggie, I want revenge, but not like this."

Holding onto the tree with both hands, he quivered and his mind spun in disbelief. He shouldn't be standing there, still breathing and feeling the wind blowing through his jumper. He studied the picture of the grave in his mind that had called for his death and knew that providence had denied the request, keeping him alive.

David ran down the pathway that the skinhead had told him to follow. His mind and his body were tired, but sheer fear maintained enough energy in his lungs to keep going.

The gun fell from his belt and he stooped to pick it up.

"Ray, I won't give up on you. I'll find the men who killed you and they'll pay the price. I won't let you die for nothing."

The rain stopped falling and he slowed down, holding onto a bricked wall to regain his breath. He stared at the unfamiliar streets and peered behind him, exhaling a breath that released the angst of the skinheads returning and this time showing no mercy as he battled to keep his life.

David touched his skin and imagined the permanent scar that would have told the world that he'd failed to live by the gun. In a gang it meant power, but in his belt, alone in the early hours of the morning it left him with fear and apprehension.

He took it from his waist and smelled the barrel. It had an aroma of being used before and it was in his hands, making him a suspect of a crime that he was convinced had been committed.

"God!" he shouted, placing the gun in his back pocket and covering it with his jumper.

***

Headlights flashed and the blue siren of the police car whirred in the distance. It was too late for him to run, so he kept walking, hearing the car draw nearer and it stopped in front of him. He moved his right hand to touch the gun in his back pocket and his stomach began to churn. A sensation of wooziness went to his head and his legs pleaded to give way to the nervous vault that electrified terror at another encounter with the law.

The policeman on the passenger side wound down his window and the driver got out the car. His colleague joined him and held onto his truncheon. He looked at David, who stood with his hands by his side and his face towards the ground.

"Hey you! What are you doing walking the streets at this time?"

They slammed the car doors and slowly advanced towards David. He raised his head and watched one of the policemen remove his truncheon. The other policeman touched his Darby handcuffs and David whispered in his mind, *this is it, I'm not going home tonight.*

"Did you hear me, we're talking to you. Why are you walking alone on the street?"

They stood in front of him and one of the policemen lifted David's chin and looked into his eyes.

David bit his trembling lip and his breaths mirrored the shivering of his body with the intimidation and menace debossing in his mind, that they had the power and it was better for him to keep his mouth shut.

"What's the problem, can't you talk? I'm asking you a question. What are you doing out here alone?"

He was locked in a cage of anguish and overpowered by fear. The tears fell down his cheeks as the truncheon was placed against his forehead. He had no authority to fight back and stood, squirming in helplessness. Cramps in his stomach pulled aggressively at his intestines and as the policeman's hand went on his shoulder, he knew that he was about to be searched.

God, no, they'll find the gun. I'll be arrested and locked up in a police cell.

"Disturbance at Holgate Road! Officers in the location get there now!" shouted the man through the radio in the police car.

"Shit! That's us, we'd better get out of here."

"You, go home, the streets are dangerous, do you understand, go home!"

David watched them jump into the police car and speed along the road with the siren screaming. He removed the gun from his pocket, quickly putting it back.

"Imagine if they would have searched me. What the hell am I doing out here!"

David threw imaginary punches in the air at his own stupidity. He kicked the wall, trying to break through the concrete and ignored the pain that shot through his foot.

"They're right, the streets are dangerous, I need to get home."

David began to run with fright and relief exchanging places in his mind. He could hear his bed calling where he pulled the sheets up to his chin and knew that he was safe. Blind anger had made him think with his heated emotions and he hit the side of his face to wake himself up and remember that Reggie's way of life, would take him to prison or hell.

He slowed down, back in familiar surroundings and he touched his back pocket.

"I need to get rid of this gun."

***

Stepping towards the entrance of the youth club, Reggae music bombarded his eardrums with a banging bass line of, "Rude boy gone to jail." Whiffs of Ganja and mixed herbs, flavoured with a 100% proof rum, mingled with the air at the doorway and he shook his head at the misapprehension, that the problems of ethnicity were solved on one draw of weed or a shot of rum.

His mind meditated on the psychological drop, when the effects wore off and reality came crashing back until the next inhale that went into the lungs and fuzzed up the brain with an irie sensation.

It's not real, one minute high, one minute low, I don't want a messed up mind.

David opened the youth club door and walked into the smog of flying high on the cloud of peace and love. He stepped on the Gold Label beer bottles that were strewn over the floor, drained to the last drop and in his mind symbolic of a celebration. He anticipated that victory must have been sweet for Reggie and his gang as they protected the small piece of earth, they called a territory or knuckled the skulls of their opposition.

"What de bumbaclaat! Fuckery! De devil is playing fucking black magic. Fucking black magic man!" shouted the youth club leader.

David covered his eyes from the dim lights that got brighter and the music reduced to a gentle vibration of the bass line. Eyes peered through the broken glass window, and the making out stopped as the youth club leader's reaction, focused attention on David who stood in the centre of the room.

"Bloodclaat! This must be a fuckin ghost."

The Rastafarian youth club leader walked over to David and touched his shoulder.

"Where's, Reggie? I want to see Reggie!"

David cushioned the fear through his aggressive tone and his body stance gave the impression he was ready for war. He glared at the two gang members who put their beer bottles on the table and stood bravely in their territory.

Looking at the faces of other gang members, he was prepared to challenge and fight his corner if he had to. He remembered, *they left me in the backyard of the skinheads to die*. David reached into his belt to retrieve the gun and he heard the metal against metal being drawn.

Reggie walked out of the backroom.

"Wait! Put your weapons down."

"What de fucking bumbaclaat are you doing back here!? You should be fucking dead, not fucking living!"

David stood fearlessly in the presence of Reggie and the gang members who whispered and reasoned with each other.

"I don't need your gun or your gang to make me someone."

He gaped at Reggie's eyes as he walked around him, knowing that an opposing enemy would have been taken outside and beaten until his brain spilled out on the pavement, yet he sensed that he had Reggie's admiration.

"This situation is not fucking real! A black man can't be left in skinhead land and come out alive," said one of the gang members.

Reggie took the gun from his hand and opened up the chamber. He wiped the gun with his red handkerchief and gave it to one of the girls to conceal.

"Go back to de bloodclaat church. You're not a fucking gangsta and if I see your face again, I'll be the one, dat pulls the trigger."

David stared at the charm bracelet around Reggie's wrist and gazed into his eyes. All of his nervousness was replaced by grit and after what he'd just endured he had nothing else to fear except himself.

He wanted revenge, but not on the terms of the gang code, a gang that he saw living on shekels. He didn't want to fight in this way to be heard and granted an existence because the white man allowed him too, living in the full knowledge that if he became an animal then eventually, he would be destroyed.

"Get out of here! Get de fuck out of this pussyclaat club and never come back or you're a fucking dead man!"

Reggie walked away and turned his head. David stood his ground.

"Why are you still here? Get the bloodclaat out of my house or I'll fucking kill you myself, God man!"

He's just like me. We all fear something and right now he's afraid.

David turned around and walked towards the exit. His ears twitched at the footsteps behind him, but he kept his eyes on the door handle. He twisted it and stepped out into the dark night, stumbling on the road and placing his hand on a car roof as he took a deep breath and walked away.

"This isn't over. Somehow, I'm going to find a way to make sure that you didn't die for nothing, Ray."

Chapter Nine

"David! Wake up, Elaine and Angela are on the phone," Mary said.

She waited at the bottom of the stairs, expecting him to stir from his sleep, pondering, *how can I get through to him and show him that God still loves him.*

"David, phone, come and answer it!"

"Get up."

She grabbed the banister, her knees knocked together and she gasped for breath when she reached the landing.

"David!"

Her voice repeated his name and refused to be ignored. She raised her hand and thumped the wood, knocking incessantly on his bedroom door and eventually barging into the room. She wanted to disturb the world that she saw as sin with him right in the middle of it and bring him back to the path of salvation.

"I don't want to speak to them."

Mary took hold of the cream bed sheet and ripped it from his head. She stared at him with an expression of measured anger.

“Don’t be disrespectful, these girls were your friends and they still care about you.”

Her eyes conveyed the disappointment in a wayward son. She’d prayed to God about his struggle and that he would find his way back to the fold instead of slipping down the slope that led to the gates of hell. Her heart was heavy that his passion for the church had been obliterated and his conviction for fairness and equality, no longer an ambition. Steaks of sadness had wormed its way into her soul, but her love for him couldn’t grow cold.

Her prayers had been heard the night that he came back in the early hours of the morning. She said in her mind, God*, thank you for sparing his life, so I didn’t hear the knock on the door that I was dreading.*

Charles came to David’s bedroom door and gazed into the room. Mary shook her head, pointed her finger and he kept his mouth shut.

Her shouting and berating worked when she had David’s respect, but now it was a thankless task, trying to save a son ablaze with vengeance. She wanted to get inside his head and assure him of a better future. It was pointless for the words of Jesus’s love that she repeatedly mentioned, left her wondering, *why can’t I get through to his heart.*

“Can’t you at least say hello to them? They’re not your enemies.”

David kissed his teeth and she could only shake her head rather than give him a friendly slap across his face. He barged past her and she helplessly watched him storm down the stairs to answer the phone.

I don't know him anymore. He was once filled with the Holy Ghost, but he came back from that torrid night filled with a legion of demons.

Her eyes watched him and her heart moved with joy as she reflected on him walking into the house and hugging him with her tears soaking through his jumper.

But he had no emotion and the way he looked at me through those angry eyes as if he despised what I am.

"What do you want?"

Mary walked down the steps stealthily in hope that Angela and Elaine could persuade him to receive spiritual help. She sat on the bottom stair, listening for one word from his lips that would confirm they'd made the breakthrough she wished for.

Mary clasped her hands together and touched her cross.

"Please, Lord Jesus, bring my son back to me, I'm afraid for his life," she whispered.

"David! Is it you? David, David!"

The sound of Angela's voice brought a smile to Mary's face. She was her desired daughter in law and she'd observed his attraction to Angela, and she saw the affection in her eyes when David stood at the pulpit and gave an uplifting speech to the congregation.

He could have his pick of any of the girls, but she's the one I want him to marry.

"David, I know your parents told you that the skinheads held in custody have been let go without charge. Ray's killer is still out there. We're having a vigil at the church, please come."

Mary reached out to touch his shoulder, mad at God for allowing demons to walk free without charge. She feared that with the killers still at bay how it would affect David's state of mind.

She knew that the shadow of light had quickly turned into a dark shade. Her dream of freedom and power overturned, leaving pandemonium in her mind.

The pulse in her wrist with a coordinated beat had responded to the revelation by racing faster than a motorbike speeding on the highway. Justice was within her grasp, but overpowered by a lack of integrity of the law that stamped its fist on her head and ignored her plea for the killers to be locked up.

"I can't believe they let them go! They arrested the killers! It has to be one of them," David said.

Mary held David's arm and misunderstanding and unfairness deepened her mistrust in a society where some lives mattered and others didn't.

David dropped the phone on the floor and the brown spiral cord dangled. She picked it up, hearing the whimpering of Angela and Elaine and accepting that even their bond with David, couldn't soften his heart.

"I should have pulled the trigger. I should have killed that skinhead, they're all guilty."

His declaration sent a thunderous shudder through her head that was already reeling with pounding tension. She was trusting God to avenge the death of Ray, but it seemed that he didn't care about her plight. He'd forgotten her and the faithfulness that she'd dedicated to the church. It seemed he preferred to let the wicked man continue to run riot, whilst her heart of oppression remained battered and tortured day and night.

"David, come to the vigil, we need to stand together and pray so Ray's killer will be found."

Mary understood David's pain because her prayers hadn't yet yielded God's vengeance.

God, when will you wake up and give us justice and bring my son back home to me?

It was a façade where a strand of hope was kept dangling in front of her eyes to create an expectation that appeared impossible to realise. Her faith was being challenged. Uncertainty and doubt took over and sprinkled her mind with thoughts of, *does God love the evil man more than the young black man, and has he neglected David?*

David took the phone from her hands.

"Don't call me again. I told you before to forget that you know me. I hate everything that's black, it's just an evil curse."

David slammed the phone down and disconnected it.

Mary touched his arm.

"So, what now, you hate your parents? We're black and proud of the colour, God made us."

She looked into his eyes, empathising with his sentiment. She'd studied the history books and read about black enslavement. The experience of the white man feeding her morsels and allowing her to enter his country and exist as a second-class citizen, rose up from her subconscious and she remembered, *it killed my hope of being so much more.*

She'd asked God repeatedly how it was possible that an entire race could be suckered into believing, that they had equal status when they controlled nothing and lacked power to create change in a white dominated society.

Her recollection of the moment that she'd entered the UK and being subjected to racism resurged in her memory. The chants of, *nigger go home on your banana boat*, resurfaced. She recalled feeling fooled by the myth of streets being paved with gold, when the reality of renting a dilapidated house in a poor area was all the white man would allow her to have.

"I don't hate you as people, I hate the colour black and everything that it symbolises. Poverty, disease, powerlessness and all that is dark and gloomy."

Mary knew that he had a point. Her mind had been conditioned into accepting that being rich and successful was only for white people. There were no examples of anyone she knew in or outside the church who was black and enjoyed the same benefits as the white middle and upper class.

The blacks that she knew couldn't assist their children in education. They lacked the money to pay for private schooling and a university education as she did. Their ambition to be anything else above working class, destroyed, just as her desire to go further in life had been killed by a weight of persecution.

She grabbed David's arm, preventing him from running up the stairs.

"David, what happened on the night when you came home late?"

She followed him up the stairs to his room, blocking his escape from the fifty questions that were firing through her head. She desperately wanted to know the confrontations that he'd been involved in, and if the police were going to break down the door and make her faint when they informed that he was involved in a serious crime.

"That was the night when I finally realised what it was like to be black and be completely powerless."

He walked around her and she grabbed the door handle, gazing into his eyes. Hope faded in her heart and she was unsure whether to hug him or go to her room and pray for a miracle.

Mary refused to move and now she knew how it really felt to have a child that you'd lost, rather than listening to the pitiful son and daughter stories of other church goers.

"Come to the vigil, I'm pleading with you to come."

She let go of the door handle and he walked into his bedroom and turned around to face her.

"Ray's killers were let loose and it has to be one of them. They're roaming the streets, knowing that they can kill a black man and get away with it. So, what happens now? What can you and your other black folk do? Pray!"

The truth hit Mary squarely between her eyes and she had no answer. Prayer was always her solution despite not seeing the immediate impact and her petition to God answered.

The just will live by faith and not by sight, she thought. It was the mantra that had been hammered into her brain by the priest until she believed it.

"Don't you get it! I don't care about your stupid church. You're foolish black people, brainwashed by a white man who doesn't even like you!"

Mary's facial muscles tightened and then twitched with a cutting sensation under her skin.

"If I'd dared to speak to my mother like this, my face would have been stinging for two weeks and my body lashed by the thin tree branch."

She wanted to slap him and apply discipline as she'd received. Her hands were clenched behind her back, because she wanted to put her fist against his head and ram sense into his brain, but as she looked at his face her heart hummed with compassion.

"Get out of this house! Get out! Mary, tell your son to leave today!"

She watched the door being shut in her face and stood in solitary confinement, gazing at the piece of wood that separated her from smothering David with an embrace of kindness.

Her tears didn't fall and she longed for the child she knew to come back home. He was there, hurting like a wounded tiger, but still her son despite the misdemeanours she assumed he'd been involved in.

"Let him be, Charles. There's nothing we can do for him. It's all up to God now," she shouted.

Mary walked down the stairs and joined Charles in the living room. All she had left was her faith in God. She tried to keep believing that he would hear her lamenting and be merciful.

But God is merciful, she thought.

What about the time when Charles had cancer and the church brothers and sisters came to the hospital and prayed for him.

Her lips curled into a smile of gratitude for God had answered her prayer and brought healing to his body. As she reflected on the miracle, she recommitted David into the hands of the lord and intensified her belief that the killer of Ray would be found and brought to trial.

She looked across at Charles, recognising the glare when his blood was running high because of David's impudence.

"Charles, let it go. We need to go to the vigil and pray for Ray."

Judge not less you be judged yourself. The seeds that you sow, that is what you reap.

Are we reaping what we've sowed?

Her reflections took her back to the generations of her family where history had repeated itself. She reminisced on her brother who'd been murdered in Kingston by a Yardi gang, and a cousin that was put under a curse from the Obeah man and died in his own vomit. Terror struck her mind and caused her body to shake with panic that David was next in line to fall under a spell of witchcraft, unless she could persuade God to break it.

She went upstairs to her bedroom, removed her wig, grabbed the yellow headscarf from the chair to cover her head and prostrated on the floor.

"God, I remember giving birth to David at twenty-four and I knew he was special then, and you had a purpose for his life, you've got to help him."

Her body quivered from the thumping on the wall and items being dropped on the floor in David's bedroom. She raised her head from the intercession and wondered, *which demon is tormenting him now.*

"I'm not black, I don't want to be black, I hate the colour black!"

"Lord, what can I do to help David? Is it my sin why these curses are also on my family?"

The anguish in his voice stirred every emotion in her body. She wanted to open the door and assure him that things would work together for good. The line from the bible that had sprung into her mind right now was a lie. She couldn't guarantee that Ray's killer would be caught. She couldn't affirm that if he came back to the church, then suddenly God's power would be manifested and the unfairness to the black race changed forever.

Her spirit became numb from the brain tension. Questions kept coming and attacking her knowledge of what she believed to be true.

"God, why do black people suffer so much across the world? Why did you let a racist skinhead kill Ray, a child of God?"

Her toes danced with the dark blue carpet as she waited for a revelation. Her lamentation opened up challenges to the doctrines of, "God is love and he will deliver you from your enemies." Her emotions were the same as David's. She couldn't dismiss his cry that opened her memory to despise that not only came from white people, but also from black people in Jamaica.

Mary recalled that in the parishes of St Elizabeth, the Jamaicans who were light skinned called her a quarchi because she was dark. They saw themselves as superior to blacker complexions, and she remembered, *some of them even called themselves white.*

"God, don't you see, not only is David in danger because of the white racists, but he's also in danger because of other black people. You've got to deliver him, please save him!"

She got up from the floor and went to the olive brown dressing table, placing her fingernail in the chipped wood and gazing at her face in the mirror. Picking up her small King James Bible, she turned the page to Romans chapter eight verse twenty-eight.

"All things work together for good, for those that love the lord."

"Will it, God? Will all things work together for good?"

Chapter Ten

A light bulb switched on his mind to a woman with a gentle touch. David walked over to the brown wardrobe with the door that slightly hung off its hinges and rummaged through the suit jacket pocket that he wore at Ray's funeral, removing the note and gazing at the name Abbie and her phone number. His fingers ran over the letters of a stranger and he remembered the rough edges of his heart being soothed, and a serene running stream that replaced the volcanic eruption in his head.

"Abbie, a white girl!"

A lot of white people are evil and she could be evil.

His heart didn't connect to the thoughts of her being a person of malevolence. He looked at the phone number, in two minds of whether to make the call. The motivation of finding answers pushed him to seek help, despite his reservations of confiding in a white girl who he knew nothing about and didn't trust her intentions.

He walked down the stairs, picking up the phone and dialling the number, quickly ending the call.

Mistrust crept into his mind as he imagined that she had a fascination with black people, driven from a heart of self-pity and ulterior motives. Yet, the more he thought about her, his curiosity increased and he tentatively picked up the phone and rang the number again.

"Hello, can I speak to Abbie please?"

David's heart strings fluttered with excitement, but also with fear. He saw her as a potential wolf clothed as a sheep, but was mesmerised by her inquisitiveness. He moved the phone away from his mouth and breathed into his jacket to stop his nerves from escalating and turning him into a babbling fool.

"Hello, who's this?"

He dropped the phone that clanged against the small table, hearing the continuous hellos that sounded like she was singing a love melody in a solo dedication to him. He picked up the phone, his heart panted and he listened to her perfect and pronounced speech. He didn't know why he'd called her and tapped his head in annoyance at becoming a fool, for ringing a white girl who had nothing in common with him.

David ended the call and stepped on his left foot with his right. The pain reminded him that black had no relationship with white. Within a few minutes, he plucked up a blade of courage and rang again, pressing the phone against his right ear and nervously waiting for Abbie to answer.

"Hello," he said with a soft tone.

Silence was at the end of the phone and he tried to breathe quietly, but his gasps were a clear indication that he was nervous. He waited like an obedient pooch, anticipating the command of the master to move and fetch the ball. His mind had thoughts zooming from one end to the other and he clutched the banister to keep his body from becoming a trembling wreck.

"I recognize your voice, who is it?"

David picked up the brown figure numbering telephone, stretching the cable and walked into the front room with a bounce in his steps. His skin itched and his shoulders jerked sharply at the key turning in the lock and Charles and Mary returning from a prayer group meeting. It was all in his imagination and he was still alone, listening to the birds tweeting and watching the branches of the trees blowing in the gusts of wind. He lay down on the sofa, stretching his feet that exposed his right toe through the hole of his grey sock and he smiled at hearing her voice for the third time.

"It's, David, we met at my friend's funeral."

"David! I never thought that you'd ring me!"

He reflected on Abbie who'd come to his rescue, rather than cross the street and pretend like a black life wasn't important. He found her attendance at the funeral bizarre, almost as if fate had cast her into his pathway. He turned to his side and then onto his back. David stiffened his body with his mind messaging his lips that curled into a broad smile as he pressed the phone against his ear to talk to Abbie, who previously would never have got his attention.

"So, how are you? What have you been up to?"

He heard a man bark an instruction and slam the door. A woman, who he assumed to be her mother shouted goodbye. His chest released heat and the sweat stuck to his fingers which he wiped on the plastic cover of the sofa. The nerves started to run up his spine and his throat was parched and in need of water to soothe his vocal chords.

"I'm so sorry about your friend. I saw on the news that the police had let the skinheads go, it's completely wrong!"

"This is an injustice and it needs to be made right."

Her voice sounded genuine and David closed his eyes, at last experiencing a connection to someone since Ray's death. He listened to her tone and her words of empathy that were like a tonic to his inflicted mind. His breathing became gentle patters, and he bathed in his emotions of intrigue that began to spark different sensations over his body.

"I made a promise to Ray that I won't rest until his killers are captured. I want all of them to die, I want them to die!"

He heard Abbie's footsteps in the background and listened for a response. Soft breaths drummed against his ears and whispered a gentle breeze of calmness into his mind. He sat up, waiting for her to answer. A blend of emotions quizzed him to respond to why he was looking for help in the wrong places when he could stand on his own two feet, but that belief didn't seem true when he was at a loss of the next steps that he should take.

"Your anger is your worst enemy. You need to be calm rather than exploding like a volcano. I can help you if you want me to."

I was right, she's a sympathiser, looking for a cause to belong to.

Putting the phone down on the sofa, he went to the kitchen and drank from the bottle of orange juice in the fridge. Charles had told him to never trust white people and that he had to be better than them. All white people deep down are racist, were the words he'd overheard at different functions, until they sank into his subconscious mind.

But it's not true. There's good and bad in all races.

David walked back to the front room and picked up the phone.

"How can you possibly help me? You don't know me or know anything about where I come from."

The silence resumed on the phone, except for her footsteps that reminded him of someone trampling on a wooden floor. He heard a door close and pondered, *why am I still talking to her when she hasn't answered my question.*

"How can you help me to find Ray's killers?"

"Shush! You've got too much tension and hate and it will destroy you. You're like a time bomb that will explode and Ray's death will never be avenged, because you'll be dead."

"Who are you to give me advice. You probably came from a wealthy background and were born with a silver spoon in your mouth."

His teeth clenched to suffocate the anger and he wanted to put the phone down and tell her to go to hell and stop meddling in matters beyond her power to change. Yet, her words were spoken with a clarity that resonated in his mind, and he couldn't resist being drawn into a web where he desired to know more of who she was.

"Why don't we meet up for a coffee? You can come over, near me."

"I don't know where you live."

The tussle began in his mind, taking him down a lane of placing his trust in a girl where he had no idea of her story.

I should just put the phone down. Why am I still on the phone talking to you.

"There's a cafe on Newman Road, Hampstead. I can meet you in two hours and then we can talk."

He banged the phone against his forehead, knocking sense back into his distorted mind and remembering, *black and white don't mix and she's a means to an end, that's all.*

"David, are you still there? So, I'll meet you in two hours then?"

"Yes, I'll be there and don't waste my time."

Chapter Eleven

The Brut Faberge cologne, a present from one of his many admirers from the church dripped down his neck. His face, coated with astral cream gave a gloss to his brown skin. A girl called Abbie, with an attractive smile wouldn't leave his mind. He knew that Charles would experience an aneurysm if he established that he was somehow entertaining an interlude, with a white girl.

David's attention focused on his great, great grandmother who'd been raped by a Scotsman in a drunken state.

My God, she even had a child, half black and half white.

"Dad told me about the graphic details of a white man abusing her and when she fought back, he punched her in the face and ripped her tights and knickers off and raped her."

The story stirred up a passionate rage and a vow to never let white intrude into his personal life. His mind went back into past conversations that had shaped his views of the world and that he believed were true.

"I'll never forget the lecture at age thirteen when dad told me, never bring a white girl home, black sticks with black."

"But those words were strange, considering that he's serving under a white priest in the church. God must have put him there to deal with his reverse racism."

David understood Charles's anger and shook his head that he'd been coaxed into believing that you should love all men, even those who were evil and had left him and his family with a lasting painful memory. It seemed to him that in places the human body with its emotions that had been affected by tragedy could never be healed by the spirit.

He was aware of many other black families, who carried similar stories in their hearts and passed down the misfortune of an unfortunate victim, and infected the minds of their children with hate.

Black people can never be branded as racists, but if you hate someone because of their colour, doesn't that make you racist? David had considered this question before, but the possibility of ever being connected to a white girl was unfathomable.

"I'm daydreaming. I must stop behaving like I'm in a relationship with her. She says she can help me to capture Ray's killers and that's it, nothing more."

***

As he turned the key in the front door, he wrapped his blue scarf around his neck. He'd never been to Hampstead and neither did he know any ethnic minorities living in that location. The vicinity, he recalled was inhabited by the wealthy business people, such as doctors and lawyers and they were all white.

He compared it to East and South London, with its high-rise blocks, graffiti on the buildings and under-privileged communities.

The deliberation stopped him in his tracks and it brought him back to the great divide of who she was, and the lack of choice that he'd been given about which family he was born into and where he grew up.

David turned back around to go home, but urgency pressed his will to forget his pride and at least hear what Abbie had to say.

***

"A return ticket to Hampstead please."

He looked into the black attendant's eyes, observing mystification as he took the ticket from his hands.

David headed towards the underground and turned around. He gazed at the black man and his light skinned colleague.

His mind dwelled on the mistake of black and white committing a crime or another rape that produced half cast, a race of no identify.

Getting on the tube, he visualised two people who seemed satisfied with their place in society, merely printing tickets all day and accepting that life would never get any better than this. It gave him confirmation of the status that black people could reach and any ambition to pursue a bigger dream, a massive no.

The accidental step on his foot by the woman sitting next to him, switched his focus back to Abbie and not condemnation of a man and woman that he didn't know.

This is crazy. Why am I doing this?

David checked the tube stops, looking out for the signs to Hampstead. He mulled over Abbie's claim that she could help him in his quest for justice. *Maybe she knows the killer, maybe it's a trap.* He had nowhere else to turn except follow his instinct and trust that it would lead to peace.

The tube slowed down and the doors opened. David watched people exiting. He left his seat and pressed the open button before the tube doors closed and the driver drove to the next destination. Walking slowly towards the steps leading to the High street, he ignored the awkward stares that seemed to suggest that he might be lost.

David jumped at the beep from a driver of a red Mini Cooper and gazed at the red double-decker buses, black cabs and cars streaming along the High Street.

The late morning air blew on his face. Tall grey lampposts seemed as high as the stone washed buildings, with their long slender windows and business addresses that tempted him to have a peek inside. He watched the busy road with trees nosing the electric cables and bustling with people of different sizes and shapes, that like him he assumed were looking for a destination point.

I don't belong here, I need to leave.

He looked around for just one brown face, but all he saw was a sea of white.

Turn back. I don't mix with white people, I can't trust them.

His stomach swilled with gas as he walked along the High street. He stopped at Sam Cook's grocers, watching the shopkeepers in their white coats busily serving customers. They reminded him of doctors in a hospital and the only difference was their healing potion was food and not medicine.

David followed the directions that Abbie had given him. His insecurities made him believe that some passers-by deliberately crossed the road, because a nigger had been loosed from his cage.

He saw the Coffee Lounge next to Speed Queen Coin Wash and headed towards it. Patrons sat outside on the green padded wooden stools and he wondered, *should I wait outside or go inside*? He looked behind him at the pub reading the word courage and thought*, I need a strong dose of that now. I'll wait inside, I don't want people staring at me.*

***

The server took the customer orders and a woman smiled at him as he sat down in the corner. A nervous energy ran through his body and he was uncertain if her smile was one of friendship or shock. Never had he felt so alone and so vulnerable in a country that had been his home for almost eighteen years.

Cups and saucers chinked together and coins rattled in the cash desk, creating more unease in his mind.

Customers took away their crisps, cakes and coffees and scurried to the empty tables. He had an impression that some were trying to sit far away from him in fear of catching a contagious disease, whilst others gazed at him with welcoming smiles.

David breathed in the aroma of an unaccustomed ambience and searched each corner for Abbie. He couldn't see her anywhere in the Coffee Lounge, and became annoyed that he'd taken the bait and put himself out in the open to be viewed as if he was some weird spectacle.

He closed his eyes and blocked out the uncomfortable stares. Ray came back into his mind and he imagined the cussing that he would be giving him right now for contemplating switching to the other side. He recalled the conversation about the dilution of colour. The lecture reminded him of being black through and through and never losing sense of his identity.

David's face radiated a glowing smile as he remembered the dreams that he and Ray shared when they tumbled down the hillside freely as lambs, bounding across the fields.

***

"Hello, David, how are you?"

The sweat behind his ears ran down his neck and mingled with the Faberge Cologne aftershave that he'd sprayed on to create an alluring fragrance. His backside felt like he was sitting on hot coals being stoked to make the fire even more intense. He stared at the table and then at the menu board, unable to look at her face that emitted confidence and an unassuming arrogance that she knew best and he didn't.

"How can you help me to find Ray's killers?"

The coffee cake being eaten by a woman caught her attention. She wouldn't stop smiling at David, which impressed upon him that she was rather comfortable in his presence, just as if they were familiar acquaintances. He wasn't in the mood for idle chatter, he wanted to get the facts and then get out of an environment where he didn't belong.

"Let me buy you a cup of coffee and you can share a slice of coffee cake with me."

Abbie walked to the counter and his head turned in her direction. He gazed at the blue jacket that she wore and the matching headband. His eyes wandered to her three-quarter length jeans and cream coloured flat shoes. He stopped at her slim waistline and stared at her small, but firm looking backside that turned his mind into a mixing pot of erotic thoughts. David knocked his knuckles against his forehead and pinched his skin to cancel any entertainment of dicing with the enemy.

He moved his legs closer together, experiencing a rise in his underpants that refused to obey his command. These were feelings that he'd been warned about that always seemed to be a great man's downfall, but he was the same, unable to resist the artistry of her body. He was attracted to it, desired it and his emotions were confused. He hated what she represented, but magnetically was being drawn in with a diminishing desire to leave.

She reminded him of the forbidden fruit from the tree of knowledge of good and evil. The warnings to stay away and to not mix made it even more difficult with the opportunity sitting right in front of him. His mind wanted to stay focused on the reason for meeting her, but his heart desired to know how it felt to kiss a white girl, touch her breasts and caress her milky white skin, until she intertwined her body with his and took what a black woman had been unable to take.

"You know, you could do a lot better than that," muttered the male server.

She took her change, wiped her hands on a tissue and dropped it in the bin next to the counter.

The server peered over at David and shook his head. His look of disgust made it clear to David that white had no place with black.

Abbie turned and smiled at David before turning to face the server.

"I know exactly what you mean, but the difference between you and David, is that he's a real man and you have no idea what he's been through."

She walked back over to David and placed the two cups of coffee and coffee cake on the table. David watched her pour the milk into his cup without asking if he wanted milk. She cut a piece of the cake and bit into it, licking the traces of the cream off the knife and then offering a piece to David who said, "No thank you, I don't like coffee cake."

"I don't have a lot of time and I feel uncomfortable sitting here with you."

Abbie slurped her coffee and ate another piece of the coffee cake.

David gazed at her face, checked his watch and puffed his cheeks.

She doesn't care about anybody's opinions. Who is this woman. What's wrong with her.

She reminded him of being a free spirit, untarnished by the expected conformities of society and she portrayed a character that drew David in with intrigue. He shook his head in resignation that she wasn't the type of person to be rushed into a discussion. The terms were hers and he either liked it or he walked away.

"Why do you feel uncomfortable sitting at this table with me? Who are you, David?"

The irritation began to burn in his brain. He became psychologically unseated at the intense digging into the depths of his mind. Yet, she made him think more than anybody else had done, and his brain searched for the subconscious emotions that created his feelings of uneasiness.

"I'm a black man called nigger by you white people. I'm sitting in a Coffee Lounge surrounded by white people who are all wondering why I'm here. How would you feel if you were me?"

"Hmm. Has every white person you've met called you a nigger? Have you asked all the white people in the Coffee Lounge if they're wondering why you're here?"

She kept her head down and he mused on the debates being stirred up in his head. He remembered who he wanted to be when he read through his dreams which didn't reflect how he'd described himself to Abbie. It was true that he didn't know what all the customers were thinking, but had made an assumption that it was all about him.

The penny dropped and his mind became alight by reasoning of what he was and who he didn't want to be. He wanted a much better life where he soared beyond his reality. With Ray's demise the sludge was trapping his feet in the mud and as he looked at Abbie, he recognised how broken he was, without an idea of the path to take that would lead to greener pastures and help him to make right out of wrong.

"David, your race has a major chip on their shoulders. You think that the world owes you something and it doesn't. Yes, there are racist people in the world, get over it. You are downtrodden because you choose to be. Life gives you what you create in your thoughts. To have something different, think and act differently."

"It's deplorable what happened to Ray, but anger and bitterness won't bring him back. The question for you is, what will you do that breaks down racial barriers and makes the world a better place to live in?"

His eyes never left hers and the passion of her words felt like they were eating into his mind. He'd never experienced anyone challenge his thinking in such a way before. She ignited his imagination with the memory of his mission that had set his soul on fire to destroy inequality.

He wiped his lips. His eyes stared with anger against her portrayal of years of oppression that still existed today. He couldn't forget the chains of slavery and the beatings of the past that still manifested in the present day, with a different shade. His blood became overheated at a white person trying to tell him what he should do when she'd never been in black skin.

"I don't know what your game is, but I don't have time for your lectures. You're a white girl, born with a silver spoon in your mouth and you behave like you know the plight of the black race!"

Abbie sipped her coffee, took another bite of the cake and licked the knife again.

Who the hell does she think she is. She can't help me and I need to get out of here.

Abbie smiled at David. His rage was at boiling point and his nostrils flared as he fastened his jacket. He kicked himself for not listening to Charles's warning and staying away from white women.

"There you go again, making judgements and characterising me by your limited understanding of who I really am. You're a nigger because that's what you believe yourself to be. You've allowed yourself to become what others have decided that you are."

His hands trembled on the table. His mind was blazed with fury and he wanted to shout his dissent in the Coffee Lounge.

Marked by patronisation, he couldn't understand why he was finding her increasingly fascinating. He wanted to leave and stay. Fidgeting in his chair, he became calm and then incensed again as condescension pricked his pride. David kissed his teeth, tied the blue scarf around his neck and pushed the chair back against the wall, standing up to leave.

Abbie placed her cup on the saucer, grabbed his arm and said, "Where do you think that you're going? This conversation is far from over, just sit down."

She tugged his jacket and to avoid a scene that gave the impression of two lovers having a disagreement, he begrudgingly sat down. The veins pulsated in his brain at the disrespect that she'd shown him, but it was the truth that pierced his heart and inflamed anger, because he knew that every word that she'd spoken was right.

"Just say what you have to say and I'll leave."

He was convinced that she had psychological issues. David stared into her green eyes and thought, *go on, what are you going to say now to try and humiliate me even more.*

"Let's start again. My name is, Abbie Butler, and I live with my parents Clive and Rose who are barristers. I'm 19 and I'm at the London University studying history."

She held out her hand and David waited for a few seconds before responding.

"I'm, David Morgan, the friend of a murdered black man and I will get revenge for his death."

Abbie reached into her handbag and removed an envelope.

She opened the envelope and removed pictures of two black girls and a young black man. She pointed to a makeshift grave on another photograph that was engraved with the words, "They shall never take our freedom."

"I was raised in South Africa and these were my friends. The two girls were raped and murdered by white men, and the young man who we buried was gunned down by the white police unlawfully."

She ran her fingers across the faces of the girls and the man on the photos. A tear trickled down her face and landed on the envelope.

David leaned towards her, opening his mouth to express condolences, but the words that he thought he couldn't speak. His mind aligned to the torment of innocent blood being shed, and his emotions of dissent towards her changed into feelings of sorrow and compassion.

David sat quietly; lost in a myriad of deliberations at the first white person he'd met who just might be able to relate to him. He wanted to take her hand and stop the quivering. He reflected on the horrific experience that she'd shared and tried to imagine how it must have felt for her to lose three friends so brutally.

That was a curse that he could relate to and he recognised that they did have common ground.

"I'm really sorry that your friends were murdered."

David took her hand and unashamedly stroked her skin. Now he appreciated the sorrow and pain that was still lodged in his heart.

Gazing at Abbie, his affinity grew towards her for she was like him, using tragedy as a motivation to arise and fight against hatred.

“You see, I do understand your situation. I know what it feels like to lose friends that you love to racism. I knew that the national front party and the Skins for Life would be there in Skegness and I’ll always make my stance against injustice.”

“So, what are you? Are you a freedom fighter?”

The barriers that he’d built up fell down. He found himself emotionally gravitating into her space, standing in her shoes and without care for whispers or disapproval of patrons in the Coffee Lounge. Now he understood her circumstances, he regretted judging a book by its cover. David loosed himself from his misperceptions and he was happy that he’d allowed humility to keep him in the Coffee Lounge.

“Yes, David, It’s about freedom, freedom from injustice and oppression. It’s about taking a stance against those who think that they can abuse, because they don’t like the colour black or any other skin colour.”

David was still holding her hand, locked in a place where their paths had been strewn with a similar casualty of life. His attitude changed towards comradeship rather than a fight between black and white. He was drawn to her and embracing unity, dropping the barriers and respecting their similarities and differences.

Dad's wrong about white women, they're not all the same.

"Abbie, I'm sorry that I misunderstood you. Can you help me to find Ray's killers and bring them to justice?" he said, letting go of her hand, writing his number on a piece of paper and giving it to her.

His persona became subdued. He had a nervous confidence that he wasn't on his own and help was available to him if he enabled trust to be his driving force, rather than hate.

Raising his head, a broad smile stretched across his cheeks and he was relieved that even though he was unsure of his direction with Abbie, there was a lantern where the light had grown brighter and he decided to follow his heart rather than his head.

"David, we've both suffered wrongdoing at the hands of evil people. I'm glad that you met me and I believe we can help each other."

He smiled, gazing into her eyes and the tenseness of his body that was there at the beginning of their conversation had gone. The wall of divide had been pulled down and he concentrated on the moment where he'd made a connection with Abbie, and he wished that he could remain longer to become more acquainted with who she was.

"I apologise again. I misunderstood you and I'm really sorry for the murders of your friends."

The heat emanating through his skin was intense. He looked at her face and turned away as the embarrassment of his increasing attraction stole his tongue.

She put her hand on his arm.

"We have to break down the racist institutions. One of those is the police force in the UK, its racist to the core."

He nodded, reflecting on the stories he'd heard about police brutality and the racial abuse people in the church had talked about.

"It's true. There are racist policemen in the force."

His eyes locked in a gaze and his mind swirled with information that began to showcase the police for who they really were.

"The question is, David, what are you going to do about it?"

She called the server over and he cleared the table, leaving David mesmerised, but in deep concentration on the challenge she proposed.

She's right. The police made arrests of suspects linked to Ray's murder and then let them go due to insufficient evidence, so they say.

He analysed the facts and they didn't line up. He found it inconceivable that a black man could be murdered in the dusk of the day, and the police to this point were unable to find the perpetrators of the crime.

"Let's go."

David followed, watching her small pert backside, but putting the physical attraction aside. He caught up with her and she linked her arm with his. The awkwardness had gone and he fearlessly rejected the stares from a man and a woman who quickly walked by them. She'd opened his eyes and he saw the only colour that existed was colour.

"I'm glad that I came to meet you, what do we do now?"

She placed her other hand on David's arm and squeezed tighter. He began to smile and the weight in his heart lifted. His mind was free of pressure as they strolled leisurely through Hampstead. No plan had been formed, but he had hope that arose with a belief that Ray's death wouldn't merely fade to the back of the Evening Standard and The Illustrated London News.

They arrived at the tube station and she let go of David's arm. She leaned over and kissed him on the cheek.

"I want to see you again. Remember, the police force is a racist institution and they know what's really going on with Ray's killers."

She left, making her fingers into a signal of a phone and pointed at David.

He watched her walk along the road, transfixed on her movements and hoping that she would turn around. He knocked his head with his fist to check if the real David was still at home. He'd gone away and he knew that he had an ally in Abbie.

Sliding down the railing he almost lost his balance as he landed on the floor. He laughed and mimicked Abbie's skip, acting like a complete idiot, but without a care for who was watching.

"Here's my return ticket back to South London."

He walked through the barriers and went down the escalators to the tube.

"She's different. I've never met anyone like her and I have to see her again."

"Sorry, did you say something to me?" said a man.

David shook his head, got on the tube and took a seat, staring out of the window at the darkness that broke into light. He reflected on the challenge that Abbie had laid down and he agreed with her perspective that the institutions, whether they were schools, colleges, the police force or the workplace all bred racism. The desire of retribution for Ray hadn't left his heart, but something kept stirring and imprinting into his mind that there was a bigger cause.

What am I going to do about it? What can I do about it?

The tube driver pulled into South London and David got off the tube. Walking quickly, his mind was churning with Ray, the Skinheads and the police.

He arrived home, turned the key in the lock of the front door and bounded upstairs without acknowledging Charles and Mary. Laying on the bed, he clutched the dark brown and blue bed cover, thinking, *it's evil what happened to Abbie's friends. We both have suffered and she understands me and I understand her.*

After their conversation, he had clarity that he couldn't take an approach of blood and guts. *I need to be calm, find a hole and rip it open to find Ray's killers. Someone knows something and I've got to find out what it is.*

"But how do I do it?"

Chapter Twelve

The knock on his bedroom door startled David and he pulled the cover over his head to block out the repeated yelling of his name. He murmured, looking at the time and dreading having to go back to St Andrews College.

Mary opened the door gently and switched on the light.

"There's someone called Abbie on the phone, she sounds like a white girl, who's Abbie?"

Tiredness and fatigue suddenly left his body and he ran downstairs to answer the call. He saw Charles reading the Jamaican weekly Gleaner newspaper and peering over at him. David closed the sitting room door and picked up the phone with his heart beating with excitement.

"Hello, Abbie, how are you? I wasn't sure if you were going to ring me."

Turning around he looked up the stairs at Mary, anticipating the harsh discussion that would come after his phone call ended.

"Why didn't you think I would ring? I don't believe in breaking my promises. Anyway, I want to see you again."

David's skin began to burn and he rubbed his neck, lost for words and acting like a little boy who'd just wet his pants in the classroom.

"Well, I didn't know if you would call, that's all."

His knees knocked together uncontrollably and he curled his toes in his blue socks. A drip of sweat ran down his chest and he tried to scratch the irritable itch in the centre of his back.

Charles opened the door and stared at him. David looked up, his body shivered and the message of *white is evil* thumped in his head as Charles pointed his finger and closed the door.

"I want to see you today. What time can I come over to see you and I'm not accepting no for an answer?"

"What! You want to come over to where I live? I have to go to college today and I'm not sure, hmm, I need to think about it."

It was one thing when he had to pluck up the courage to go over to Hampstead where he was an unknown entity, but Abbie coming over to South London in his backyard put stress on his brain. He didn't want to entertain the implications of being accused of selling out.

He put the phone receiver on the phone stand, stood up and walked along the hallway, brushing his hand along the light grey and pink wallpaper and considered the characteristics of Abbie that he'd observed. Musing on her brazen display of confidence and lack of care for what others thought that deeply concerned him, put his mind in a state of dread. He twisted his head from side to side with the accusing eye ramming *you're a traitor,* into his brain.

Back at the phone stand, he sat down on the step and listened to her purring breaths as she waited for an answer. His mind struggled with being out in the light rather than being hidden in the dark. He toyed with telling her no and preferred to take the coward's way out to save himself from the inevitable scrutiny of judgement.

"David, I can read your mind and I anticipated this. I thought that after our conversation, your eyes would have been opened, but I was wrong. You're not the person I thought you were, goodbye."

The dialling tone persisted and he banged the head of the phone.

"Abbie."

His eyes opened wider and his top lip touched his nose.

"Did she just put the phone down on me!"

She did.

He wasn't in the mood for a joke. David put the phone back onto the receiver, waiting and drumming his fingers against the wall. He picked the phone up, unscrewed the head and replaced it, hit hard by a dose of reality. The truth in his heart filtered into his mind with a reminder that he was apprehensive of being associated with a white girl and one pleasant day in Hampstead, wasn't going to dislodge it.

David slowly dialled her number and his fingers twitched. The fear and the opinions and judgements of others bit into his head with a visual of looks and glares.

Ridicule and abuse painted his imagination with the fallout of being a coconut, and he could hear the nagging voice in his mind that told him, *walk away and forget her*. The magnetism that had enticed him wouldn't allow a simple ending of the call, when he was still experiencing a strong pull to follow the path and see where it led to.

"Can I speak to Abbie please?"

The silence continued and he wanted to end the call, but stopped, resisting his desire to disconnect. He disliked the picture that whirred in his mind of cowardice. It accused him of being happy to go to Hampstead where the chances of being spotted by a black person that he knew were remote. His body juddered at the notion of walking through South London, in predominantly black neighbourhoods with a white woman, when black sticks with black was a principle that had been driven into his soul.

"It's Abbie, what do you have to say to me?"

"I'm sorry. All I could see was every black person I know hating me. I just panicked. We can meet in the Battersea Country Park at the Guinness Festival Clock at 1.00pm."

His heart was still beating at pace as he listened to her wittering. He pondered, *have I lost my mind.* David knew he should probably heed the call of doubt to not taint himself with the Milky Way.

"So, I'll meet you at 1.00pm then and don't be late," Abbie said.

David put the phone down with his heart skipping and twirling in anticipation. He began to smile, reminiscing on the cordial Abbie, who didn't care about the discriminations of others and who fearlessly walked into situations of contention.

"I'm going to need a double dose of courage," he whispered.

"Wait a minute, young man."

Oh what now.

David stopped in the middle of the stairway and sighed, sensing the heat to come and a tutorial of history.

"I have to get ready for college, I don't want to be late."

Charles opened one of the letters and looked up the stairs.

"Please tell me that you're not involved with a white woman, the very people that enslaved and abused us."

Charles walked up the stairs and the lectures came back into David's mind. They seemed like words of wisdom at the point that Charles had counselled him, but now they didn't count for anything.

"She's not like how you've described white women. She's bright, intelligent and brave. She too lost black friends to racism and murder. She understands our situation better than most other black people."

Charles placed his hand on David's shoulder and lifted up his chin.

"It was white men that raped your grandmother in Jamaica. I'm telling you, don't get involved. What's wrong with the black girls in the church? They're your colour, your creed. Stay away from this white girl, it will bring trouble, big trouble!"

Mary came out of her bedroom, walked to the top of the stairs and sat down.

"Your father's right. You have no business with this white girl, its poison. Do you think that we want a bastard child in our home that doesn't even have an identity?"

David turned away and Charles gripped his arm. The intense staring continued until David bowed his head in submission. He was isolated from Charles and Mary and the pressure to obey Charles's instruction, mounted an attack on his place of clarity that he began to mentally acquiesce.

"End it now! Remember the white skinheads who murdered Ray. Stay away from this white girl and stick with your own."

For a moment, his words reasoned practical advice to David when linked to the death of Ray. A flashback of that day returned and David held onto one of the wooden posts supporting the banister. He nodded his head in recognition that he should despise the skinheads who were guilty, but he couldn't hold Abbie accountable for the race crimes of a few.

"I'll never forget Ray's death and neither will I rest until his killers are found. Abbie's different, there's something about her."

Mary stood up and walked down the stairs, trapping David between herself and Charles. She placed her arm around his shoulder and turned his head towards hers.

"Walk away now. A white woman only wants a trophy to make her feel special. When she's had enough, she'll chew you up and spit you out. Stay away from her."

David struggled to move from the stairs to the comfort of his bedroom. He finally managed to wriggle free and Charles grabbed his arm.

"Listen, we'll never accept a white woman in this house, never! We don't want a half cast child who'll struggle to know whether to be black or white!"

The mutterings continued in David's head. The tension of the atmosphere caused his skin to perspire. He evaluated their advice, prayers and a dead God whose ears were still on mute.

"I have to go to college," said David, having confirmed in his mind that Abbie had won the battle of difference.

He bounded to his room, selected clothes to ensure that he made a mark of distinction in his dress and rushed to the bathroom. The lavender soap on his hands and face felt like smooth silk and it brought an aroma of freshness to his skin. He gazed into the mirror and stared at his face. Pursuit of the cause encouraged him to cross lines if he had to, and take the oppression on the chin if it led to the truth and that was what he wanted above anything else.

He skipped down the stairs after getting dressed. Excitement turned his brain into a melting pot of poetic potions, misgivings and nervous emotions.

David slammed the front door and Mary ran towards the hallway.

"David, stay away from that Jezebel, she's evil!"

He turned back for a moment, pierced with the cry to avoid a slut and a tramp of a woman. His head told him to go back and ease Mary's anguish, but his heart desired to entwine with Abbie again.

She was in his blood, his heart and under his skin. He was unable to shake her off and purge his mind of her presence. He didn't want to put the brakes on, despite the guilt of being the same as the black men he'd criticised for rejecting where they came from.

***

Studying law and economics was the least of his interests as he got on the bus to take the twenty-minute journey to the college. He chuckled to himself and thought about his involvement with an older woman. *Well, a year and a half older than me isn't that bad.* His smile enlarged across his face and all he could see in his mind was Abbie, standing defiantly and throwing out her commands that he complied with.

"Have you come into some serious money or something?" said a black girl, sitting two rows in front of him.

David cast his eyes on her long French plaits and red glasses. He'd seen her before at college and had overheard someone mentioning that she fancied him. He watched her chewing and blowing gum into a bubble that popped and covered her lips, but he had no interest in her question.

"Sorry, are you talking to me?"

The girl nudged her friend and he turned away to look out of the window, occupying his attention with the rendezvous at 1.00pm and bunking off college to find love, rather than study the deep ridges of law.

Nearly eighteen and thinking about love and with a white woman. Why am I thinking about love?

"St Andrews," shouted the driver.

David got off the bus and walked through the open gates.

Two young men in his law class caught up with him at the entrance of the college.

"Hi, David, have the police caught those skinheads who killed Ray?" asked one of the men.

"No. They arrested several suspects and then let them go."

He watched them walk ahead of him and one of them turned around.

"That's the problem with the Babylon, there're damn racist. If it was a black person who'd murdered a white person, they'd already be banged up."

David slowed down and watched the men enter the college. Their views resonated with his. He reflected on the case and inertia demonstrated by the police, finding it unbelievable that they hadn't been able to gather sufficient evidence to apprehend Ray's killers.

"That's why Abbie's right. The police force has to change, because it's full of bigots."

He went to classroom 103, rather than wander to the hall where he anticipated being asked the same question repeatedly.

The law teacher arrived and opened the door.

"Hello, David, good to see you again, how are you?"

David raised his head and looked at Mr Watts, unsure if it was a good idea for him to come back to college when his head was still firing on all cylinders and many issues remained unresolved.

"I'm fine, thank you."

Mr Watts stepped into the classroom and shut the door.

David stood in the corridor and rubbed his fingers across the beige painted walls. His mind switched sides between Abbie and law. Usually the precepts of the legal system would win the battle for his attention, but the expectation of seeing her again was dominating his thoughts.

He imagined her arriving early at the Guinness Clock to check what time he turned up and if he was one second late receiving a lambasting. Even her anger stirred up emotions inside his chest and he smiled at her eventually calming down and greeting him with a huge smile. He touched his cheek, remembering the way she flagrantly grabbed his face and kissed him. His body and his mind were both in a place of remembrance from her gentle touch that he could feel through his fingertips and he wondered, *what would it would be like to kiss her lips?*

"I should leave now and just wait in the park."

Before that decision could occur, the classroom door opened and Mr Watts beckoned him to enter. He walked into the classroom, remembering the wooden lectern that Mr Watts stood behind and sat in the front row, removed the law book from his bag and placed it on the desk that contained scribbled black ink in the etches of the wood.

I'm meeting her in the park. It would be good to kiss her lips. Why am I thinking about kissing her, we're just friends, he thought.

Turning towards the door, he watched the other students enter the classroom, physically in the room, but mentally in the Battersea Country Park where he was drafting his own amendments that forced change, whilst enjoying the pleasure of constant flirtations with Abbie.

Mr Watts tapped the blackboard, bringing him back to earth.

"Now, who can tell me about, The Prevention of Corruption Act, 1906?"

Two of the students raised their hands and Mr Watts walked in their direction.

David answered the question silently, but his response was an act born out of common ground and it certainly wasn't corrupt. As one of the students answered, the only cohesion he could draw to "The prevention of Corruption Act, 1906," was black and white coming together and forming a new law of unity.

"David, David."

He jumped up out of his daydream and back into reality.

"Sorry, are you talking to me?"

The other students sniggered.

David sensed the eyes of the students behind him, staring at the back of his neck and raised his head to face Mr Watts.

"I missed the question, can you repeat it please?"

Mr Watts went to the blackboard, took up a piece of chalk and wrote, "Can the planet Jupiter, please release David from his dream of a damsel in distress."

The students banged their desks and erupted with giggles which then became loud jeering. A student at the back threw a crumpled piece of paper at David's head and whistled.

"Wake up, daydreamer, she doesn't love you, she loves me."

I should never have come back to college today, it was a mistake.

He listened to the jabbering about relationships and men being the superior sex, shrinking in his chair and raising his head to Mr Watts to bring order and get him off the hook. Looking at his brown strapped Zenith watch, he willed the bell to ring to end his embarrassment. His infatuation was exposed and his skin reacted with a burning heat that he couldn't wait to get outside and into the cool air.

Finally the bell rang and Mr Watts walked back to the lectern.

"Make sure that you study, The First Offenders Act of 1960, particularly, David please."

A boy tapped David on the head with a ruler and flew out of the door before he could respond. The other students followed, chuckling and staring at David as they left.

David quickly put his books in his satchel before Mr Watts called him back and gave him a round of ten quick fire questions. College was over and he normally didn't miss lessons, however, today was an exception with mission and Abbie ordering his footsteps and he had no will to resist, but walk in the direction of the calling card.

***

Wandering through the college, he avoided the recreation area where he didn't want to engage in differing conversations and face interrogation that would open up reminders of his suffering. His pace quickened and he exited the college, heading for the bus stop. He looked at his face in the mirror and blew his breath into his hands, resting his head against the glass and contemplating how he could find a quiet spot to remain inconspicuous.

Abbie, I'm meeting Abbie in the park.

The bus arrived and as he got on, she was there again in his mind and teasing him as she giggled and frolicked on the grass. A vivid picture passed before his eyes of him chasing her and tickling her sides until she screamed for mercy. Her eyes, her smell and her sweet perfume lured him to the mountain top, and he pouted his lips that met with hers and the second kiss was an explosion of melting moments.

Stop being stupid. I'm being crazy. She's just someone who can help me and that's it.

"Battersea Country Park," said the driver.

***

The butterflies started to flutter in David's stomach. He watched the cyclists, cycling along the path and the two lovers holding hands. He gazed at them again with a close eye and saw normality in a black couple being together and it registered that if he was thinking about Abbie as girlfriend material, he'd better banish the thought from his mind.

"This is crazy! My parents are right. She's a danger and I need to walk away."

How can I back out now, he thought.

The strong tone of Abbie's voice, merciless in her counsel of weakness and cowardice drummed in his brain. He strolled along the path, having arrived before her and sat on a park bench. The ducks in the pond chasing a piece of bread were disinteresting, but he still watched them fighting whilst mixed emotions flowed through his mind.

C'mon, David, be a man for once. Ok, she's white. Is it so bad that she's white.

The self-reasoning drew no firm conclusion. Comparisons of their characteristics lighted up his brain. *She's cocksure and I'm not. She doesn't care about the opinion of others and I do*. He began the last battle mentally, debating flight or to remain and just let nature unfold the plan.

"Ok, you win. Let me go and meet Abbie."

***

He strolled towards the Guinness Clock on a warm afternoon checking in all directions for a recognisable face. A group of black youths played football and he stopped walking to watch the game for a few moments. He raised his hand in celebration as a goal was scored and chuckled at the debacle of the offside rule.

The football landed at his feet and the youths leered at him, waiting for the ball to be passed back. Eventually he got the message and was greeted with a loud jeer.

There she was and in his line of view. He gazed at her standing at the Guinness Clock and admired the light brown summer jacket that complemented her jeans and cream blouse. He quickly veered towards the bushes and waited for a woman to pass by. The feelings to run returned, and he sat on the grass trying to encourage himself that it wasn't forbidden for black and white to mix.

"She'll kill me if I stand her up!"

Returning to the pathway, he waved at Abbie. His heart wouldn't stop beating with panicked thuds and he looked around the park, sensing accusing eyes watching him and he knew it was too late to run for cover.

She didn't wait for him to arrive at the clock, but began to walk towards him. David's fingers played the game of shakes and he clung to his satchel to bring his nerves under control.

"Hello, David, it's been a long time."

He gazed at her face and smiled, quickly turning away as heat under his skin burned through the pores and a trickle of sweat ran down his nose.

"Hi, Abbie, it's good to see you again."

Abbie stepped closer to him and touched his arm. She leaned forward and kissed him on the cheek.

He didn't know whether to look right or left. The pangs in his stomach became stronger that he wanted to run to the toilet to spew, clear his head and stop acting like he'd never been alone with a girl before.

She wrapped her arms around his shoulders and joy and uneasiness oozed at the same time as she embraced him. He studied her green eyes and then her brown hair for five seconds, standing in a familiar neighbourhood, but in peculiar circumstances and a sense that he was being watched from all corners of the park.

"Hello, David, it's been too long, since I last saw you."

He remembered stroking her hand and ventured to hold it again. A streak of nervousness ran through his body and reminded him that he was in a black neighbourhood, where he would have looked twice if he saw black mingling with white.

She wouldn't stop looking into his eyes and he smiled under the blushing heat of his skin.

Her hand slipped from his and she took it again. He didn't know whether to pull away or just stand there, and let the mood have its way with his emotions that turned upside down and inside out.

The colour of her skin doesn't matter. Love doesn't recognise black, white, or brown.

For once his mouth struggled to find the words to break the silent awkwardness and he could only utter, "Abbie, what do you want to do in the park?"

This is so embarrassing, but she doesn't seem to care. What if someone I know sees me with her?

He didn't hear Abbie's voice bleating instructions in his ears and he wondered if she was having the same reservations and would smile, shake his hand and walk towards the exit. His mind twisted one way and then the other, wanting her to leave and then happy that she was with him in the park and if she didn't care then why should he.

He looked up again and she moved closer to him, putting her arm through his and making his heart beat faster with intrigue and angst for crossing over to the other side and making a public display of it.

David touched his lips, reminiscing on the image he had of kissing her lips and convincing himself that he wasn't committing a crime, because he chose white instead of black.

His eyes were glazed and his heart quivered, cancelling the words that he wanted to speak and he allowed his body language to convey his emotions. He reached a point where he was contented to be right by her side for he remembered that pain and murder had no racial barriers, and it was murder that acquainted them.

They walked pass the clock, along the pathway towards the Festival Gardens and David put his arm around her shoulder. She responded by placing her arm around his waist and now he knew what it was like to be a young potential lover strolling into a moment of beauty, with no desire for it to end.

"Ah, David, this is perfect. You've been in my mind constantly. I just knew that when we met again it would feel right."

His mind envisaged no truth in the statements that Charles and Mary had made about Abbie. All he could see was a beautiful person inside and out and didn't believe that she had any desire to hurt him.

As he gazed at Abbie, her white skin was inconsequential. It was her heart and her characteristics that was drawing him in deeper; deepening his attraction without reason to retreat and forget that she existed.

***

“Bloodclaat! Look at this. A coconut. A white nigger. He must be fucking mad!” said a black youth walking past them with his black girlfriend.

The girl turned around and spat on the ground. She tossed her hair and the sunshine that David bathed in became a reality where the evil daggers made his heart sing with a fearful murmur. He interlocked his fingers tighter with Abbie’s and held his tongue rather than engage in a battle of words. Her boyfriend tapped her arm and they walked along the path, looking back at David.

“Don’t let that bother you, they’re just small minded,” Abbie said.

She let go of his arm and skipped along the pathway.

David waved hesitantly, wanting to look behind him in expectation of another person expressing their dissent with his decision. He scanned the park, no longer in the place of innocent infatuation, but now realising that he'd made himself vulnerable to not only white haters, but also black haters. Intuition pushed him to find an exit away from the persecution, rather than tightly embracing with Abbie and becoming a target.

He walked slowly and she stood before him. His heart took dominion over his head and began to skip to a beat of love and terror at the same time.

Her gentle stroke of the back of his neck was sensual, but didn't stop his head screaming, *what have you done, you should never have met her here, its suicide.* A slight tremble went through his legs at the blaze of venom in the environment at the audacity of his mingling with a white girl in the park.

This is bad, this is really bad.

The stares and whispers of the small crowd gathering behind them got his attention. He clutched her hand and wiped the drip of sweat from the tip of his nose, looking at Abbie.

Doesn't she see that this is bad. How can she still smile and be so cool when this is about to get really nasty, he thought

"Abbie."

The boys who argued about the offside rule wandered towards the pathway, kicking the ball towards David who trapped it with his right foot. He wished that he'd followed the wisdom of his mind and snuck out of the park with Abbie, rather than getting carried away with blissful romantic imaginations.

One of the black youths took a cigarette from his pocket and lighted it, blowing the smoke into David's face.

"Brother, this is wrong. Black has no place with white shit! Have you forgotten the enslavement of our people? You're making a mockery of our suffering."

One of his friends walked around David and touched Abbie on the backside.

"Don't you dare put your hands on her! Don't you dare touch her."

He clutched Abbie's arms. Fear whistled through his body and foolish bravery made him stand his ground, instead of walking away from the confrontation.

"Raasclaat! To bumba. Get the fuck out of the park. You're a fucking disgrace!" screamed the boy.

David's eyes burned with anger and the warning from Charles and Mary flooded back into his mind. He was isolated, trembling on the ground and still holding Abbie's hand. He'd never felt unclean and dirty before, but the scourge of the youths made him a leper, an outcast and his thoughts told him, *you've forgotten who you are and where you come from.*

Abbie gazed at the boy and smiled.

She's fearless. She's not even afraid of them.

Abbie let go of his hand and stepped forward.

"No Abbie, don't be stupid, come back," he whispered.

"We're no different. Cut us open and you'll see blood and pink flesh," she said.

David watched some of the crowd walk away. Others didn't speak out aloud, but he heard their mutterings of repugnance. The boy with the football stared at David and Abbie and shook his head.

"Go back to your upper-class life. We don't need your bullshit and your patronising comments and take your white nigger with you. He's not a true black man, he's a coconut, a fucking bloodclaat coconut."

He kissed his teeth and beckoned the other boys to follow him.

They walked away and David touched his forehead. His mind swilled with madness and stupidity.

You're an idiot David. Why the hell did you agree to meet Abbie in the park? Idiot.

His knees trembled and he grabbed the waste bin and spluttered profusely. His soul awakened to a cruel taste of reverse bigotry, hated by white people for being black and hated by black people for mixing with white. He didn't want to go through this experience again and be challenged on his beliefs of who he was and where he originated from.

"David, I'm sorry, I should never have come and put you in a situation like this. I'll leave and we don't need to meet again."

Momentarily, he considered her proposal of options. He watched the black boys returning to their game of football and the other black people dispersing. He was at a crossroad, with fear telling him to follow her advice and whispers in his head of *don't be a coward* that compelled him to hold his nerve and not faint in the face of adversity.

The uncertainty filled his mind and in one way it seemed right to sever a relationship that spelt trouble.

"Yeah, it would be the right thing to do and I'm not a traitor or a coconut."

The insults rained on his mind and he looked around at the park knowing that he belonged, but as he stood alone gazing at Abbie, he pondered, *should I walk right and let her walk left?*

She walked towards him, taking his hand and resting her head on his shoulder.

Embarrassment drizzled over his face and he tried to pull his hand away, sighing deeply as his head spun with fate and foolishness for believing that they could walk together in the open and not be a target of abuse.

"Thank you for standing up for me, I know that you didn't have to and I know how hard it was for you."

His fingers closed around hers and he knew that he'd lost his mind with infatuation binding him with a rope so tight, that in the face of danger he chose white rather than black.

He was back where they'd started, standing on the pathway and overjoyed to be meeting Abbie again.

They walked towards the exit. His mood was sombre and many reservations still fired through his head. He looked at Abbie, reflecting on cause and purpose that brought him back to why they were standing together in an environment of hate.

Abbie held his arm, stopped walking and clutched his face.

"You see, David, this is why we have to be brave and do things that others aren't prepared to do. Today, you made a powerful statement, but to bring about real change you must cut out the heart of racism. Join the police force and find Ray's killers and at the same time destroy the root of racial hatred. Destroy it now!"

Chapter Thirteen

His unconscious mind batted the statement from side to side. Concealed pain was easily sparked by his thoughts of the moment when his life changed forever.

David let go of Abbie's hand and the memory of the police stopping him in the early hours of the morning when he'd been left at the mercy of the skinheads, jolted his brain with a sharp reminder. He took a few steps away from her, puzzled and surprised. His heart pounded with an unsettled rhythm and seemed that it was about to burst through his chest.

He contemplated the blue uniform and the flashing lights of a siren that made people jump. The authority of power that he'd experienced sent shivers through his legs. He saw the warped power that white police adored so that they could strike fear into the black communities. The more he considered the antics of the police, a rage began to rise at an institution built on thuggery and hatred.

He looked in her direction and knew that she must be on a crusade for personal vengeance and he was the pawn.

"You've absolutely lost your mind! No black man would ever dream of joining the police force, a racist organisation."

He walked further away. His head began to scream with frenzied anger at being a puppet on a string and being pulled in a direction, which his reflections confirmed was a suicide mission.

Gazing back at Abbie, his mind confirmed that he was dealing with a crazy woman, thinking beyond the impossible and looking to recruit the dumb into her outlandish plan. He turned to look back at her and she hadn't moved from her spot. She kept smiling and he had the impression that she knew something that he didn't, or was truly a psychopath.

She walked towards him and vexation ran through his veins at the smile that was still on her face. Bemusement was in his mind of how they'd gone from being vilified in the park, to him becoming a man dressed in blue. A realisation formed that they were on different planets and her suggestion, a complete death wish and he wasn't prepared to put himself in the firing line, only to be gunned down.

The burning in his face was a visual contortion of exasperation. David nodded, reassured that she was completely delusional. He wasn't prepared to give her a second chance and this time, it would be hello and goodbye.

This is it, I'll never see her again. She's absolutely lost her mind.

"David, you didn't even let me explain. You stormed off, seeing only hatred, getting irate and that's the point."

Why's she acting so cool? Does she believe that she can flutter her eyelids and I'll say yes to her ridiculous suggestions.

She touched his face and he swiped her hand away. She tried again and held his cheek. His anger simmered and his mind opened to having a discussion, even though he believed that it was futile.

"Have the police found Ray's killers? Do some police hate black people and abuse their power? Has anyone black ever joined the police force that you know?"

Her questioning sparked a debate in his mind. He remembered when the police cars screeched and they deliberately stopped the black youths to hound them.

They enter black communities, create chaos and then leave the residents to clean up their mess.

He was still waiting for them to confirm that Ray's killers were behind bars and awaiting trial for murder.

"Can you imagine the abuse I'd get? Not only would I be abused in the force, but the black people that I have grown up with would hate me. My life would become a living hell!"

A sheet from the Daily Mail newspaper blew across the path and he stooped to pick it up, reading the headline statement with an imagination, *Police force recruit their third black policeman, David Morgan.*

He could hear the shouts of, *there's monkey in a police uniform,* in his head. He could see the black people cross the road when he was on the beat and hear their mutters of, *a black man, a Babylon, to bloodclaat.*

Trying to uncover the positive, his mind drew blank after blank. Sitting on the grass and mulling over all the implications, he got up and walked away with a strong desire to be back home in his community, where familiarity and acceptance was what he knew.

He stopped, looking at the exit gate and behind him.

"What would Ray do if he was alive and I was dead?"

He couldn't answer for Ray, but he did have to answer for himself.

Astley Lloyd Blair joined the police force and then there would be me. He had the courage and I've got to do this to find Ray's killers.

The other half of his brain woke up and he concluded that they would never allow the very vermin that they hated to be one of them.

"I'll be despised by black and white! They'll see me as a pig. I'll be a disease. I'll have to arrest my own black people and listen to racist policemen hurling abuse, how am I supposed to do that?"

The fear oozed through his words. His imagination revealed a young man with great potential, but who'd sold his soul to become the disease that he despised. He could hear the chants of condemnation and envisaged being covered in so much shame that he was afraid to walk through his front door.

He had no idea why he walked back to Abbie when she'd created the explosion in his head.

Abbie pulled him towards the grass and he followed, without the willpower to resist and blindly ambling towards a road filled with challenge, but offering the solution to his unfulfilled desire.

"Open your mind to the impossible. Something doesn't seem right why the police still haven't convicted someone for killing Ray. Are you going to spend your life waiting for justice or will you make it happen?"

David pulled his hand away from hers and walked away.

"You're crazy! This is some type of white crusade you're on to compensate for your guilt, because you let your friends be raped and killed," he replied, going back to the grass bank and searching her eyes for the truth.

She turned her face away and David moved to the other side, gently lifting her chin and his heart confirmed that he'd hit a mark.

"You're right. I do feel guilty that I couldn't stop the brutality of the racist police. Don't make the same mistake I did and sit and wait for justice. Act now or you'll wake up regretting your indecision and Ray will just be another unsolved murder case."

The truth kept his head turned in the opposite direction. Thoughts came into his mind and fell out, dismissed as, *this is ridiculous, but she might be right*. Voices, which laughed with elation, were quiet. He sat, plucking blades of grass and allowed the breeze to blow on his face. Fight stirred up inside of him that acted as a propeller to do what others wouldn't dare to do.

David stood up and Abbie waited before joining him. He held her arms that slipped around his waist and closed his eyes as her breath on his neck gave him a warm sensation. He wanted to speak, but struggled to say the words floating in his mind. His heart and soul were entwined in a conviction for certitude that slowly merged his incongruity to Abbie's way of thinking.

"Say something, David?"

His eyes blazed like a burning bush. She let his hand go, but he gripped her fingers, refusing to let go and preferring to stand in solidarity for a cause that was hurling him to break down the strongholds of lies and hidden secrets. He knew that somewhere in the police files the truth was stored. Ray's killer's name had to be in the police records and only his courage could unearth it.

"I always wanted to be a lawyer and fight for those in need. I trusted in God, but he failed me and now I no longer believe in him. I promised Ray that I wouldn't rest until his killers are dead and I must keep that promise."

His hand had to move for something to be done. The magnitude and ridiculousness of becoming a police constable blazed him with scorn and derision. Hesitancy and terror reeled in his head, but as he bit his lip, the choice of expecting a racist institution to put black before white peeled away the option of him just sitting there and hoping for a conviction.

I need to do this for Thelma. She's tired of waiting for the police to knock on the door and tell her that Ray's killers have finally been arrested.

The image of Lorna in distress, because her brother's soul couldn't be laid to rest until the offenders had been incarcerated, hadn't left his mind.

"We should go to the station now and get an application form, you've waited long enough."

This wasn't the afternoon that he'd been expecting. He remembered his reservations and embarrassment and trying to decide whether to stay or go.

The racist slurs against her had strengthened his bond with Abbie rather than break it apart. He'd stood in her shoes and protected her, resisting the pull of the crowd to come back over to the black side and leave her standing in isolation.

As he mulled over the events of the day, his heart was totally convicted. To stand and do nothing wasn't a viable option. He had to act, or live in regret when the hunt was over and the police file closed.

Holding her hand, he walked on the grass and then back onto the path. The looks and gazes of opposition hit the wall of resolve that he now shared with Abbie and David knew that every word she spoke carried an arrow of truth.

There was no disconnection in his heart that he and Abbie were of one accord. Single minded and driven by memories of prejudice and racial brutality, his fingers tightened around Abbie's hand. The opinions of black or white dissenters to two people, fuelled by purpose and a strong emotion of equality, fell to fragments in his imagination.

"You do know that my parents will disown me."

Shaking her head she said, "They won't, David."

They reached the exit gates of the park and he watched the traffic zooming on the busy road. The honking of car horns appeared to be for them, and he experienced the exposure of a misunderstanding world, yet to come to terms with an interracial relationship.

He had to look beyond being a leper condemned to the caves, knowing that this was a taste of things to come. *Me, a policeman and having a white girlfriend.* The very thought rocked his brain, sending a violent tremor through his legs with the light bulb switching on in his head and pleading for him to wake up from the unthinkable.

"David, where's the police station? This is bigger than your parents, you and me."

"We need to get the train to Croydon, it's about forty minutes away."

"Then let's go, David, we can't delay anymore."

They waited at the zebra crossing until the light turned to green, walking to catch the train. Passion had knocked and he answered, misjudging the extent of the fiery flame. There appeared to be no stopping to the momentum so that he could pause and take a breath to understand the immensity of his assumed commission.

Silence was on the train, but not in his head and as they arrived at Croydon, his apprehension began to amplify.

They got off the train and David looked across the road, knowing that taking the walk to Fell Road was a defining moment. Fear pulled at his conscience and he didn't want to walk through the doors and ask to become one of them. He imagined walking on the beat next to a white policeman who hated him and the leers from the black people, giving him a dressing over with their eyes of hate.

I can't do this. I can't become a policeman, a traitor, no way.

"David, David."

He stood and gazed at the dreary grey stone washed building that wasn't welcoming him with open arms.

I don't want to become the Babylon.

It's a big mistake.

A police car pulled up to the entrance with its lights flashing and the siren blasting into the atmosphere. Two policemen in the back threw open the doors and pulled a black man out with short dreadlocks. The man was handcuffed and one of the constables pushed him towards the door. David glimpsed his eyes and quickly turned his head, for he was sure that he recognised him from the community club.

"Forget it! No way can I join the police force. This is your crazy idea. Forget it, no way, no Abbie, no."

He began to walk away from the Croydon police station, fuming that he'd allowed himself to be carried away with the idea of being the saviour of the black race.

What power and authority will I have, he thought.

His perception of himself switched from a warrior to a young man barely out of his nappies and he stared at Abbie.

I won't be an idiot. Me, a black man in blue, it's ridiculous.

"Find another black fool to become a martyr. I don't want to be part of your crusade, because you failed."

Now he appreciated the advice of Charles and Mary.

They're not stupid, he thought.

If they've told me to stay away from white women, then there must be a good reason.

He realised that he had to have more dignity as a black man and stop dancing to the white man's tune. David shook his head in annoyance and frustration that he'd allowed all his common sense to disappear, because of his fascination with Abbie.

David looked behind him and she pointed to the entrance. Anger fuelled in his mind that he was being compelled to walk into the station and demonstrate that at least one person was prepared to take on the system, irrespective of a lack of support.

"What is it with this woman? She won't let go. What's wrong with her?"

He didn't move from his spot of stubbornness and refused to be reeled into a plan of absolute ludicrousness.

David watched the policemen pouring out of the station, observing their lack of disturbance by her presence, even though she could be a criminal or about to bring some other threat to society. He recognised that her skin colour made her exempt from curiosity and questioning. His mind created a different picture of himself if he was standing there. An image of police reaching for their truncheons and ramming his head against the wall swirled in his head.

He ambled back towards her, looking for a friendly smile. Instead he received a stare of determination that confirmed this was his moment. He embraced her and she hugged him.

The clenching of his fist was to quench the angst and make his confidence rise to do the impossible. The doors opened, two policemen walked out and eyeballed David. Their expressions screamed, "Nigger on the loose," and he swallowed his spit with his left and right brain playing a game of fight and flight.

"Go inside and don't be afraid. You're doing this for Ray, remember that."

***

David looked up at the black lamp with blue glass and the words police station written on the outside, still in shock that he was entering a police station for the first time, not to report a crime, but to ask to become one of them. Cautiously, he walked up the three steps, through the wooden doors and into the police station.

The policeman behind his glass window and writing in his notebook finally raised his head, whilst his colleague continued dialling the telephone.

"Can I help you?"

David gazed at the three girls who sat on the bench. Their lack of clothes reminded him of women who roamed the streets and sold their bodies for money. The white girl winked at David and opened her legs. His face flushed with embarrassment.

They're the type of people that I would have to arrest, prostitutes.

All of his heart, mind, body and soul were in complete agreement, *run and get out before I make the biggest mistake of my life.*

"I want to join the police force," whispered David, drumming his fingers on the glass.

You don't want to join the police force. Don't be stupid, leave now.

"Is this a joke?"

"I want to talk to someone about becoming a policeman."

This time he raised his head and looked straight into the eyes of the policeman. His mind centred on Ray and his slashed throat, bloodied face and battered head. He remembered, *the police arrested fifteen skinheads and then let them go due to insufficient evidence, so they say.*

Three other policemen, including a sergeant walked through the entrance and the policeman behind the desk called them over.

"He wants to talk to someone about joining the force."

David watched them through the glass as they consulted and whispered. One of the policemen walked out and came back with the Chief Superintendent. He whispered into his ear and the superintendent smiled.

Walking out through a side entrance he said, "Follow me." He extended his hand. David shook it and followed him through the back to where the other policemen sat at their desks, making phone calls or writing up their reports.

He could no longer hear the chattering conversations or the buzzing of the phones. He sensed the eyes of the police following his movement and the hairs on his neck stood up on full alert. His heart skipped with a frenzied fear as he strolled through their domain. His legs walked in the direction of the superintendent, but his mind was outside and far away from the police station.

"Back to work ladies and gentlemen, this isn't a freak show."

The Chief Superintendent arrived at his office and unlocked the door, walking into the room and beckoned David to enter.

David gazed at the immaculate office with a few files positioned neatly on the long brown desk. The photograph of the Chief Superintendent's promotion that hung on the wall above his brown suede chair caught his eye. The Chief Superintendent walked over to his desk and sat down behind it, gesturing to David to sit down in the chair opposite him.

"Why do you want to join my police force?"

The blood in David's body reached boiling point and his eyes never left the Chief Superintendent's face. His right foot refused to stop twittering under the desk and he grasped his leg to force the shuddering reaction to stop.

"I want to make a difference, stop the abuse of black people and ensure they're treated with respect."

The Chief Superintendent stood up, walked to his door, then came back and stood behind David.

He turned around and looked up at the face of the Chief Superintendent. His gaze of dissent made him want to crawl in a hole and never come out. He tried to control the nervous breaths that were hurting his chest and causing pain in his lungs. The intimidation of power and authority towered over him and his body tremored in the chair.

"Don't try to fuck with me. Nobody of your colour has ever tried to join this police force. You would have to be out of your fucking mind."

David pushed the chair against the Chief Superintendent legs, standing up to face him. He wanted to hurl abuse at him and respond to the anger emotions that were stinging his brain.

Antagonised by the abusive rhetoric of the Chief Superintendent, he clenched his fist with a strong desire to punch him in the face. His mind simmered and cooled down. He refused to hear the cell door shut, watch the blind being drawn down and be locked up as another black statistic. He held his nerve, rather than giving the Chief Superintendent the pleasure of another arrest.

David coughed, extending his fingers at the same time the breeze of calm soothed the tension in his left temple.

"I want to join the force, is it just open to white people? Does the name of the police station say, Croydon for white's only police station?"

The Chief Superintendent shook his head, walked back to his chair, sat down and put his hands on the desk. He picked up the phone and dialled a number.

"Sergeant, come to my office now and bring Rob and Mike with you."

David sat back down and kept his eyes on the Chief Superintendent. The tables had turned, and he could see the uncomfortableness in his eyes that sent a message to his mind, *If I stand up to him, join and refuse to be intimidated, I can fight against racism.*

"Everything ok, chief," said the sergeant, entering the office, followed by Rob and Mike, two of the constables.

"This young man is interested in joining the police force, what do you think about that?"

The constables erupted into coughing fits and the sergeant joined the chief at his desk.

"You've got to be fucking kidding me. You, joining our police force! Is that a serious proposal?" said the sergeant.

The two constables began to smile and then laughed.

A deluge of delusion swelled in David's mind at the preposterous and unimaginable notion of a black policeman in uniform.

"Your raasclaat and bumbaclaat community would hate you outside, and inside the force you'll just be a nigger, a black bastard and a fucking reject on both sides, is that what you want? Go home and become a bus driver or a cleaner, you'll never survive," said the sergeant.

The constable who sat on the corner of the desk removed his truncheon. He twirled it in the air and then positioned it right next to David's nose. David's lips began to twitter and the snot mingled with his tears. Butterflies stirred in his stomach and his heart pounded against his ribcage.

The constable took a deep breath and pushed David's head backwards.

"Get the fuck out of here before I arrest you for wasting police time."

David sucked up the air through his nostrils and breathed, hearing their slurs whirring around his mind. Hatred for the policemen who stood gaping at him with smirks on their faces rocked his brain from side to side. A burning desire of rage intensified and the pleasure of breaking their noses with his knuckles wouldn't suffice to make them pay for the abuse that left their lips.

Everything that he'd been taught about racist white people suddenly became true, but he had a warped respect for the three policemen, who at least displayed their true intentions without a smokescreen to camouflage how they really felt.

"The door is that way. We're pleased to have met you and wish you all the best in your chosen career," said the Chief Superintendent.

Nigger, nigger, nigger, flashed before David's eyes. The colour of his emotions changed to fear. The system was bigger than him and all he could see was an image in his mind of an ant being crushed under black leather boots. He stood up nervously, holding onto the side of the chair and unable to make eye contact with the policemen whose belittling was still piercing his brain.

Tripping over his left shoe that made the policemen chuckle, he stumbled to the door, grabbing the handle and walking into the corridor. He shut the door quietly behind him, completely slayed by the ten-minute baptism of fire that he couldn't imagine facing on a daily basis.

"Join the force, never!"

"This was Abbie's stupid idea."

I don't want to be racially abused every day.

A conclusion formed in his mind. The reality of who he was hit him with a powerful impact. He tried to dismiss the image of a minnow fighting against sharks in his head, but the picture of his bones being crunched until they were powdered dust wouldn't leave.

His forehead rested against the door.

"Imagine that, one of them, joining this police force," said one of the constables.

"Yeah, imagine that," said the sergeant.

David's eardrums sparked and he let go of the door handle, pacing along the corridor. The indecision fled from his mind and he scurried back to the Chief Superintendent's office and raised his hand. He listened to the conversation unfolding behind the closed door and became fired up by a passion that if he didn't act now, he wouldn't be able to forgive himself for failing Ray.

Grabbing the door handle he stormed into the room, enraged by their blatant expression of despise. He turned a blind eye momentarily to the cross that he envisaged would test his resistance level to the breaking point.

"You didn't give me an application form."

"Hmm, what did you say?" mumbled the sergeant.

"I said you didn't give me an application form. I want to join the force to fight against crime."

The constables looked at the sergeant and gazed at the Chief Superintendent, who sat down and took a drink from his glass of water.

"Please give me an application form," David said, stretching out his hand and refusing to leave a second time until they met his request.

His heart rumbled with hatred at their representation of human beings. He despised the stink of racism and refused to crawl like a serpent on his belly and give them the pleasure of power that was like taking a gunshot to his brain.

He had the power in that split second for they were on the back foot, looking to the chief to provide the answer, but David watched him crumbling in front of his subordinates and he realised that surprise could be a powerful defence.

"You're fucking serious! You really want to join this force and make history? You have absolutely no idea what you're letting yourself in for," said the sergeant.

The words of the sergeant whispered fear and a rush of anxiety went through his body.

He's right, it will be worse than burning in hell itself.

David quashed the thought and listened to the silence in the room. Bravery and integrity ignited in his heart and even though he didn't understand the enormity of the challenge ahead, he stood his ground.

"You're making a serious mistake, this isn't the place for you. Don't apply to join. You'll regret this decision for the rest of your life," the sergeant said quietly.

David took the application form from the Chief Superintendent's hand. He went to the door, opened it and walked along the corridor to the exit. Turning around, he saw the Chief Superintendent following him. The policemen sitting at their desks gazed at him and he held his head high, returning their gazes with a look of defiance. His stride appeared to be confident, but inside his mind was a bolt of stupidity that threw a left uppercut to bring rational reasoning to his head.

David reached the open doors and turned, gazing at the Chief Superintendent and his subordinates.

The Chief Superintendent raised his hand and stroked his chin.

“It’s a new day, ladies and gentleman. The black man going through the exit wants to join the police force. I never thought I would see a day like this in my career, but it has happened today.”

Chapter Fourteen

Abbie caught him as he stumbled down the stairs of the police station, watched by Rob and Mike. She pondered, *look at them, they're scheming to make David's life hell, if he joins the force.* Abbie walked up the stairs, confronting them with a piercing glare and the brawn of a woman who wasn't prepared to be daunted by what she saw as a couple of knuckleheads.

"The day will come when you'll eat humble pie and you'll be the one's grovelling on the street."

Mike moved towards her and Rob pulled him back.

She stood defiant in the atmosphere of dissention, despite the fear that crawled underneath her skin. It reminded her of South Africa, when the police gave her similar glares and spat in her face as a message that her loyalty was twisted and she required a lesson to remove the confusion from her mind.

"Do me a favour. Tell your nigger boyfriend to stay away from the police force. Anyway, what's wrong with you? You have thousands of Caucasian men to choose from and you choose a nigger! Get some fucking sense into your brain and get back on the white side," he said quietly.

Abbie refused to move and David joined her on the steps. She took hold of his hand and interlocked her fingers with his. She didn't need to speak. Her composure in the line of a threatening stance from Rob and Mike sent a clear message. In the past, she hadn't stood her ground, but this time she wasn't prepared to run and crawl under a bush and wait for trouble to disappear.

She stood in solidarity with David, authentic in her stance against the abusers of power and didn't have time for gimmicks or pretences.

Her belief for equality and an egalitarian society where people were judged on character and not on skin colour, murmured in her mind. She wanted change and knew that it started with unearthing the criminals hiding in the shadows and who were accountable for Ray's death.

"We'll be coming back, and David will become a policeman in your force."

Rob and Mike smiled and went back into the police station.

Abbie remained on the step and stared at the shut door, reflecting on the light that she'd seen a long time ago. Brute force and power had its place and once upon a time they sent shimmering terror through her mind. Valour and intellect were qualities that she'd refined and knew that they could shake the very foundation of a bias institution.

She squeezed David's hand, sensing the tension in his body and kissed his cheek to assure him that she was right in the middle of the battlefield by his side and prepared to fight against an establishment with its undercurrent of bigotry.

"Let's go, David, and come back today with the completed application form."

Walking down the stairs ahead of him, she waited for David to reach the bottom step. She looked up at the door thinking, *I hate that some of them abuse their power just because they wear the blue uniform.*

"David, I want to know exactly what happened in there," she said, as they walked away and entered a West Indian cake and coffee shop.

Her eyes followed his footsteps towards the table. The question, *am I letting my past dictate his future,* fired through her mind.

As she sat down she ran her fingers against the corners of the red and green tablemat.

"Abbie, it was horrible. They were really intimidating. They don't want me to join. They think it's a fucking joke."

Abbie stroked his palm softly and put her arms around his neck. She was unsure if he had the mental strength to rise to the challenge, without going into meltdown.

She looked into his eyes.

"We have to start a revolution and it begins with being on the inside of the force so we can discover the secrets they're hiding."

"David, and also, this isn't about you or me, it's about Ray. They know more than they've told us."

Abbie lifted up his head. "I'm proud of you because it took courage to walk in there and stand up to them." She leaned forwards to kiss his lips, only to stop when the old Jamaican woman behind the counter kissed her teeth and tapped the glass.

"Are you young people a-go buy sumting or just sit there trying to fix de world?"

"Yes, sorry. Two coffees and two slices of ginger cake," David said.

The server went into the kitchen to boil the kettle and returned with two hefty chunks of cake on the same plate. She smiled at them and put a napkin and two knives on the table.

"You can pay when you leave," said the woman.

"You see, David, not everyone sees colour. Some people see people for who we are."

He nodded, biting into the cake and sipping from the cup of coffee.

"It was horrible in there. They really don't want me to join."

Abbie pulled the application form from the envelope and placed it on the table. She watched David studying the form and writing his name and address in the designated section.

"You seem really hesitant. Don't do this if you don't want to, it must be your decision and your decision alone."

He continued until he reached the signature section and stopped, raising his head and looking at Abbie.

Abbie sipped her coffee and took another bite of the ginger cake, smiling at David as a cloak to hide her inhibitions. Her knees knocked together under the table to utter fear, a deep fear for David and if he would be able to withstand the burning heat of the furnace.

"David, are you sure?"

He nodded and said, "Yes, I'm sure."

Picking up the pen she scribbled on the napkin. She continued depicting her thoughts, allowing her mind to wander freely and contemplate, *what would the world be like if people let love, care and acceptance of each other be the driving force?*

The pen fell from her hand and the desire that she had when they first met in Battersea Country Park bubbled again. She gazed at him and whispered, "David, kiss me."

David peered at the old Jamaican woman. He reached over quickly and kissed Abbie on the lips.

"Not like that, a proper kiss."

Removing his choices, she grabbed his neck and pulled him towards her. She passionately kissed his lips and rekindled the flame of attraction that was burning brightly in her heart.

Letting him go, her eyes were glazed and her lipstick was slightly smeared on her chin. She didn't have a care for the outside world and was exactly where she wanted to be, side by side with David. Her eyes caught the gaze of the Jamaican woman who smirked and Abbie smiled back. Her heart whispered a flutter of romance and stern desire that together they would expose the killers in hiding and make them account for murder.

"Can I see your picture now?"

The skin on her forehead crinkled and the smile shared with the Jamaican woman became a frown. She folded the napkin twice before presenting it to him, watching him with intent as he stared at the drawing of liberation, love and power to the poor in spirit. Her face flushed, changing from pink to red and a line of sweat formed across her top lip.

"I bet you think I'm crazy, don't you? I can see you wondering, who's this girl, she's too full on!"

David folded the napkin carefully and placed it in his pocket.

"No, I don't think that you're crazy, but the fight that you expect, seems impossible to win."

Her mind spun in several directions. Her eyes widened and she studied the image in her imagination that saw the walls of hate that stood like a fortress crumbling to the dirt and the unexpected becoming a reality.

David looked at the space requiring his signature and Abbie grabbed his hand.

"Stop! Before you sign, do you really want to join the police force?"

He held the nib of the pen.

She picked up the form from the table and thought, *what will he do when he hears the racist jibes day in and day out? How will he respond when black people see him on the street and curse him? What if he has to arrest someone that he knows from the black community?*

Her mind reflected on the black revolutionists in South Africa who'd ended up in prison or were murdered. She knew that they'd made a difference, but it didn't go far enough. As she looked at David, the idea of him sauntering with the notion that he could succeed where others greater than him had failed, disturbed the airwaves in her brain.

Abbie thought, *when the fire is too hot, will he quit.*

Maybe, he'll run and regret that he ever met me or will he stick to me like glue and fight for what we believe in, even if there are consequences.

Abbie touched his face with a smile that hid the worry that was prompting her to think of an alternative plan. Nothing came to her mind that there was another path they could take.

You'll have to be really strong David. They'll do everything they can to destroy you. I hope that you can be strong.

"Ray, I have to admit that I'm scared, but I have to do it for you and me."

Abbie affirmed her pride with a firm nod.

"David, this will be hell, but we'll get to the truth and I promise you, I'll always be by your side."

Playtime was over and Abbie recognised that a new reality beckoned for the brave or the dumb. She sensed the tension of the war that was filled with disproportionate challenge and an army unlikely to acquiesce and break their system of white power.

"Shall we go?"

David didn't move.

Abbie watched him and a red-hot rage burned in her chest. Flashes of the news channels flooded into her head of how many black lives had to be destroyed, before someone confronted the policemen and put an end to their carnage. She knew that her mind housed courage and fear, each competing to be the overriding factor that would determine the final outcome, good or bad.

She placed the form on the table and David read through each section again, before signing.

"I'm ready, let's go back to the station."

David paid the bill at the counter and joined her outside.

Ripples were underneath her skin from the agonising experiences that terrible things happen to the innocent and could change the course of their lives forever. Standing on a road that she didn't know, a compelling desire burned to pay the price for justice.

Her heart and mind was with David and as she looked into his eyes, the explosion in her brain confirmed that there was no turning back from their destiny.

***

They arrived at the station and stood under the dim light of the lamppost.

Abbie looked up the steps and gazed at the brown door.

"Do you want me to come in with you?"

"No, this is something that I must do, alone."

David put his foot on the first step and Abbie held his arm and pulled him back, wrapping her arms around his waist and snuggling her head into his chest.

"I'm coming with you."

They climbed the steps and David pushed open the doors, walking straight to the counter. He banged on the glass window and the policeman who'd tended to him previously, jumped.

He looked at David and then at Abbie who gazed with ferreting eyes.

She watched the policeman's lips slightly parting and drummed her fingers on the glass window. A smile on her face expressed her determination to not be intimidated. She wanted to demonstrate that the power of two could be a force to be reckoned with, and she quelled the attempt of fear trying to rise up and overtake her confidence.

"Can I help you?"

"I want to see the Chief Superintendent. Here's my completed application form, I want to join the police force."

The policeman dialled through to the Chief Superintendent who arrived quickly. He walked through the side door, shaking his head and stared at David and Abbie, whose hands gripped the counter with zest and zeal to not break in the sight of conflict. She steeled her nerves and she held David's hand to show her solidarity and that she wasn't going to run.

Her mind raced into overdrive of the nervous disposition displayed by the Chief Superintendent.

She took David's hand and stood steadfastly by his side, waiting for the Chief Superintendant to receive the application form to process it. He reluctantly took it from David's hands and she kept her eyes focused on his face. Her heart bounced that retribution was one step closer.

"Thank you. I look forward to hearing from you very soon," David said.

The Chief Superintendent went behind the glass window and drew down the blind.

Abbie placed her ear to the window. She couldn't hear their assumed conversation, but knew that they were conspiring and conniving.

No retreat and no surrender flowed through her mind. Raising her head, she looked at the high ceiling and thought, *how high do we have to climb to win the battle of fear.*

"David, it's not too late, you can still walk away. If you do, I'll understand."

A chink of light appeared from the covered window and the policeman serving unravelled the blind. The Chief Superintendent was still there, reading through David's application form. They both mumbled and the chief approached the window, directing his attention towards Abbie.

"Do you know this young man?"

Her eyes widened and the skin on her face stiffened like ice had been placed on her cheeks. She grasped David's hand, dwelling on the question and allowed her imagination to wander down the lane of present life changing circumstances.

"Yes, I know him and he's one of the bravest people that I've ever met."

Abbie locked her arm with David's, gazing at him and then turned to stare directly into the eyes of the Chief Superintendent.

"Ok then. We'll review the application form and be in touch."

David and Abbie left the station and went back to the high street. They kept walking until she saw the tube station.

Abbie's lips pursed together. With a furrowed brow she thought, *even if I'm afraid, I can't show it to David.*

They stopped at the tube station and Abbie checked the time. She moved her head towards his ear and whispered, "When you're in the force, you must keep your eyes peeled and listen. You need to find the clues."

She grasped his waist and kissed his cheek. A moment passed before she met him halfway, closing her eyes and waltzing on a bed of leaves. She unashamedly expressed her commitment and zeal and she had a half drunken look again, but didn't care if the outside world were watching from a distance.

"You have to trust me, I'm a woman of my word. We'll need help and I know people who can help us."

Walking down the stairs of the tube station, she turned around to make the shape of a heart and whispered murmuring words of, "He's the one, he's someone I could have a life with and we've both suffered. Maybe this can be more than just two people fighting for justice."

"Wait! Abbie, what do you mean? You need to tell me more!"

Chapter Fifteen

"Who's that trying to break down my door on this peaceful Saturday morning?" Mary said.

She put the rolling pin on the table, washed her hands, walked to the door and twisted the latch.

"Oh my God! Father God almighty, what has David done?"

The two policemen, with jackets buttoned and helmets in their hands stood at the door. They gazed at Mary's face and smirked.

"Sorry to disturb you, Mrs Morgan, but we're here to see your son, David," said one of the constables.

"What has he done? Are you here to arrest him?"

"Can we come inside, rather than discuss this on the doorstep," said the policeman.

Mary opened the door wider and said, "Ok, but what has he done? He's never been in trouble with the police before."

The policemen followed Mary into the living room and sat down. One of them pulled a white envelope from his pocket and placed it on the dark brown oak coffee table.

"Can we speak to David, please?" asked his colleague.

David's ears twitched at the voices he heard downstairs. He stopped his exercise routine and sat on the bed, looking over at the poster of Martin Luther King that had found its way back onto his bedroom wall. He tiptoed to the door, opened it slightly and took a deep breath. His mind was set that like his hero, he had to walk in the domain of trouble in the pursuit of freedom and justice.

David shut his bedroom door, only to hear the thuds on the stairs.

He dropped to the floor to complete his press ups and finished with a nod of his head, jumping up and touching his bedroom door. His eyes closed and slow breaths oozed gently from his mouth. Courage flowed into his mind and gave him mental preparation to go downstairs and face the music.

Turning the handle, he opened the door.

"Boy, you'd better tell me what you've done? Isn't it enough for you to leave the church and now you bring shame to my house because of your crime!"

David left his bedroom, brushing past Charles after looking at him with squinted eyes. He held onto the banister and stepped on the stair, listening to the conversation ensuing between Mary and the two men. Emotions of hate and despise arose in his mind and a gust of fear knocked his knees together as he reached the living room door.

Their voices, it's them.

He put his hand on the door handle and the wisp of Charles's breath on his neck stimulated a greater depth of apprehension. David pushed open the living room door, walking over to the sofa, sitting down and staring at Rob and Mike with a gaze of anger.

"Good morning, David, good to see you again," said Rob.

Rob stood up, walked over to David and offered his hand. He held David's hand tightly and stared into his eyes. It reminded him that white power would never give way to the ideology of becoming a servant to the inferior.

"I was explaining to your mother that we have a special project and recognise that we need policemen who are from an ethnic background. At the end of the day we are one force for everybody."

Rob went back to his seat and smiled.

David's Adam's apple wouldn't stop gulping in his throat. He glared at Rob and Mike, recalling their bigotry with a special warning.

Their arrival at his front doorstep was a sign of the promise he recalled them stating so vehemently, if he followed through with his plan. The rigid expression remained on his face, but his heart was palpitating with a mutter for a way of retreat rather than being incinerated in a cauldron of hate.

"David came to the Croydon police station and expressed a desire to join the police force. We're really excited and that's why we're here to confirm that he's been selected for a physical and could be the first black policeman to join," said Mike, picking up the letter from the coffee table and handing it to David.

"Wait a minute, David isn't going to join the force! He wants to be a lawyer. You're mistaken," said Mary.

Rob and Mike smiled. David put his hands underneath his legs. He squeezed his thighs and resisted the urge to run to the toilet. His heroics brought a steam of regret and he mused on the reality of the war ahead. The first stone had been thrown and as he raised his head, he knew they were here to finish what he'd started.

The misgivings came back to haunt him. Now that the glaze was off his eyes, the swirling in his stomach confirmed a truth. *They've accepted my application form and soon I could be one of the men in blue.*

Mary looked at David and then back at Rob and Mike.

"I'm sorry, Mrs Morgan, but that's not correct. David came to the station and asked to join, and we're here to confirm that he needs to go through a physical and a medical, next week."

"David, this must be a mistake, yes? Why would you want to join the police, when you want to be a lawyer?"

David stood up and calmly faced Rob and Mike.

Look at their smug faces. You're not going to stop me.

"It's the truth. I want to join the force to fight crime and stand up for justice."

Mary shook her head and David looked at her face, not wanting to hurt her, but his mind focused on going through with his plan despite the fear that was eating him up inside.

David studied Charles's expression, seeing how powerless he was in the presence of the police sitting in his house. He didn't want to be the tail with his voice silenced by an authority that had no respect for him, or Charles and Mary.

The contempt for Rob and Mike surged through his body. He hated their brazen attitude and sensed their determination to swat him like a fly if he dared to tread into their territory.

David raised his head to Rob and Mike, receiving their message loudly and clearly that affirmed in his mind, *they're out to get me.*

"Thank you for dropping by, I'll show you to the door," Mary said.

"Nice to meet you both and I'm sure David, will make a great policeman, fighting against crime," Mike said.

David left the room, opened the front door, walked down the pathway and stood at the black gate, waiting for Rob and Mike to follow and get into the blue and white Ford Anglia Panda car. They brushed past him and he refused to be intimidated by their scowling. He planted his feet with a mindset of devising a new game of rule to exploit any chink in the armour that he could find.

He knew that time had been their friend. Unsure of the details of their conspiring, one thing was certain in his mind, it was about to become even more hostile if he swallowed the terror and turned up at the station next week.

"You won't break me. I'll be at the physical, you won't break me."

Rob put his helmet in the car and returned to the gate.

"Leave it, we need to get out of here," Mike said.

"Listen, if you think that we're going to let a little brat like you make up the rules, you're fucking mistaken. You have no idea what you've done and the price that you'll pay," said Rob under his voice.

Rob eyeballed David and he clutched the fence to prevent himself from collapsing under the pressure that increased the angst, snapping in his head.

Mike walked to the gate, touched Rob's arm and gave David a fierce stare.

He said quietly, "C'mon, we need to go. Leave the bumbaclaat until next week and then we'll see what black shit is really made of."

David held his nerve until they drove along the road and turned the corner. He wiped the tears from his eyes, summoning courage to rise and override trepidation. Walking back towards the open front door he saw Mary who said, “David, come inside, we need to talk.”

He walked into the house and into the living room. The admonition, lecture and correction from Mary, he didn’t need it right now.

I know exactly what they’re going to say.

Charles stared at David and walked around the living room. He went upstairs and slammed the bedroom door.

David leaned against the brown cold paraffin heater, staring through the window at the spot where the police car had been parked with a fire set alight by Rob and Mike’s intrusion in his heart, and no disagreement from Charles was going to make him change his mind.

“David, why do you want to belong to a racist institution that has nothing but hate for us?” asked Mary.

Charles came down the stairs and walked into the living room. David turned and gave him a fleeting gaze.

He stood at the window, his mind unchanged and even more determined now that Rob and Mike had dared to bring another threat to his doorstep. He watched the neighbours trundle along their garden paths and into their homes pondering, *did they see the police car parked outside our house?*

"Someone has to stand up for Ray. The police have no intention of ever finding his killers, why should they? To them he's just another dead black man whose life doesn't mean anything. Well I won't stand by and let this happen."

Mary sat in the chair opposite Charles. David observed her slight nod of the head. He braced his shoulders for the big speech to persuade him to stand down and see reason.

Charles pawed at the pages in the bible and David's heart hardened even more against any biblical message that tried to point him to another way of truth.

The quietness in the room gave an impression of stalemate with David, undeterred from his quest for justice and not a care if Charles and Mary were confused by his rush of blood to the head. No more words were required and he said in his mind, *even if I'm scared, I have to become a man in blue.*

He peered at Charles and Mary, resolute that he wouldn't say that he'd acted impetuously and tomorrow he would resume college to focus on his real purpose.

Turning around to face them, his eyes had a strong look of determination. It was a message of intent that irrespective of their opinion, he was going to the medical and physical.

"It's that white girl. I told you not to get involved with her and now she's filled your head with this ridiculous nonsense. You can't beat the police. You're just a child. You can't win, you can't beat the police."

Charles walked over to David and rested his hand on his shoulder.

"Son, your mother's right. Whether Abbie influenced you or you made this decision on your own, you can't beat the police, they'll crush you. To them you're filth, nothing but dirt and they'll make your life a living hell. Is that what you really want?"

David brushed Charles's hand off his shoulder. He pondered on the faith that he was supposed to have and understood why the sinners called church people hypocrites. He now held the same view, recalling them practicing the bible when they were with the congregation, but convinced that when outside or in their own homes, God became a pastime and forgotten until next week Sunday.

"How strange, mum and dad. Doesn't, Philippians chapter four versus thirteen say, I can do all things through Jesus Christ who strengthens me?"

Now he had their attention, he watched their persona change as his bombshell hit them squarely in the face.

"But everything must be done in accordance with God's will," replied Charles.

"But nothing, you're Christians, preaching the bible and that's what the bible says."

David stormed out of the room, into the hallway and rang Abbie. She picked up the phone and he whispered, “Mum and dad, they’re trying to change my mind about joining the police force.” He listened to her reassurance and encouragement and she said, “Don’t back down, it’s obvious that the police are nervous.” He smiled at the sound of her kisses and promise and repeated, “So you’ll meet me at the station next week Monday at 9am?”

“Yes, I’ll meet you there."

***

He found the next few days confrontational, with Mary constantly lamenting at him and Charles providing all the justifications why his decision was wrong. He stayed in his room, training and preparing for the physical and becoming inspired by the feats of Martin Luther King. The gaze at his fear was constant and he whispered, “Get away from me, you can’t stop me.” It was his way of psyching himself to persevere until he found the truth that allowed his mind to move from strife into rest.

“I can do this, I don’t have a choice. I have to do this for Ray and for me.”

Tomorrow, he knew that the police would be waiting, having created their camouflage to break his will. He considered Rob and Mike, bold in their entry through his front door and he brimmed with hatred towards them. Terror raced up and down his spine and he repeatedly heard the words of Charles and Mary, *you can't beat the police,* pounding his brain.

Switching off the light he reflected on the words of Stokely Carmichael.

We have no choice but to say very clearly, move over, or we goin to move over on you.

It was the determination that he needed to survive. The room darkened and he closed his eyes. He could feel the terror, but pulsated with the will to do what other great black men had achieved in playing their part to succeed in changing the affliction of the black race.

He heard the footsteps of Charles on the landing, his bedroom door opened, but he didn't enter. David pulled the blue cover over his head and clutched the fraying threads, allowing sleep to dominate and take his mind, body and soul into a peaceful state. He accepted that the feud with Charles and Mary would continue tomorrow, but as he floated away to his dreams, he confirmed mentally, *they won't change my mind, I'm going.*

Chapter Sixteen

The morning light invaded his sleep and he jumped up, banging the bells on the head of the brown wind alarm clock. David yawned at the early rising of 7.30am and he held his shoulders in a tight embrace, to simmer any doubt of not turning up at the Croydon station, in ninety minutes.

A cramp in his stomach and the rumbling wasn't for a hearty breakfast. He got off the bed and touched the picture of Martin Luther King with a pledge, "I'm not going to run, I'm going to fight."

"Martin, help me to be strong."

David ran to the bathroom, got undressed and filled the sink with cold and hot water, washing himself as if trying to remove the skin from his body. His mind wasn't clear, but jumbled with clashing thoughts of foolhardiness and wilful intent.

Blue sirens buzzed in his head as he took the blue towel from the rail and slowly patted his body. He kept it over his face for a short while, wrestling with the shudders in his legs and the nervousness that wouldn't let his mind find any respite from the attacks of fear.

His stare in the mirror revealed a solemn face staring back at him and no elation set alight his enthusiasm for a new job. He could only see a picture of the lion's den and their mouths wide open to devour him.

Quickly cleaning his teeth he shaved, put on his bath robe and went back to his bedroom to get dressed.

As he walked to the passageway with his packed duffle bag, he stopped on the middle of the stairs. His ears twitched to the opening of Charles's and Mary's bedroom door and the footsteps coming towards him.

"David, please don't go. I'm begging you, please."

David turned around and gazed at Mary. He turned back and walked down the stairs. His hand grappled with the blue coat on the stand, but he took it, walked to the front door and swiftly closed it behind him. Feet stuck to the doormat as he heard her plea vibrating in his head, but he closed his mind to the wrenching in his heart that desired to walk back inside and close the chapter on a silly idea.

Seeing the bus coming, he ran to the bus stop, stretched out his arm and dismissed all reservations that the way forward was the way back. His fare was paid and he deliberately sat at the front, reminiscing on Rosa Parks who made history in the USA, because she refused to give up her seat to a white passenger.

Rosa Parks stood her ground and I've got to stand mine.

His thoughts dwelled on fate and purpose that had arrived with a blistering introduction. The key to open the door was in his hand and he had to unlock it, knowing that the answer wasn't to run away, but walk through and enter a world of abhorrence.

The bus driver got nearer to the stop for the police station sooner than he would have liked. He got up, rang the bell and got off. Turning right, his legs became like wet plasticine. The urge to spill his guts screamed in his mind and as he approached the station, the voice of reasoning compelled him to turn back, before he was smashed and torn from limb to limb.

Abbie waited at the station steps. His mind was indifferent as he strolled towards her. She clutched his face and kissed his lips. He smiled, putting on a persona of bravery, whilst he thought, *don't you have a different plan.*

Abbie took a pendent from her neck and placed it into his hands.

"This was my grandmother's, I want you to have it for good luck."

David didn't open the pendent, but ignored the moment for sentimental reflection. He kissed her forehead and bounded up the stairs to the police station front door. The choice to still turn back remained and he held the door handle for a fleeting moment, before pushing it down and walking into a zone with the unwritten words ringing in his ears, *blacks aren't allowed.*

***

The white recruits sat on the bench outside in the hallway. Some of their gazes rained unacceptance in his brain. Others made him think, *they look completely shocked.* David walked over to the bench and sat down. The stench of hatred sent his nerves into freefall. His muscles cramped and his left leg developed free will with a twitching vibration that forced him to grab his thigh to bring it under control.

The lump in his throat became larger and he gulped, swallowing his spit that had no effect on the swilling fear in his stomach. A blazing furnace of racism in the reception area became hotter as he gazed at the faces of two of the recruits and received the same message, *fuckoff, nigger.*

David held Abbie's pendent, wanting to pray, but still out of love with God, and too proud to ask him for help.

"Well, well, well, what do we have here, a group of pussies. We're going to find out how tough you are," said the sergeant who David had met before.

The young men walked to the desk to collect their information packs and locker keys. They followed the sergeant along the hallway to the male changing room.

"Get changed now, the gym is just along the corridor and second door on the right."

One of the recruits walked past David and accidentally shoulder barged him.

"Oh, I'm sorry."

He sniggered as he walked to his locker.

David tried to muster the confidence that he had earlier in the morning. He watched the expressions of the recruits and it enlarged his doubt that he was an outsider.

Sitting on the wooden bench, he stared at the ground and wondered, *where did the hallucination come from that I could take on the might of the force?*

David stood up, opened his assigned locker and a Golliwog fell out. Some of the recruits roared with amusement and the victimisation upon difference increased his realisation, that in the hostile white environment he was nothing, but dog shit on the pavement that even the flies refused to settle on and eat.

David reached into the locker and took out the note.

Go home, nigger, this isn't the place for you. Go home, Kunta Kinte.

David picked up his duffle bag, stormed to the corridor and slammed the door behind him. He heard the sniggers and a comment, "Good riddance, the black bastard has gone."

The sergeant peered around the corner of the door of the gym and smiled at David.

David walked to the end of the corridor, reached the door and kicked the skirting board. The power of agreement with Charles and Mary hit his mind with a wakeup call that he couldn't beat the police because they were too powerful. Mary's words rang aloud in his head, *what did we tell you about this racist institution.*

Whispers of *fool,* defined his name. Anger burned in his chest and overwhelming discouragement showered him with a firm confirmation that he was nothing more than a weakling.

"Fucking hell! Ray, help me!"

David leaned against the wall, bit his bottom lip and clenched his fists.

The courage of purpose found a light that ignited his soul with a compelling reason to face the fear. Walking back to the changing room he pushed open the door with force that clattered into one of the recruits. He threw open the locker door and kicked the Golliwog across the floor.

David changed into the white tee-shirt he'd brought, pulled up his white training shorts and laced up his white plimsolls. The picture of England beating Germany four goals to two on the wall in the world cup final didn't motivate him, but added to his doubt that he wasn't on the winning side. He clutched the pendent and patted his chest, commanding the nerves to be calm and he whispered, "I have to do this, I can't go home."

***

The walk to the gym was slow and he opened the door to face Rob and Mike who'd visited the house and twelve other young men. He didn't know which one of them would embrace him as a colleague and who had the same impression as himself that he was lost.

"Give me fifty push ups right now. You're not special, you're not an exception, no one turns up late," shouted the sergeant.

David dropped to the floor with Mike crouching down beside him and counting each press up that he did. He clenched his teeth together, forcing his body to respond whilst the other trainees commenced their physical with a gentle run around the gym. He reached number fifty and fell to the ground. His chest muscles pulsated from the tension and his arms were deadened by the pressure of exertion.

"C'mon, is that all you can do? Is that all you've got? You'll never make it in the force, never!"

David got to his feet, pursed his lips and clenched his fists behind his back. A visual of hitting Mike so hard that his jaw broke in several places and he had to stay in a coma for one week, came into his head. He breathed slowly, letting his fingers uncoil and bringing his fired-up emotions under control, knowing that if he lashed out, retribution would continue to exist as a dream.

He joined the other trainees and ran around the gym. The pace began to quicken and will kept him running, until he was directly behind the leader. The man in front began to pump his arms faster and David responded by letting anger push him to another gear.

"Ah, ah!" he screamed, as the medicine ball hit his stomach.

“That is why on the street, you must always be alert of your surroundings as Mr Morgan, has just experienced,” said the sergeant.

David writhed on the floor, rolling from side to side, holding his stomach with no air coming from his lungs and through his mouth. He tried to breathe, but only spit dribbled from his mouth and down his chin. The excruciating pain curled his body up like a hedgehog on a busy road.

The sergeant walked over to David, crouched down beside him and whispered, “What’s the problem, David, get up, quit now and go home, before we destroy you. I don’t want blacks in my force.”

The winded pain subsided from his body and David staggered to his feet. He watched the constables dropping medicine balls onto the stomachs of the other recruits, who yelled out on the impact against their flesh. He fought to follow the commands of press ups and repetition of squats that tested his will and determination.

David turned his head, gazing at the recruit who got up and left. He wanted to follow him, but destiny kept his backside in the gym.

“Anyone else want to leave? Do it now so we can separate the men from the boys,” Rob said.

David joined the other trainees on the training mat. He watched the constables demonstrating how to apprehend a violent criminal and turned away from their glare. Intuition whispered continuously in his mind, *walk to the door and don't look back.*

He studied the men, who one by one went up to act as the criminal and learn how to hold a potential suspect in a painful arm lock, before placing handcuffs on him. It deepened his apprehension as they all completed their turn and he sat on his hands with an alarm bell bellowing in his head.

The constable said, "David, you're up next." He got to his feet gingerly, still feeling the pain in his stomach from the medicine ball, and beginning to regret his decision to ignore the instruction of his intellect.

"Attack me!" shouted the constable.

David lunged towards him and the policeman grabbed his arm, swept his feet and took him down to the ground.

"This is nothing, nigger. Your stench from the floor is sickening. You smell like shit," he said under his breath.

David got up and began to walk back to the other trainees. The policeman grabbed his shoulder and pulled him back.

"We're not finished, attack me again."

David stared into his eyes, seeing the contempt in his expression and sensing the annoyance that he was still there and fighting for survival.

The policeman circled him and David charged at him, burning with an evil intention to rip his head from his body and stamp on his face.

The constable caught his flailing arms and brought him to the ground, placing him into a stranglehold, until he felt like his Adams apple was going to burst through his throat. The policeman kept him on the floor and he began to see silver stars and pass from one cloud of darkness to the next.

"That's enough for the physical. Go to the changing room and get dressed for your medical examination," said the sergeant.

Two of the trainees gawked and one of them stepped towards David and said, "Can I help you?" before being told to go to the changing room.

The other recruits left, leaving David squirming on the ground and gasping for air. The door slammed and his head shuddered against the floor. Despondency crawled up next to him and muttered that he should go home with his tail between his legs and dismiss the notion of becoming a man in blue.

David got up, hurting, but not defeated.

In the pain, desire filled his mind and soul, quenching the thirst of fear that tried to leap above his mild vibe of confidence.

"I'm joining the force. I'm not going to quit. I won't quit," he said, hobbling towards the door.

"What the fuck is wrong with you? Don't you get it? You'll be hated in the force and hated by your own communities," said the sergeant.

David opened the door to the corridor and Mike shut it. Rob and the sergeant walked towards him. The cold baton on the back of his neck chilled his vertebrae. Heavy laboured breathing from the policemen whispered condemnation in his mind. He turned to face them, bruised, but with a passion stronger than before to find out the truth.

"You can't win. The force is bigger than you and you'll end up broken. Ok, you took it today, but what about the next day and the next. Go and enjoy your future and forget about joining the police," said the sergeant.

David turned away from them and the constable moved from the door and let him through. He staggered towards the changing room door. His body felt like he'd been put on a medieval torture rack until his joints became dislocated. The tears poured down his face and he fell against the wall, being bombarded by the proclamations in his head of what he couldn't do, but through a grimace he steeled his mind with determination.

Placing his hand on the wall, he dismissed the chants of the police. Charles and Mary had chastised him for being dumb and blind and he used his power of resilience to quieten the criticism. The all-consuming fire blazed in his spirit. Their words of defeat lost strength to deter him from a mission that had kept him going through the pain of the physical.

The sergeant, Rob and Mike, watched him from the corridor and he turned back and met their stares with a look of fortitude.

"You won't stop me, I will, join the police force."

Chapter Seventeen

David gazed at the blue uniform that hung on a hanger outside the wardrobe and the helmet with the silver shield sitting on his small dressing table.

He wiped the smear of his breath from the mirror, and studied his wrinkled brow with his heart pounding from exhilaration and angst.

"Constable, 5503."

David picked up his letter from the table that confirmed he'd passed the medical and the physical examination and was now officially, a trainee policeman.

Sitting on the bed he picked up one of the black leather boots, smelling the polish and gazing at his reflection in the steel toe cap that came from the light bulb. His stomach rumbled as he mused on the day ahead. Speaking softly he said, "They'll be really mad that they couldn't stop me from joining." The moment his sentence ended, his hands juddered as he thought, *what's going to happen when I arrive?*

David remembered the look they gave him as he left the station and their murmurs that made a vivid statement that more was yet to come. Ripples went through his flesh as he considered, *I'm their special project of embracing black policemen and the chosen one.* Terror switched on in his head that hell was waiting for him and if he wasn't strong enough, then his backbone would be broken.

He contemplated Mary's attitude of conversation on mute and Charles, who just grunted and expressed his disappointment through small shakes of his head and gazes of pity for a lost son. David heard them praying excessively loud at night and in the morning, committing him before God that his eyes of blindness would be opened.

"Oh my God, this is it. There's no turning back. I'm in the police force," he said, putting on the uniform.

He picked up his jacket and the helmet, stepping into the hallway.

Charles opened his bedroom door and looked at him.

Mary waited at the bottom step. He walked confidently down the stairs. She touched his face and he held her hand and nodded to express that there could be no surrender or backward steps.

"My son, David, a policeman, may God be with you in the hell that you've chosen."

David walked into the kitchen and sat at the table, rubbing his fingers against the red plastic tablecloth and waiting for one of the policemen to pick him up. The heels of his boots trembled against the kitchen floor. He mused on the rumours that had spread from house to house and the usual greetings that had turned into quick acknowledgements, and a hasty getaway.

And now I'll be the one arresting the blacks and throwing them into the police vans. They're all going to hate me.

Whichever way he looked, he saw himself as a man with no home. He had power in his hands to make arrests, but was now a reject from his own community and dreading the first time he had to arrest somebody black after his training.

The front door thudded with a knock that quickened his heartbeat. He remained seated. *Am I mad?* The answer didn't come to confirm that he wasn't suffering from psychosis.

Adrenalin pumped through his body that in fifteen minutes, he would be sitting in the classroom surrounded by hate and as if vermin had entered the station and needed to be decimated.

Walking to the front door and opening it, he held his hand out to be recognised as a fellow policeman.

"I'm David, what's your name?"

"I'm Greg, are you ready? Let's go. Everybody knows about you, you're the special project."

David followed him, turning back and looking at the window of his front door before he got into the car. Inside was warmth and in the car the iciness chilled his nerves with a stark reality.

It's not a surprise that the entire force knows that a black policeman is joining today.

Looking at Greg from the corner of his eye, he shook his head at the mantle that suddenly enlarged.

I'm just trying to fight for justice. Surely they'll be at least one policeman who'll be on my side, he thought.

David felt the seatbelt clip. A strong voice preached in his head, *just hit the dashboard and tell Greg to take me back home.*

He heard Abbie's lecture of the reason why he was joining the force, strongly rebounding in his mind. He began to smile, reflecting on her bloodied mindedness and passion for the truth. A sense of realism formed before his eyes. No games or fun, it was real, with a clear mission set before him to unearth the darkness and establish the secrets that would lead to Ray's killer.

***

They arrived at the Croydon station and Greg parked the Panda car in the rear car park.

David looked at the station. He slowly unclipped his seatbelt with a whispering thought, *don't go in there, just don't.*

Getting out of the car, he stumbled on a jagged piece of concrete.

Greg pushed open the side entrance and David followed him into an office of white policemen. He watched some of them talking in their cliques and others working at a frenetic pace at their desks.

David studied the light brown desks, hanging lights surrounded by glass bowls, the grey swivel chairs and the off-white blinds that blocked out the sunlight.

Greg's nudge of his shoulder disturbed the assimilation of his new working environment.

"You need to go through there, into the classroom, good luck."

David nodded.

Why good luck.

He sensed the eyes watching his footsteps and turned around to heads dropping towards the desks. The whispers, the murmurs and the shuffling of paper, played a game of cat and mouse in his head. A baptism of suspicion submerged him as he the unthinkable, was now a part of them.

David closed the door quietly, standing outside and leaning against the wood to let his mind acknowledge where he was. Even the white walls when he touched them appeared to become tarnished by his black handprints. The fight of courage and fear began to battle in his mind. He'd never been in this type of atmosphere, except when confronted by the skinheads on that fatal day where every person was his enemy.

Pressing the door handle, he entered the classroom.

"You must be, David Morgan," said the training officer.

David nodded and walked to the front of the classroom to the only spare seat next to the young man who he recalled had got up from the bench.

The training officer found David's name on the register and tapped the desk.

"When I call your full name, please answer me."

David looked around the classroom, sitting amongst, but isolated from the other trainees. He had no sense of belonging as one of them. He saw the glares from the other side of the room that confirmed no allegiance between black and white. His mind tingled with the abhorrence and the disgust that they had to sit in the presence of what they saw him as, a nigger.

The Chief Superintendent walked in with the sergeant.

"Good morning and welcome to the Croydon police force. Whatever your perception of being a policeman is, forget it. You'll learn over the next few weeks what it is to be an officer of the law, we'll make sure of that," he said, staring at David.

The sergeant stepped forward and picked up a piece of chalk. He began to write on the blackboard.

David looked at the words that the sergeant had written and thought, *why do I want to be a policeman.*

His left boot heel began to clatter against the floor and the trainee next to him looked over and smiled. The pressure on his bladder increased and he clenched his fist, looking around the room and turning back to meet the eyes of the sergeant.

"For the next few weeks, you'll know me as hard bastard. I'm going to push you until you want to scream for mercy. I don't like any of you, I'm not your friend and you're all shit."

The sergeant threw the piece of chalk on the desk and walked around the room, gazing at each young man.

"What's your name and why did you join the force?"

The man stood up.

"I, hmm, want to fight crime and arrest criminals."

The Chief Superintendent left the room and the sergeant walked back to the front of the classroom.

"That's right. It doesn't matter if it's the Richardson gang or the Kray brothers, we'll get them eventually."

"We got Charlie, and Eddie Richardson and we'll get Ronnie and Reggie."

"We're here to fight crime and bring law and order to the streets. There are many criminals, black, Indian and white that must be stopped. You're going to stop them for you are the law and don't forget that."

"What's my name?"

"Hard bastard, hard bastard," replied the young men repeatedly.

David muttered the words, "Hard bastard." They didn't have the same ring of power in his ears as the trainees who chanted. He tried to stir up his emotion to fight and exude passion, but his heart didn't feel the same motivation that appeared to inspire his fellow policemen.

"Enough. I want you to add one more word to my name and call me Fucking hard bastard!"

David's tongue was silenced by the frenzy and banging of the desks. He tried to close his mind to the venting and their screams. His backside was stuck to his seat by their collaboration that subdued him in the euphoria of power. Turning around, his eyes met with their eyes and he murmured, "Fucking hard bastard, Fucking hard bastard." It was a feeble attempt to align himself to the multitude, rather than remaining as the solitary soldier.

He looked at the man next to him, watching him waving his hand and saluting like a hardened soldier. A strike of angst hit him squarely between the eyes that he wasn't in the playground of his neighbourhood, but in the middle of an army that would swallow him up, leaving him marred and never the same again.

The police sergeant held up his hand and the trainees stopped chanting. He walked behind David and gripped his chair.

David's sense of fear bloomed through the twitching of his lips. The imprint in his mind of being the anomaly in the classroom enlarged. His shoulders were tense and his breaths laboured. A cold draft of air on his scalp that interrupted the brainwaves, murmured, *hold up the white flag and surrender* now.

"That shouting and screaming that you did was for good reason, fucking get familiar with it. It's nothing compared to when you face a group of drunken lads on a Saturday night, or you have to deal with trouble in a black neighbourhood."

He let go of the chair and walked around to face David.

"And yes, let's not pretend, you, David, are in for double trouble. On the streets, you're a fucking nigger, black bastard and from the blacks in your communities, you're a bumbaclaat, a raasclaat and the fucking Babylon."

The men sniggered and elbowed each other.

David's confidence began to wilt strip by strip. The gaze of the sergeant made him gulp and his throat became parched. His words ruminated in David's mind and the enormity of the feat compressed him into the chair with a vision of being a tadpole amongst sharks.

"That's enough for this morning. Take a break outside and come back in thirty minutes."

The trainees got up, walking out in their pairs except for David, who walked in front of the man sitting next to him.

The man leaned forward and said quietly, "Did you enjoy your morning, fellow policeman?"

David watched the other trainees waltz outside into the crisp air and wandered to the toilet. He looked at his face in the mirror, shaking his head and blowing a mist of his breath onto the glass. A depressing sentiment hit him hard that he would drown under the pressure without anyone who was prepared to grab his hand and pull him out of the boisterous storm. All the bravado, courage and willpower couldn't stop him searching his heart and concluding, *they'll destroy me, or I'll destroy myself.*

He went into one of the cubicles and left the door slightly open. The mixed message of Charles and Mary and Abbie's belligerent stance for the truth, confused his mind. Shudders were in his legs at the fight against an establishment too big for him. To face the bigotry, the isolation and hatred everyday was a cross too great to bear on his shoulders alone.

"I'm sorry, Ray, I just can't do this, I just can't!"

He sat on the toilet seat with his head in his hands, completely deflated as he mulled over the pointed comments from the sergeant. A strong recognition that they were serious and no way were they prepared to let a nigger fuck up their system, panged his brain.

David removed his badge in complete submission to his experience of white power and decided that they would never see his face again.

***

"Can you believe it? A fucking black bastard in the force?" said a man, as he entered the toilet.

His colleague joined him and they both stood at the urinals.

"It's fucking unbelievable, a fucking monkey in uniform."

They both walked to the sinks to wash their hands. One of the policemen went to the cubicle doors and pushed it open with force. He went to the next one and did exactly the same.

David climbed on the toilet seat, holding onto the pipe and listening to the footsteps that got closer to the cubicle that he was hiding in.

With no control over his racing pulse, he tried to nullify the pounding in his chest by holding his breath and pressing his hands against each side of the cubicle.

"The chief and sergeant are pissed. I can tell you this much, he won't last beyond a week and we can all go back to the way it was."

His colleague laughed as he combed his hair.

David climbed down from the cubicle with twinkle toes and opened the door slightly wider to look at the two policemen. He didn't recognize them and quickly pulled his head back into the cubicle, climbing back onto the seat.

"I was talking to, Ben Harrington, from Hayes. He said the meeting is still on at the basement, 10 Colney Lane, East London, 9.30pm, 11th October. You should have seen it in the codes. You're still coming, aren't you?"

The fellow policemen nodded and washed his hands.

"Yeah, I'll be there. The Chief in Skegness, Richard Broker, is under serious pressure to find the killer, and Croydon are involved in the case as well, we all need to be careful."

They both walked out of the toilet.

David climbed down from the toilet seat, holding his stomach and rushing to the sink. He splashed the water on his sweaty face and loosened the tie that felt like it was deliberately trying to take his life by asphyxiation.

His mind popped with surmises and inconclusiveness. He placed the badge back on his blazer and knew that policeman 5503, had to live to fight another day.

“What’s going on?” he said, wiping the vapour from the mirror and watching his lips twittering as if they’d been bathed in ice.

David wandered to the office inconspicuously, where the two constables sat at their desks. A barrage of nervousness licked the soles of his boots with stumbles and stutters. He ambled towards them, pretending that he was on an errand and registered their names in the forefront of his mind.

“What are you doing in here? Shouldn’t you be with the other trainees?” asked Simon Logan.

David raised his hand and nodded. He ran to the outside yard and stopped, watching the other trainees milling around. Ignoring the conversations he bowed his head, preferring not to make eye contact with anyone.

Alone, in a secluded area of the yard, his chest and heart raced at a frenetic speed.

His mouth opened and his eyes widened at the snippet of information that he saw bigger than him and much bigger than the Croydon police force. He mulled over the conversation that he'd heard between the two policemen in the toilets. His mind concluded that there was a double side of the blue uniform and he knew that he had to turn the screwdriver into the hole and bore at the wood until all the pieces fell into place. David's intellect clicked into first gear. He thirsted for more intelligence and any inclination to resign was no longer an option.

The name Ben Harrington came back into his mind. He knew that he was a policeman at Hayes police station, but had no confirmation he knew anything about Ray's death. His thoughts wandered to the two policemen he'd seen in the toilet. *They said the chief at Skegness is under pressure to find the killer and Croydon's involved. What else do they know?*

The Chief Superintendent came outside and spoke to two of the trainees.

David observed him looking in his direction and he began to walk over towards him.

"So, David, how has it gone this morning? Do you still feel that you made the right choice in joining the police force?"

The saying repeated by Joyce resurrected from his memory, that a right eye with a crooked chink was a sign of a dishonest person.

I wish I could press my knee into his groin until he tells me everything he knows.

David took a deep breath, letting his head cool down and quelling his emotions that were ready to burst out. He knew that this wasn't the right time for him to erupt.

"I'm fine. I made the right choice. I want to be a policeman."

He turned his eyes back on the Chief Superintendent, with a firm conviction that behind the false enquiry of his wellbeing, was a dark secret that he had to uncover with dexterity.

"I'm really glad about that and it's my pleasure to be leading change across the forces, you're our special project."

His hand fell from the wall and brushed David's shoulder.

"We'll make the project a success and you'll be famous."

David watched him go back into the station.

What does he mean I'll be famous?

The Chief Superintendent's words rocked his mind back and forth into a conundrum of plight. Fame and fortune wasn't his pleasure. Being singled out as the special one whispered a cold blast of steam into the centre of his brain.

Two minutes passed by and the sergeant aka Fucking hard bastard came outside.

"Back to the classroom now ladies, it's not a party out here."

David followed the trainees back inside, entering the classroom last and taking his seat.

The man next to him stared, pushing David to engage in a battle of intimidation. David maintained his gaze until Fucking hard bastard tapped the blackboard and stopped his battle of who blinks first.

Another two policemen who were part of the training programme entered the room to run the next part of the day.

David didn't listen to their words and his mind kept spinning. He looked towards the back of the room and then adjacent, pondering on, *who can I trust, no one*. It seemed that the conspiracy net was widening, and he read the words in his notebook, *Ben Harrington, Simon Logan and Andrew Blake.*

***

David looked at the black plastic clock. The hours that had passed by seemed like he'd been locked in a prison for days.

Fucking hard bastard clapped his hands and said, "Ok, ladies, that's it for the day."

The trainees put the workbooks in their desks and moseyed out of the room.

David sat for a few moments and as he got up, the man next to him also moved. He followed him out of the classroom to the reception area of the police station.

Quietly he said, “Hope you enjoyed your first day, see you tomorrow, David, or maybe not.”

“I’m not leaving. There’s nothing that you can say or do that will make me leave,” whispered David, going through the station doors and walking towards Abbie, who waved from the open window of her car.

“So, how was it?”

David got into the green Austin Morris and strapped the seatbelt across his chest. He opened the window to let the breeze cool his flustered mind and his throbbing heart. His body moved with anxious vibrations to the hostile intentions that he couldn’t get out of his head.

“This isn’t good. I heard two policemen, Simon Logan and Andrew Blake, talking in the toilet about a meeting they’re going to and something about Ben Harrington at Hayes police station, I wrote it all down”

“None of it makes sense.”

Abbie reached over, kissed his cheek and then touched his thigh.

"I know that you're afraid, but you must be strong. Whatever they're hiding, we have to find out."

"Yeah, and they also said that the chief at Skegness, Richard Broker, is under pressure to find the killer and they all have to be careful. Ray was my best friend and they talk about him like he's nothing!"

Abbie drove along the road, taking a right and heading towards David's house.

He looked across at her, still trying to figure out how he'd ended up in the fast lane and hurtling at lightning speed in an unknown direction. One minute he was contented to dabble in the law of the land and now being the law he pondered, *how do we fit into the equation,* when all he could see was him taking the risks.

"This isn't the right turning."

"I know it's not, but you look so sexy in your uniform."

Abbie pulled into the dark alleyway, dimmed the lights and switched off the engine.

She kissed his face, his neck and his lips.

His resistance levels became weaker and the trials of his day paled into insignificance. He succumbed to a desire that he'd been counselled was the lure of Jezebel. His lips moved out of motion with hers. His heart beat faster. Skin began to sweat and his trousers bulged with a burst of testosterone.

"Let's get in the back seat."

Abbie climbed over the front seat and into the back. She unzipped her trousers and pulled them over her boots.

David looked at her pure white skin and her black knickers. Doubt and desire dispelled from his mind as she pulled him into the back seat, and he touched her nipples and moved his hands all over her body.

"Put it in me, I want to feel you inside."

But isn't sex before marriage wrong and an abomination to God?

His flesh was weak and he pulled his trousers and white briefs down, slithering on top of her and placing his left hand under her backside.

The spiritual reasoning didn't have the power that it used to over his emotions and he slid inside of her, gyrating his hips and falling into sexual pleasure that he'd fantasised about and in earnest, dismissed as a wrongful act.

“Ah, that’s it. I want more of you, I want more, more!”

David moved up and down, looking into her eyes until he couldn’t hold it back.

“Ah, ah,” he muttered, falling on her body and shivering from the physical and emotional release.

He crossed a line that he’d vowed he never would until he put a ring on the finger of the one that he loved.

“That was good, David, that was good,” she whispered.

David buried his head into her chest. The Eighth commandment, *Thou shall not commit adultery*, reverberated in his brain.

He expected the pleasure of elation after losing his virginity, but experienced disapproval and a sense of shame.

He couldn’t move, only lay still.

Abbie’s wet lips on his cheek reinforced that what was supposed to make him feel good, didn’t and he closed his eyes and thought, *I can’t do this again, I just can’t.*

Chapter Eighteen

"Look at them, they're back for more punishment."

The trainees stood in front of Fucking hard bastard dressed in white gym gear and looking at the obstacle course ahead of them. Fucking hard bastard walked up and down the line, staring at each young man and pointed at the tee-shirt of the trainee closest to the door, who dropped his head.

"What's that fucking black mark?"

Heads turned to look at David who thought, *you can't intimidate me.*

The door opened and his head turned to see Simon Logan walk in, go to Fucking hard bastard and hand him a note before leaving.

Simon Logan, Ben Harrington and Andrew Blake, yes, the meeting at Colney Lane.

"If you want to be a great policeman, then follow in the footsteps of Simon, he's one of the most respected officers in the force," said Fucking hard bastard.

Respected, but what about the meeting at Colney Lane, what are they up to?

Fucking hard bastard read the note, put it in his pocket and clapped, bringing David's attention back to the training session.

"Soon, you'll be on the beat if you're successful in passing the training programme. No one's going to like you. In fact most people will hate you, but don't give a fuck about that. You're in the uniform and you have the power."

David looked at the man standing by his left side, knowing that at the right time, he and Paul Broker would be walking the beat together.

He turned to face him and engaged in a battle of who blinks first without giving any ground.

"You're a fool," Paul whispered.

"Right. Move your backsides around the course and don't stop running until I tell you to."

David followed the trainees, sprinting around the gym, jumping over the obstacles placed in his path and dropping to the floor at the instruction of Fucking hard bastard to do press ups and sit ups.

He watched two of the trainees wheezing from exertion. A smile stretched across his face as they collapsed on the mat and held their stomachs, which inspired him to push harder and prove that he was the ready for the beat and fitter than any of his compatriots.

Fucking hard bastard walked over to the mat.

"I didn't tell you to stop you pair of pansies, now get up and work!"

He allowed the obstacle course to continue for one hour and then raised his hand to bring it to an end.

Fucking hard bastard walked behind David and placed his hand on his shoulder.

"David and Paul, you're up first for self-defence training."

David got up slowly, walked to the mat and watched Paul limbering up and cracking his knuckles.

Before he could blink, Paul ran at him and knocked him to the ground. He raised his foot to stamp on his body and David quickly rolled out of the way and jumped to his feet.

"This is a fucking training session, not a real fight, save that for the street."

David circled Paul, knowing that one of them was supposed to play the assailant and the other the policeman who had the responsibility to apprehend the attacker. Paul charged again, pulling David to the ground and wrapping his arms around his chest. David elbowed Paul and heard him wince from the blow to his ribs. He nodded his head to send a message that he was the boss and had the combat skills to deal with any attack.

"Fucking keep it clean, you'll have enough shit on the street."

David grappled with Paul on the ground, getting the advantage and grabbing his hand to hold him in a wrist lock. He lacked the strength to bring Paul into submission, who flipped him on his front and applied a choke hold.

His throat was squeezed until the air could no longer be exhaled from his lungs.

David's arms became limp and Paul said under his breath, "Remember, who the police force is for," before Fucking hard bastard pushed him off.

David held his throat, gasping for a puff of air, but with restricted lungs he could only choke. He tried to stand up, reaching out for someone to help him, but no one came to lend a helping hand. He coughed and spluttered. His bravado was in battle with confidence, and he took a psychological tumble with a clear message resonating in his mind that the hell wasn't going to end.

"That's it for this morning, get changed and get back to the classroom."

The other men left to get a shower, except for one trainee who went to the training mat and helped David to his feet.

"What are you trying to prove? You get more abuse than anyone. People hate you, but you put yourself through this every day, you must be fucking mad!"

David stared at the man with his eyes on fire.

"Thank you, but you'll never understand, I can't leave," he replied, stumbling to the door.

He walked into the changing rooms, stuttered into the bench and fell to his knees.

"Whatever you might think, I'm not quitting, I will be a policeman!"

He gazed at the trainees as they left one by one.

The door slammed and his left foot kicked out and danced to its own tune without an instruction to move to the silent music of sound that he wanted. He raised his head and saw Paul standing and holding the blue flowered plastic bin.

David stood up. Fear rumbled in his stomach and churned his intestine. The hello and kiss between his two knees buckled his body and he leaned against the wall, fighting for strength, but vulnerable and at the mercy of a man who he knew that he couldn't get the better of in a physical fight.

"You've got big balls and you're harder than I thought. I'll see you on the beat real soon David, bright and early," he whispered.

"In a way, I have to respect you, you're tough."

David nodded with a wry smile.

Are the tables turning?

Going to the shower he let the water soak through his curly black hair.

"God, you need to help me!"

Quickly remembering that he and God weren't allies, he turned the shower off and allowed his heart to become full of pride again. His cry to God for assistance was dismissed as a knee jerk reaction to fear, but a dart of conscience pricked his mind.

If I've destroyed all association with God, then why did I feel dirty when I had sex with Abbie and why am I calling out to God to help me now?

After drying his body, he got dressed and made his way back to the classroom, visualising himself as a martyr and fighting with his religious beliefs that were still haunting him from the past.

He took his seat next to Paul.

"Welcome back, David, I'm pleased that you decided to join us, now where were we?"

He heard the sarcasm and ridicule in Fucking hard bustard's words, but dismissed them.

Opening his book, he stared at the names that he'd written without any evidence that they were guilty of a crime of murder, or knew who Ray's killers were.

"You at the back, wake up. Get to the front and explain what it takes to be a good policeman in Croydon."

The trainee got out of his chair and walked to the front.

David released a small sigh, relieved at the respite that took the attention away from him and put it on someone else.

He watched the man receiving jeers and derision. The mockery of another person didn't resonate with his spirit of justice, and he was glad when Fucking hard bastard released the man from the embarrassment.

The door opened and two constables walked in. David turned his head and quickly looked to the front. He crossed his feet under the desk and squeezed his pencil with power and repeated in his mind, *they won't break me, I can't let them break me.*

"Simon and Andrew, will take over for the rest of the day. They are two of the best constables in the force and you'll learn a lot from them, so pay attention."

Fucking hard bastard left the room. Simon shut the door and Andrew stood at the blackboard, holding a piece of chalk.

"One of you will definitely quit straight after the training and half of you will quit in the first six months. The police force isn't for girls, it's for men who can take shit and give shit."

A kick of his boot under the desk and the vibration of the word quit, messaged David that he was hanging on by a thread.

All I need to do is get up and walk out of the room. Nobody here will blame me after the torture that I've gone through, he thought.

Defeat kept swarming his mind. He shuffled his chair backwards, looking around the classroom and then at the door.

Just a few steps and I'll never have to see these racist bastards again.

A picture of two chameleons floated into his mind as he gazed at Andrew and Simon, but he was incited by their passion as he listened to them talk about the murders of fellow constables, Geoffrey Fox, Christopher Head and David Wombell and the arrest of their killer, Harry Maurice Roberts.

Their fervour was a passing breeze as he thought, *if three white policemen can be shot in Shepherd's Bush then what chance do I have?*

His mind couldn't absorb any more mental pressure at the thought of being murdered.

David looked up at the ceiling and breathed as red for danger became blazing orange and cemented his decision. He stood up and walked towards the door.

“Hello, what’s this? I spoke too soon. Make it today that the second person quits. Goodbye, Mr Morgan,” Simon said.

David’s hand rested on the door handle. His forehead touched the glass window. He didn’t need to turn around. He could sense the atmosphere of the trainees and Simon and Andrew willing him to open the door, step out and slam it shut.

“If you walk through that door, your career as a policeman is finished,” Andrew said.

Chapter Nineteen

The dustbin lid that clattered on the pavement and the screeching cat burned David's ears with an emotional strain. Silver stars lit up the black sky and the full moon that shone on the building gave him an impression of a normal and calm night. The whispering wind blew on the back of his neck and he pulled up his collar, gazing at the solitary tree bending over and nearly kissing the cobbled stones. Houses without light, or the smell of a cooked meal coming through an open window and romanticising with the dense atmosphere, made him stare more intensely, for one address, number 10, Colney Lane.

Abbie grabbed his arm and he winced. A cut into his flesh from her fingernails caused him to stutter on the dark cobblestones.

"David, I'm scared."

David pulled her closer to him, covering her mouth and holding his breath to stop the sound of his panic breaking the stillness of the quiet night. He gripped Abbie's hand and pulled her into a garden of a decrepit building. David clutched his chest to simmer down the fearful convulsions that ebbed through his body and threatened to reveal his place of hiding.

His heartbeats throbbed and he commanded them to be silent. The danger overrode the instruction and they continued to pound in response to the terror that brimmed inside of him. Putting his finger against his mouth, he watched the faint lighting and the black metal steps that led to a basement.

"We have to get inside, Abbie."

Two men appeared and David pulled Abbie down to the ground behind the wall, surrounded by bushes. His lungs cried for air to be released and he put his hand over his mouth and nose to quieten his breaths, lest the ears of the skinheads were pricked. He peered through the small gaps, gazing at the skinheads and their blue jeans and red Doc Marten boots as they headed towards the metal steps.

"Fucking Skins for Life, we live on," said one of the men.

David watched them walk around the vicinity before going down the metal steps and opening the black door.

He raised his head and dropped it quickly as a van pulled up, shielding his eyes from the bright headlights. A frenzy of fear clawed at his nerves and palpitations strummed his heartbeats with a sound of anxiety. David clutched Abbie like it was the final goodbye, before the world that he knew changed forever.

The door opened, a man coughed, threw his cigarette into the bushes and farted.

"Don't say a word, at least it doesn't smell as bad as a dead nigger."

David peered through the bushes at the swinging baseball bats. He couldn't stop the quivering in his legs and a pressure of panic attacked his mind.

To run and forget the idea of discovering what was behind the black door, appealed to the pulsations of fright that kept telling him, *if we get caught, we're dead.*

"David, let's leave, it's too dangerous. There has to be another way," whispered Abbie.

His thoughts tossed and turned, settling on a remembrance that he'd been here before and survived when a gun was held to his head. To walk away and let Ray die a second time when the clues appeared to be unfolding was inconceivable. He reflected on Martin Luther King, visualising his hero's bravery and motivation that anchored his refusal to concede, despite the threat to his life.

"I can't be a coward and run. If you want to leave, then leave, but I can't," he said, letting go of Abbie's hand.

He stood up and parted the bushes, peering through the gap before walking onto the pavement to make sure that he was alone. The blue and white Commer van in front of him blocked his view to the basement building. He put his hand on the door handle and pulled to open it and then tried the other door, looking through the window in an attempt to find the secrets, being hidden in the dark enclosure.

"David, quick! Get back, get back, there's a car coming!"

The bright lights of the car in the distance beamed and he dropped to the ground and rolled underneath the van. He heard the car come to a screeching halt behind the van where he lay. The opening and slamming of car doors registered in his mind that the occupants weren't here to play games. His head turned to the footsteps of the black boots, and he knew that they were one of a kind who would show no hesitation in pulverising his body until he lay motionless in the dirt.

"Good, the others are here. Let's get to the meeting, we have issues to discuss. Power to the skins," said one of the men.

David saw the glint coming from the handcuffs of the policemen. The footsteps stopped and a coin dropped on the floor, intensified his banging head tension with a flurry of terrorising trauma.

Hearing the footsteps coming towards the van he sucked in air and held his breath, seeing the boots that were near his head. David grabbed his throat. *Don't look under the van.* In his mind he said, *Abbie, don't scream* whilst his foot trembled, despite his command for it to be still.

The policeman tapped on the van. His taps got closer to the bottom of the driver's door and David pressed his hands into the ground. His heart perpetually missed beats. Every nerve responded with an attack of angst that shook his brain with an image of blood, his blood, running into the cracks of the pavement.

"What's the problem? Leave it. We need to get to the meeting," said one of the policemen.

"I'm sure that I saw something. It must be the fact that I haven't cracked a nigger's skull for a long time."

He drummed on the window and went back to the black metal steps. He looked back again before stepping down the stairs and joining his fellow policemen, walking into the house and closing the door.

"David, David," Abbie said softly.

She came out from the bushes, laying on the pavement and stretching underneath the van to touch David's arm.

He laid still. His head was diced with a baptism of blood in his imagination. His hair brushed in the gravel and the small stones were stuck to the palm of his hands.

Darkness surrounded him and the terror of hatred pelted his mind with whispers of defeat. He wanted to move, but he couldn't. Fear kept him impaled to the ground and revealed pictures in his head of death at the hands of the traitors to the uniform.

"David, please, let's just leave!"

He reached over and wiped the tears from her eyes, letting go of her hand and rolling from underneath the van. He stood up and pulled Abbie to her feet.

The dread ate into his mind and he could only see risk and endangerment. He held Abbie's face. The image as they took it in turns to rape her before his eyes and then cut her throat whilst he watched and was unable to save her life, was a recurring film in his brain without the ability to turn it off.

"Abbie, I'm scared, I know you're scared, but we have to go in."

His hands encased hers and he kissed her lips. He looked over at the steps that led to the basement and nodded, knowing that they were cemented in allegiance for the cause of justice and not even the scent of being killed could deter him.

"I've got my camera, let's go," she said.

David pulled her back and put his forehead against hers.

"Whatever happens in there, don't ever forget that I love you."

***

David scampered over to the black metal steps with Abbie and crouched down at the top stair, pointing to himself and then pointing at the door. He climbed surreptitiously down the steps, peering through the keyhole and beckoned Abbie to follow.

He could feel her breaths on the back of his neck. The speckled hairs on his chest spiked and he stood on edge. He grabbed her hand whilst he stared at the door. Fright told him, *run*, but pluck forced him to stand, despite knowing what could happen to him, if the skinheads and the policemen smelled the infiltration of their environment.

"Don't make a sound," he whispered.

He turned and placed his back against the door, freezing in the chill and holding onto Abbie. David squeezed his thighs together, resisting the pressure in his bladder and the desire to turn back. Fear was outside and inside him and looming with intent to rip apart his bravery and he let out a deep breath.

I have to go in, I can't be a coward, I have to go in.

David turned back towards the door and peeped through the keyhole, gazing into blackness. He pulled back. His heart jumped. Nerves caused a riot in his mind and the valour dismantled.

"You're right, this is too big. Did you see their baseball bats? I don't want to die tonight! Let's get out of here."

He climbed up two steps to run to safety, rather than face the terror that had ripped into his courage. His hands sweated furiously despite the cold temperatures, and his mind was imprinted with a coffin and him in it, as another murder victim.

"Can you live with your conscience, knowing that Ray was murdered by racists and you stood by and did nothing? Can you sleep at night if you walk away like a coward?"

He stood still on the stairs. Her words enveloped his heart like a terminal cancer. He contemplated *what would Ray do? He'd fight for the truth, even if it meant losing his life.*

To run, that was definitely his desire, but a picture of Ray's face pierced his brain and stabbed purpose into his heart. He stepped backwards into the arms of Abbie. His soul turned upside down and his spirit compelled him to walk into danger and hope that this wouldn't be a red night.

"This is for Ray. Abbie, let's go and get out, God help us."

***

David twisted the doorknob and opened the door to the dark and spooky hallway. He brushed the cobwebs from his hand and reached out for the walls that were damp. His heart hammered to a beat of fright and his mind whispered, *you're going to die, exactly the same way that Ray did.*

Abbie held David's jacket.

The darkness blinded his eyes and he led the blind, taking careful steps and using his police training to listen for sound and movement. *Skins for Life*, a definitive echo, he could hear in his mind.

He visualised the cowards and the next tranche of evil that they were planning, knowing that they would rather kill than be exposed. Their thirst for murder made angst crawl through his veins and he was afraid of their warped minds and stumbled on the step, at the dismembering of a black man and a white woman. His feet desensitized and he was glued to the stairs with a heart that twirled with a vibration of trepidation.

"Wait, do you hear that noise? It sounds like chanting," whispered Abbie.

The intensity of David's terror grew bigger. He could hear voices without understanding the lyrics. His hands clutched Abbie as he listened to the aggressive shouts from upstairs that contradicted his constant silent proclamation, *be brave, be brave.*

David put his foot on the third step. It creaked and he stopped. His bones rattled together in his body and his mind screamed with internal cries of dread.

Abbie stepped ahead of him and he grabbed her jacket as the chanting became louder and mixed with stamping and clattering of chairs.

He pulled her back, musing on his foolishness to enter a remote house without the cavalry to watch his back, believing that he could unearth the enigmas of racism, bigotry and outwit the Skins for Life. He could only see one thing, a tombstone with his name on it. He placed his hands over his ears to shut out the celebration of white supremacy, and extinction of the nigger resounding through the walls and striking at his heart with a death sentence.

He crept pass Abbie and followed the cries of hate, placing his back against the wall. His body was frozen into a musical statue and his mind was in a state of pandemonium.

"Fucking niggers. Death to the blacks and power to the skins," shouted the men.

Abbie tiptoed to David and pulled him down to the floor.

He banged his head with his knuckles to knock out the fear and pulled the string of her standard single lens camera.

She grabbed the ledge of the window and took the first photograph.

"We'll never let niggers achieve equal status to the white man. They're inferior, they come from monkeys and they belong in a pile of shit," shouted the man, leading the chanting from the front.

"That's right. We're the skins and I say death to the fucking black bastards. Death to every nigger that walks the planet," said a skinhead.

Abbie took another photograph.

A place of remembrance, executed a twinge in David's head to recall when the mob screamed out their racist obscenities. The clapping, cheering and stamping caused anger to rise up in his heart and burn through his flesh with a compulsion to leave no man standing.

David clenched his fists, rocking on the ground with no control over his upper body. Hostility, hatred and the desire to kill took over him like an epileptic seizure. He dug his fingers into the cold stone floor, biting his top lip and all of his emotions desired to explode and enact a blood bath.

"I want to fucking kill them. They're murderers, they're killers, I want revenge."

He stood up, peering through the window and covering his ears to drown out the noise of death coming from the room. He watched the skinheads and policemen throwing up Hitler salutes and thoughts of, *get in there now and kill them,* coerced him to burst through the door and cause a stampede of justified retribution.

"David, let's go, we have enough evidence. Let's go before someone comes out."

He pushed Abbie's hand off his leg. His reflections swilled around in his mind.

The skinheads and the police are the same thing. They're killers and their roaming free to kill again. I can't let that happen.

David put his hand on the door handle with rage and fury driving him, rather than a cool and controlled emotional intellect.

They all have to die before another black man is murdered.

***

"There's a nigger, who thinks that he's above us and he needs to be brought down," said a man.

His voice was familiar to David, but still unclear through the continuous shouting. He let go of the door handle, patted Abbie on the shoulder and returned to the window. The noise in his brain began to simmer down and he craned his neck to see the man standing at the front.

"This monkey wears my uniform and thinks that we don't know his plan. I say death to him, the same way his friend died alone on the memorable day in Skegness," said the policeman.

Simon Logan, it sounds like him.

David dropped to the ground, clutched his jacket and banged his fist into the ground until it bled.

"David, I'm scared. Please, let's go, please!"

He pulled himself up to the window again, this time seeing the face of the policeman standing at the front. His heart incited murder and war. He fought with the swelling in his mind to burst through the door and tear the man's head off and trample on his body, until there was nothing left, apart from a bloody pulp.

Clutching the window frame, his heart seemingly pumped blood through an enlarged ventricle and his head was frazzled with a picture of Ray's dead body. The boasting and venom coming through the mouth of the policeman made his body shake in horror and his eyes popped with tears, fuelled by a cocktail of sorrow and anger, that turned his mind into a haze of aversion.

"It's him! Paul Broker! I thought that he was just working for the sergeant and the chief to force me to leave, it's him!" David whispered.

Abbie stood up at the window and took photographs of Paul Broker.

"David, c'mon. We need to get out of here now! C'mon, David."

David nodded and pursed his lips, cut at the heart and squeezing his fists together. He turned to leave and then came back to the door with every thought driving him to strike now, or leave in remorse that he dishonoured the death of Ray, because he let fear rule his heart and mind.

"I still remember that nigger, pleading for his life when I slashed his throat. We'll never show mercy to a nigger, they must all die."

David's mouth fell open, his arms limped by his side and his foot kicked out into the air at an imaginary foe. Tears welled up in his eyes and fell onto the stone floor, each one a cry for Ray. He clasped his mouth and each silent scream felt like it splintered the bones in his body and made incisions on every inch of his skin.

"I want him to die, I need him to die!"

Abbie pulled at his arm and whispered, "We must leave now!"

He covered his ears to shut out the applause and the celebration, but it penetrated his brain with derision.

Abbie tugged his arm and he walked stealthily to the stairs, searching for the banister in the dark. David took one step at a time, feeling for the stair that creaked. He stopped. His body started to dance and his Adams apple locked in his throat. He looked back up the stairs and watched the light coming from underneath the door that flickered on and off.

"Death to the niggers and keep the skins movement alive," said a man.

His feet trampled on the landing and he pounded the wall. Belching, he took a step down the stairs and beat his chest.

He kept coming down the stairs, getting nearer and David stood, frozen on the step and holding Abbie's shoulder in a tight vice grip.

His lungs contracted, desperately requiring a gush of air. He stretched his hand into the darkness and his fingers trembled. The vibe in his head sensed that the man was close to his face and he tensed his hands to reach out and strangle him until his feet stopped kicking and his heart stopped beating.

The man took a box of matches from his pocket and lit a cigarette. He took another step down the stairs.

David looked up at the light, waiting for him to get close enough before knocking him out cold.

Abbie coughed and instinctively he grabbed her hand and ran down the stairs. He fumbled to find the door handle as his brave heart melted into a terrorizing agony that they were about to be murdered.

"Fucking hell! There's someone here, we have fucking intruders!"

"Quick, run! We need to get out of here, now!" David said.

He grabbed Abbie's hand and threw open the door that clattered against the metal railing. As he sprinted up the stairs, Abbie tripped and gashed her leg on the sharp jagged metal.

"Ah, my leg, David, my leg!"

He ran back, putting his arm around her shoulder and pulling Abbie to her feet.

"Forget the pain, just run to the car or we're dead!"

David ran down the cobbled street, dragging Abbie with him and turning the corner. The voices that cut into the night caused his heart to sing with frantic wails.

"Abbie, hurry up, get the car keys, quick!"

Abbie got the car keys, opened the car doors, got in and switched on the ignition.

David dived into the seat, panting, his brain throbbing and his body trembling.

"Drive, just drive!"

Abbie put the car in reverse and sped out of the cul de sac. She changed the gear stick into first gear with David's right foot pressing on an imaginary accelerator, as they sped out of the Skins for Life location.

"Ah, the bright lights, I can't see!" shouted Abbie.

She pressed on the brake and jerked David towards the windscreen, jolting his head against the car seat.

"Don't stop, go, go," said David, grabbing the steering wheel, swerving around the van and narrowly avoiding a collision with another car.

"Drive, Abbie, just bloody drive or we're dead!"

She took hold of the steering wheel, driving down the road and onto the pavement.

David looked behind, with his body convulsing and his brain frying up a plate of terror which fired gunshots into his mind that their lives were within a whisker of being snuffed out.

"David, they saw us. David, they know who we are!"

Holding onto his seat, he looked behind through the back window at the beaming lights that seemed to be getting closer.

"Quick! Pull down there and switch off the engine."

The screams of the skinheads were still in David's brain and slamming it from side to side. He sat and shivered in the seat. His composure was in complete disarray and he looked at the end of the road, gripped by panic.

"Ah, ah, it's them!"

A van flew by and David grabbed Abbie's mouth to silence her voice. She bit his hand and he gritted his teeth, taking the pain, rather than sending out an alarm that they were here, exposed and vulnerable.

"Calm down. They won't find us, they didn't see us, are you calm?"

Abbie nodded.

He removed his hand from her mouth and let his breaths tranquilise the boisterous storm, but kept his brain alive to the threat of danger.

She unclipped her seatbelt and threw her arms around his neck.

"David, they're evil. Why doesn't God destroy them?"

David closed his eyes and quickly opened them, reasoning with the words of Paul Broker. He reminded himself, *God wasn't there in Skegness and he let Ray die*. His heart had no confidence in the creator that he would act now to save them.

But yet we've escaped, he thought, almost conceding that it could be God who'd intervened supernaturally.

A wave of sorrow enveloped his soul and he cried relentlessly. He could see Ray again in his head, not alive, but dead.

The confession of Paul Broker taunted him that he saw the killer and heard him talk with relish as he murdered Ray and he just stared, rather than rush into the room and kill to settle the score of a life for a life.

A rampage of guilt filled his mind. He tried to stamp out the cries of a thirst for blood, but they kept ringing in his ears. Trust in his fellow policemen to make the arrests and bring the guilty parties to trial, was a risk that he wasn't prepared to take, and he knew wholeheartedly, that he had to be the one to apply justice.

***

The cool chill of the night brushed across his face. He pointed to the street for Abbie to begin to drive, now he was sure that they were out of the woods.

She drove to the end of the road, taking a right turn and driving towards the traffic lights.

“Wait! You said his name is Paul Broker.”

David shrugged, visualising Paul’s face and reflecting on his gloating of being there on the pavement and inflicting the fatal strike. He despised him, wanting to hold up his head, look into his eyes and cut his throat.

The only rhythm in his mind was a chant of death and he squeezed his hands, seeing the killing, smelling blood and feeling anger of retribution which still didn’t release him from the pain.

“David, Paul Broker. The name of the Chief Superintendent at Skegness police station is Richard Broker, they could be related!”

His mind began to churn and he reflected on the police arrests that hadn't resulted in a confirmed suspect remaining incarcerated, now he knew why. Their slow responses and perceived attempts to bury the case and leave the matter as unsolved began to string together. He recognised that they had no intention of finding the murderer, because he was one of them and under police protection.

"He did it! He killed Ray. Paul, it was him that plunged the knife into Ray."

Abbie held his hand and his body shuddered against the seat. His eyes glazed and his brain under a trance, fixed his mind and locked his thoughts onto a singular mission where his soul couldn't rest until the deed was done.

"David, David, listen to me. He said it, but we can't prove that it was him. We need evidence. Think, David!"

She arrived at his house and he watched the dimming lamppost lights, shutting his eyes when it became black and opening them when the brightness hit his eyelids. He had no great speech to make and repeated the word, *evidence,* in his head. Paul's lips was the proof and silent night the only verse that whirled around his mind.

He held out his hand and she took it. Fear had come and gone and he was back to torment his troubled spirit that switched between bravado and terror.

Abbie touched his face.

"David, I'm not a Christian, but once upon a time you knew who God was. We need his help. These people know that someone was there and if they find out that it was us, they'll kill us."

David pushed down the handle to leave without a care for his own life. He opened the door and then shut it.

"My friend, Ray!"

His emotions uncurled and he hit the dashboard, hating God even more than the skinheads. He recollected, *God was supposed to send angels who excel in strength, listen to his voice and protect his children from harm.*

"Abbie, never talk to me about God again, he's dead. Let, Paul Broker, enjoy his little victory. I can promise you, he's a dead man."

Chapter Twenty

"You can still say good morning to us."

David stared at Charles and sat at the table, pouring a cup of tea from the white china pot.

Mary entered the living room and he looked at her face, lost in a sandstorm and breathing in the air of reprisal. Images of riotous behaviour were in his mind. A gentle hum of lyrics toughened his resolve and criminalised his record of being the perfect policeman.

"Aren't you going to work today?"

He didn't need to go to the station to see Paul's face, it was etched in his brain. He drank the tea quickly, debating his moment to strike without the perpetrators guessing his intent.

Mary buttered a slice of toast and placed it on a plate in front of him. David smiled, hiding the hate and the pain rumbling in his body through the first bite and the slurp of his drink.

"I'm still your mother and I know something's wrong. Whatever our differences, you're still my son, what is it?"

David looked at her face, aching to confide and trust the plea for her help. He questioned, *should I tell them my plan and make them accomplices?* Doubt shook his head at their belief in God that would prevent him from convincing them to agree to his intent to commit murder.

"When's the last time that you heard anything about Ray's murder? Everyone has given up, nobody cares anymore."

His ears responded to the rustling of the newspaper. The banging of the cutlery on the table alerted his senses that he had their attention.

"The killer won't escape, David. If he or they aren't caught in this life then believe you me, they won't escape the final judgement. Hell awaits them where they'll burn for eternity with Satan and his demons," Mary said.

David got up from the table. To wait until the final judgement was a major problem. He couldn't reconcile that in the Old Testament when the enemies of God's children were attacked, he destroyed them.

He reflected on the story of Joshua and the kings that amassed an army like sand on the sea.

Yet God threw hailstones from heaven and killed more than died by the sword.

"Ray can't wait for revenge until the second coming of Christ, he needs revenge now."

"Son, vengeance isn't yours, it belongs to God, he will avenge Ray," Charles said.

David's thoughts screamed *wrong, wrong, you're wrong.* This was why he couldn't confide in them, because they always referred back to God, as if he cared.

Why can't they see that God is inconsistent. He does one thing at a particular time when it pleases him, and then changes his mind and does something else.

"I won't stand by and let Ray's death mean nothing or allow his killer to walk as a free man," he said, pushing the chair aggressively from the table and stomping upstairs.

"David, come back down. Come back downstairs!" shouted Charles.

David slammed his bedroom door. He leaned against it with a central image of Paul Broker laughing in his face. His hand touched his throat as he remembered gasping for breath when Paul held him in a choke hold. His mind professed that it wasn't a friendly warning, but an act of wilful intent.

His legs could barely hold his weight and he grabbed the window ledge, knowing that he had to strike first before he was swept away by a tirade of white power.

David rummaged through the wardrobe for his jacket. Nervousness ran through his body at going back to Skegness to visit the place where Ray died. The scarring in his mind flashed in intervals with the grisly reminder of a bloodbath and the painful separation from his brother that he loved.

Holding onto the wardrobe door with his left hand, he closed his right hand into a fist to stop the convulsions of his fingers, and still he had no control over the shuddering of his heart and the tears that streamed down his face. He was bleeding inside from a memory that was no longer subservient to his command to lay down and be quiet.

Musing on the Chief Superintendent of Skegness, Richard Broker, he wanted to see his face and look into his eyes. His ears heard him confess that he knew the murderer and his involvement in the Skins for Life. If Paul was his blood, he determined that he would make him suffer for raising a racist son and experience the pain of unending loss.

***

"Ah! What's this?"

He threw the green Corduroy jacket onto the floor, kicking it across the room and staring at the clothing as if it was a dead animal. David took his grey Harrington Bomber jacket with the tartan lining from the wardrobe and put it on.

He returned to the jacket that he wore in Skegness with Angela, Elaine and Ray. Picking it up from the carpet, he inhaled the smell of the linen with a reappearance of the events that took place that day. His eyes gazed at the speck of blood on the pocket and he knew that it was his blood.

His fingers wandered to the pocket and he felt something hard through the material. It came flooding back into his mind. The coin thrown by the skinhead when they cursed and shouted had hit him in the forehead.

“I wanted to throw it back, but I didn’t. The policeman knew what I was going to do, but took us away before I could retaliate.”

He reached inside the pocket to take out the coin.

“Wait. Fingerprints! There might be fingerprints. Whoever threw this, their fingerprints could be on the coin.”

A car horn beeped outside. He quickly wrapped the coin in a piece of paper and ran downstairs to the open front door. Contorted expressions lit up his face as he watched Mary talking to Abbie. *What's she saying to her?* He walked quickly and then slowly, hearing voices of laughter and glee that sprung the element of surprise in his imagination.

"Abbie, you must come around for dinner, it was lovely talking to you."

David walked to the car, got in and turned, watching Mary walk up the garden path.

"What was all that about? Why were you and my mum talking?"

Abbie giggled, putting her hand on his knee, whilst his mind was twisting with stories of colour and reverse racism.

She switched on the ignition and began the drive to Skegness.

"David, relax. Your mum is really lovely. She invited me for dinner and I'll be able to try rice, peas and chicken."

He looked at the sky, it hadn't changed colour and neither was the sun replaced by the moon. *I'm sure it's not April fool's day.* Staring at the front door, he mused on Mary and her hate of him being involved with a white woman. Her comments that they were trouble harassed his head with confusion.

I mean, she's standing outside, talking to Abbie as if she likes her and invites her for dinner.

David shook his head at the mixed messages that were firing into his brain.

This is just strange, what's changed, he thought.

An undeniable truth seemed like it whacked him on his forehead. He could run, but he couldn't hide. The Lord appeared to be watching his every move and playing with his conscience.

Firstly Abbie tells me to pray and now mum's pretending that she likes white women.

"I've told my parent's everything, David, they're going to help us."

His mind dispelled Mary's behaviour as he heard the word help and doubted if it meant murder. *This can only be settled by death and that I'm absolutely sure of.*

He didn't want to imagine Paul and his killing accomplices walking free from prison, having served half of their sentence only, and then going back to pick up the remnants of Skins for Life.

The scheming went through his brain and he settled on one outcome. *I won't stop until every skinhead responsible for Ray's murder is hunted down and killed.*

"You do know that this can only end one way?"

Abbie took the A1 (M) motorway, overtaking a car in the slow lane and proceeded into the middle lane.

"We can't make this right by spilling blood, even if it's deserved."

David bit his bottom lip and banged his knee against the door. He turned to stare at her and saw that Abbie wasn't for him, but against him.

Why can't she understand, that there's only one way?

David reached inside his jacket pocket.

"I found a coin that was thrown at me in Skegness."

Abbie braked and threw him towards the windscreen.

"You didn't touch it and remove any potential evidence, did you?"

He took the piece of paper from his pocket and opened it, gazing at the fifty pence coin that was stained and black. It exacerbated the torment residing in him and he knew that someone else who was there had more answers that he had to discover.

"David, someone's fingerprints are on that coin. You don't need to meet violence with violence, the truth always has a way of being exposed."

David nodded, looking through the window and observing the white Humber Super Snipe pulling out and the driver moving into the middle lane.

He watched the vehicle in the mirror and Abbie reduced her speed, moving into the slow lane.

"They're after us," she whispered.

The policeman moved into the third lane and picked up his speed. Other drivers moved out of the way. He slowed down and remained within a whisker of Abbie's car.

"Don't look at them, Abbie, just keep driving."

David kept his head straight and sustained his gaze on the vehicles ahead of him, playing it cool, despite the fright that vibrated through his body.

The driver advanced and drew parallel to David and Abbie. The blue light began to flash and the siren blared.

"David, they're after us, I can sense it. We're going to be arrested!"

The policeman in the passenger seat pointed. The noise of the siren became louder and the engine of the police vehicle revved.

"Don't look at them. Keep your nerve Abbie, don't look at them!"

The driver sped along the motorway and David jumped in the seat. He opened the window and breathed profusely to turn the terror in his mind into a gentle running stream.

As he clasped Abbie's arm, his hate towards the white men in blue uniforms intensified. A blade of encouragement strengthened his belief that he had them nerved and watching their backs.

The lie didn't seem true when his foot trembled on the car mat and his mind was perturbed by the constant thoughts, *it's only a matter of time before we're taken apart by the police or the Skins for Life.*

"David, they're watching our every move, I can feel it."

Her statement sounded the truth in his mind.

This is why I must strike first.

"Abbie, we can't stop now, even if we're afraid. If we don't stop them, someone else will be killed."

The story of David and Goliath spun around in his head. *One pebble destroyed a giant.*

I have a stone of evidence, now I have to be smart and get to them before they.

Looking up, he saw the directions for Skegness and his adrenalin ignited a thudding heartbeat.

"I want to see, Richard Broker's eyes, he's guilty, just like Paul Broker."

Every time he thought about his name, his emotions roiled. Sweat soaked through his shirt and his fingers pressed an imaginary trigger that sounded gunfire into a cold night. His nemesis was at his feet and his body twitched on the floor. David nodded his head to signal agreement with the picture that his mind had created, and locked it into his memory to be revived at the appropriate time.

Abbie followed the sign for Skegness and took a right turning.

"I'll go into the Skegness police station David, I have a plan," she said, looking across at him.

His stone-cold stare was focused on the windscreen. The prodding of his thigh brought no reaction from his body. His eyes didn't blink and his lips remained tightly shut.

He was in the car, but his mind had a visual picture, one of horror and lingering distress.

Abbie turned left and then right onto Mercy Way where Ray fell.

David unclipped his seatbelt, gazing at the flowers that were tied around the lamppost. She stalled the car and David's nerves reacted to the tingle running over his body. His eyes flickered through the teardrops that splashed onto his chest. They were reddened by a memory that leapt from his mind and turned his brain into a sea of thunderous proclamations of death and the silent wisp of breath that left a body to bathe in blood.

"David, David."

He opened the car door and ignored the call of his name. His eyes were blinded by a haze and it wasn't from the Sunday morning sun. Stumbling on the cobbled street, he heard the chants, the curses and the repeated cry of, "Nigger, nigger." He moved slowly, taking small footsteps and reaching out to the image in his mind that if he didn't run, it wouldn't be too late to save Ray.

"Ray, Ray, get up, get up, you have to run!"

Stuttering and grabbing the lamppost, he stretched his hand towards Ray's to help him to his feet. He looked at the blood on the ground that ran over his Puma trainers. His body jerked as the multiple stabs of the knife went into Ray's chest. Terror was in his eyes as he saw the blade coming towards his throat and he grabbed his neck where his mind simulated the brutal attack of murder.

David took his jacket off and pressed it against the lamppost.

"Abbie, help me, I can't stop the blood. I can't stop Ray from bleeding, help me!"

His hands slipped down the post and he fell to the ground, scratching at the dirt. He looked up and saw the marauding skinheads running towards him. The silent screams in his brain put his head into a padlock of tension. Fear ran through every nerve cell in his body and he shook profusely on the ground. His mind was in disarray and his heart bound up in unrelenting pain that killed his conscious thinking and battered his heart with more grief.

Abbie stood near the car and walked towards him.

"David, Ray's dead. He's dead and I'm so sorry."

He clutched the lamppost tighter, tears streamed down his face and his heart shook from a recollection of the murderous day. He looked at Abbie and thought, *why aren't you helping me, we need to stop the bleeding.*

"C'mon, Abbie, help me. We need to get Ray to the hospital. He won't die. He won't die if we help him."

Reaching out to the imaginary portrayal of Ray, he fought to pick up his slumped body. His hands were covered in blood and he stared at them, hating himself for cowardice and a broken promise of always being my brother's keeper.

"David, let's go to the Skegness station. You're right, Ray needs our help and we have to get justice for him, no matter what."

"Abbie, what are you saying? We can't leave Ray to die on the pavement, look at him, he's still alive. Get him into the car and take him to the hospital, we can save him!"

His heart juddered through his tears and he clenched her waist with reality finding its way back into his head. He tugged her jacket at the stamping on his heart that crumpled his body into a vision of shudders and stutters from a decision that was a choice of, live or die.

"I shouldn't have run. If I'd have gone back and fought, I could have saved him. I was afraid and I let him die. I could have saved him, Abbie."

David wiped his face with his jacket. The broken bottle that he kicked released a pit of rage for turning back when he should have gone forward. The flowers that he touched in remembrance, allowed him to see a spark of joy when they walked side by side and the air was filled with joyous laughter.

It quickly turned into a dark flame of fire.

Murder is the only language they'll understand, and murder, is what they shall have.

Chapter Twenty-one

Abbie saw the signpost for the police station. She drove towards it and found a space behind a black Ford Anglia. The engine of the car shook and she pulled the handbrake up and pressed the clutch.

What secrets are you hiding, Richard Broker.

The repeated counts from one to ten didn't sway her from the bad idea that would implicate her in a case of false identity.

"I'm going into the station to confront, Richard Broker," David said.

Abbie put her hand on his leg and said, "No, I have a plan and I'll go to meet him, if he's there."

Reaching over, she took a white plastic bag from the backseat. Inside the bag was a black hat and a pair of red glasses. She put them on, pulling the mirror down and gazing at her face that showed bravery, even when her heart was shaking and releasing terror that she might never come out the same as she was when she entered the station.

"I'm Sara Walton, from the Croydon Technical college newspaper team. Let's see the weasel's face when I ask him some hard questions," she said, finishing her disguise by donning a grey overcoat and carrying a black briefcase.

She looked at David's face and held his hand. Behind her heart was a camouflage to deflect the quaking emotions that soared through her body. Her mind twisted with failure and the panic of arrest.

She patted her chest and breathed slowly.

"Legs, stop jittering."

Abbie suppressed the motion of fear and summoned up courage to fan a flame of confidence. She stepped out of the car, staring at the police station door, wanting to stay, but recognising that she had to enter and reel in the culprits one by one.

As she approached the steps, the faces of her murdered friends came back into her mind. *This isn't just for Ray, but also for them and every other black person who's been murdered by the police and the Skins for Life.*

She pushed open the door and stormed to the desk.

"I'm Sara Walton, and I have an appointment with Richard Broker, the Chief Superintendent."

"I can't see your name in the book," replied the policeman, standing behind the glass window.

"I'm a friend of his son, Paul, and he told me he would arrange it on my behalf."

"Do you have any identification?"

Abbie opened her purse and removed a driving licence with the name Sara Walton and held it up.

The policeman checked again in the red book and closed it.

"Wait here."

So he is Paul's father, she thought.

Abbie's wry smile stretched across her face. She crossed her legs and pressed her face against the glass window to show the expression of her intent. Questions replayed in her mind. *I have to break his resistance and get to the truth.* All she had was hope that her plan would work and she could walk out unscathed from any potential savagery of attack.

The policeman signalled to his colleague and left the desk.

Abbie watched the other policeman's expression and tried to read the message in his eyes. Her pulse vibrated against the window ledge. The sound of the clunking of the cell bellowed in her mind when she was detained for siding with the blacks, and not the racist whites.

The policeman came back and said, "He's coming out to meet you."

She muffled the breath that wanted to break out from her lungs and through her mouth; grinding the heel of her boot into the carpet to control the anxiety swimming in her chest. The policeman looked over and she avoided his stare by pretending to read through some fictitious notes.

A door opened. She gazed at Richard Broker, a man who reminded her of her father, tall, impeccably attired in his uniform and with a confident stride.

"Paul, never told me about you, but that's typical, he can be scatterbrained at times, follow me."

Abbie pushed herself up from the seat and scurried behind Richard along the corridor. Her first impression was that he was a policeman, upholding the law and maintaining its integrity for all citizens. She quickly counselled herself and thought, *I can't be fooled by his outer appearance, he and Paul could be involved in the same evil and that's what I'm going to find out.*

"What can I do for you?"

She raised her head and studied his clean-shaven face, except for some grey stubble on his chin. His bull neck and broad shoulders sent a shimmer of intimidation through her body. He looked at Abbie and she whispered in her mind, *be confident and don't show any fear.*

He'll be more scared than me, once I've finished with him.

"I'm a writer for a college newspaper, and I need to ask you some questions for a report that I'm writing. Paul said it would be ok."

The temperature in the room got hotter and the sweat ran down her back. She planted her feet on the ground, poised with a pen and her notepad. The tension of the atmosphere struck at her heart rate and turned up the notch that made her brain swim with giddiness. The pinch of her skin forced her mind to respond to composure and she lifted her head and stared into his eyes.

"Can you tell me why the killers of Ray, a young black man, murdered for no other reason than the colour of his skin, are still free? Can you tell me why no arrests have been made? What are you doing to find the killers? Why did you let the skinhead suspects go?"

She sustained her gaze on his face, refusing to give ground and studying his body language that informed her, *I've hit a nerve*. She ignored her upbringing of, "When you judge, be sure of all the facts." Her emotions confirmed the guilty was sitting in front of her and even though her hand was shaking under the table, will for the truth to be revealed kept her backside in the chair.

He looked at the black phone, stretched to touch it, but pulled back and coughed.

"Who are you and what do you want? I can have you arrested for wasting police time, right now."

The tone of his voice clattered her shoe against the floor. She gripped the pen, swallowing the angst through the spit in her mouth and speaking to her mind, *don't move, he's more afraid than I am.*

Her head jolted at the knock on the door. Her mind spun with images of the cold water tap running and toilet flushing as she lay on the thin blue mattress, waiting for her father to arrive and get her out of police custody.

Abbie allowed her deep exhale to mingle with the cause of purpose.

Her brain became filled with images of police callousness. She recalled that sacrifice had to be a necessary evil to break the chains of racism and to be terrorised because of the risk to her life, wasn't enough of an excuse to run.

"Why are you allowing Ray's killers to be free? What do you know about the Skins for Life? An organisation that, Paul, your son who's a policeman is part of?"

Her mind repeatedly switched between bravery and dastard foolishness. She looked at the door. *Why aren't the police running in to arrest me?*

Fright raced through her body and she jumped at the loud slam of the desk.

"How dare you! My son isn't a skinhead or part of Skins for Life. He's a policeman, who upholds the law!"

"Put the phone down. My parents are barristers and you don't have any grounds to arrest me. Your son murdered Ray and you're protecting the other killers!"

Richard Broker clasped his hands together, stood up and paced around the room.

The notebook flew out of her hand as he came towards her and held the back of her chair.

I'm dead, she thought.

"I've no idea where you've acquired these wild claims, but I uphold the law. Everything has been done to find the killers of Ray, and the investigation is still ongoing."

She wanted to look behind. The quietness in the room shot arrows of worry into her head. A shadow of doubt if she was right to confront him or if she should have waited with patience to let the mouse come to the bait, passed through her mind.

"I suggest that you leave. I could have you arrested for false representation. Paul, had nothing to do with this murder, now get out!"

Abbie pushed the chair back, forgetting about her fear and snatching her notebook from the desk. She knew all along that he wouldn't confess, but she didn't regret throwing Paul into the fire and hoping that if Richard Broker was truly a man of honour, he would uphold the law and bring him in to answer for his crime, despite the thick bloodline.

"Your son is guilty and I have the evidence. Do the right thing and stop hiding a killer."

She left, scratching the back of her neck as the suspected stare from Richard Broker burned her skin. Abbie heard the door slam and scampered towards the reception area. Her throat was on fire and she couldn't stop gulping at the thunderstorm and the suicide mission that she'd just committed.

***

"What happened in there?" said David, as she got back into the car.

Abbie shut the door and placed her head on the steering wheel, unable to control her body that still shook from the adrenalin, flowing in her bloodstream. She looked up the steps. Her head was in a quandary from the mixture of terror and fearlessness. She grabbed David's hand for comfort and then let go to allow her mind to find the middle ground, between peace and an act of idiocy.

"I don't know if he's involved or not. I told him about Paul and he flipped. I don't know, David, I just don't know."

She switched on the wipers by mistake and a judder shot through her body at the beeping of a car horn. Her hand shook at the ignition and she fumbled with the key.

Glancing over at David, she saw two sparrows fighting against a golden eagle, with the odds of survival, diminishing by the second.

That was stupid Abbie, stupid.

As she assessed the situation, the odds appeared to be stacked against them. Uncertainty pushed open the door of her mind and left her with a thought, *the guilty culprits will never be found, they're under police protection.*

She began the journey back to London, touching David's thigh and checking in the mirror to confirm her suspicion that she now had to keep her eyes really focused, lest they struck when she was distracted.

"Say something, David."

His silence twirled her mind with another side of terror. Her imagination listened to the phone ringing and she heard the strong denial from Paul. She visualised another scene that made David and her number one targets of the police and Skins for Life.

Oh, Abbie, what have you done?

Chapter Twenty-two

David buttoned his blue shirt and put on the black tie with a mind that was still raging with a tide of brutal focus. Meditation sparked in his head on the uniform wore by upholders of the law and criminals alike. Suppressed anger, banged at the door of his heart, and his head twitched violently at the cry for it to be unleashed to settle the score and end his anguish, with one final act.

He stared through his reflection in the mirror at purpose, intent and murder.

He must die today.

Sleep hadn't been his usual companion when he went to bed and he'd tossed and turned in the night. Paul's confession spoke repeatedly in his mind and he saw Ray's eyes that were compelling him to strike out and take vengeance.

"I can't leave it to the jury."

He crunched his knuckles, focusing on one face, Paul Broker's.

"Today, Ray, today, justice for you today."

David reflected on the phone call from Abbie last night, and mused on her statement that she'd given the evidence to her parents and they were constructing a case to flush out the guilty. It made no difference to the erection of pain that filled his heart and the raging inferno, burning with a desire to trample on the head of the serpent, killing it so that it could never bite with poison again.

He pondered, *when will the Skins for Life make their move*?

"I can't be concerned about that. I'm making my move today."

David put on his helmet, touched his badge and jangled the handcuffs. The fury inside of him since seeing the imaginary Ray in Skegness kept burning like an uncontrollable fire. He heard Abbie's instruction to wait, replaying in his mind. Her request was dismissed and he determined that patience for the law to be the adjudicator of right and wrong wasn't a wheel that he wanted to spin and hope that it landed on the right number.

"Paul, you're a dead man."

He cocked his head from side to side at the banging on the door. Taking one last look in the mirror, he opened the bedroom door, shut it and walked down the stairs to answer the calling of time for him to gain recompense.

David opened the front door and took a long gaze at Abbie's face.

"David, David, this is going to be over and we'll have justice for Ray."

His ears didn't sing with music that the pieces of the jigsaw were finally coming together.

David hugged her, knowing that fate had brought them this far, but that their opinions of settling this matter were completely different.

"David, did you hear me? The killers and the Skins for Life organisation will be flushed out. If God does exist, then he's heard our prayers and justice is ours."

His mind remained unmoved. No joy or excitement turned the ace card in his favour to confirm that he'd won.

He reminisced on the nightmare that he had last night in his bedroom when Paul scoffed and laughed at seeing Ray slashed with the knife. She didn't see his tears that fell like the rain in the Amazon, as the image of Ray's face tormented him, and fired thoughts at his brain to administer the same compassion shown by his murderers.

No way could he envisage that after ten years of good behaviour and the high powers pulling strings that Paul and his accomplices, would walk free.

His heart couldn't accept that they would be deprived of life for a season, but able to roam again with an unchanged mentality. He could smell the disease inflaming his nostrils. He had the cure if he focused his mind and acted without being afraid of the outcome.

"Abbie, you're a special woman, a woman that I love. Thank you for being with me and that finally this nightmare ends," he whispered, kissing her and calmly walking to the other side of the car.

His head stayed straight and his eyes stared intently at the picture in his brain. Opening the door he got into the car, lips pursed, barely blinking and thoughts riveted on his purpose.

Abbie indicated and drove along Browning Road.

"David, promise me that you won't do anything stupid and compromise this? We're too close."

He wanted more than she wanted, he wanted Paul's blood. He patted his left jacket pocket to touch the sharp kitchen knife that he'd placed there last night. The fear of justice being denied and Paul escaping from the hand of the law because of police protection had haunted him, and he couldn't take the risk of knowing that a killer would be free to be able to kill again.

"David, you didn't answer me."

She arrived and parked outside the Croydon police station and touched his hand that was clenched.

He kept his head in the clouds, trusting that Abbie and her parents would finish what they'd started. Looking in his head at the face of his hero, Martin Luther King, he prepared himself mentally to change the history of the police force forever, and become an instigator of a revolution to bring down the Skins for Life.

"Abbie, I'll see you later, collect me at the normal time please."

He kissed her, closing his eyes and keeping his lips on hers. She clasped his face and he gazed with a message in his eyes, but without interpretation. He tried to leave and she grabbed the door. His breaths showed intensity. He blew out to regain his sense of calmness.

"David, don't do anything stupid. We must play them at their own game. Don't jeopardise any of this."

He slammed the car door, looking at the police entrance for a moment, before bounding up the stairs. Abbie beeped the horn and he turned around and acknowledged her gesture to stay level- headed. He smiled at her, having perfect clarity, knowing exactly what he was going to do and trusting that the rest would take care of itself.

***

David walked into the training room, receiving the stares, but only caring about the seat next to the one at the front that was empty.

He remained standing, searching for the one face that he really wanted to see. Opening the door he gazed along the entrance, slamming the door and uncaring that it made the other trainees jump.

David walked to the front, looking at faces for clues and held the back of his chair. His head spun with, *where's Paul?* He touched his left chest muscle and rehearsed the confrontation and the enacting of his plan. Standing motionlessly, he gazed at his imagination of a lifeless Paul, slumped in the chair with his eyes closed and knowing that the deed of retribution was done.

"Look at you fucking pussies, all grown up," said Fucking hard bastard.

The other trainees chortled and David sat down, expecting an explanation. His face changed expressions multiple times as he looked at Fucking hard bastard and pondered, *where is he, where is he* that made his heart become more enraged that what he'd planned couldn't be finished today.

David gripped the chair, clenched his teeth and hit the desk with his knee. He held the back of Paul's chair, looking at the door and then at the blackboard. His mind played tricks and surmised one possibility after the other. He could see failure in Abbie's plan and was unable to contain the rush of panic that trembled his foot against the ground and numbed his backside to the chair.

"Do you have a problem, David?" Fucking hard bastard said.

Yes, I do have a fucking problem, he thought. *Paul, where is he? Why isn't he sitting in the chair?*

His mind turned upside down, keeping him spinning on the roundabout and dismantling his coherency that the only picture he saw was a blur.

He touched Paul's seat and required that he was there so he could look into his eyes and see the guilt. He wanted to rip the badge from his jacket and watch him squirm as he recognised that his life was about to change forever.

"For those of you who are paying attention, let's get back to the lesson on the Moors murders."

Fucking hard bastard wrote the names, Ian Brady and Mira Hindley, on the blackboard and the trainees commenced answering the question posed.

The mutters around the room twitched against David's ears. He heard the mention of Paul's name, and turned around sharply to the voice that appeared to have knowledge of why he wasn't in the classroom.

David held the pen and pressed the nib onto the paper until he pierced it and indented the wood. His mind wrote a clear message, one of death and not of life. He kept staring at the door, expecting Paul to walk in and take the spare seat at the front. His heartbeat quickened, pounding against the knife he'd brought with the motive to remove at least one racist thug from the earth.

"Ten minutes more and then you can have a break, ladies."

***

Five long hours disappeared without Paul's arrival and David's focus on the refresher training dwindled into complete disinterest. He rotated his neck intermittently and turned back to face the front, opening and closing his hands and his quiet huffs incensed his mind with continuous rushes of frustration.

The door flew open and the Chief Superintendent walked in. He rushed to the front and whispered in Fucking hard bastard's ear. They both quickly departed from the room and left David to think, *what's going on, why have they gone?*

The murmuring of the trainees correlated with the bedlam that fizzed in his brain. His plan was misfiring, without ingenuity granting him an alternative. He turned around to confront the trainee who he believed had information that would bring lucidity to the turbulence, knocking at the door of his mind.

"What did you say about Paul?"

David kept his gaze on the man, gripping his hands behind his back to stop them from doing to the man's neck what his mind instructed. He hated their frolicking and Chinese whispers that stirred up his heart with more anger. He wished that he could put his hand into the trainee's brain and rip out the information, taking him one step closer, to sending Paul to the grave.

Fucking hard bastard returned and gave David a fleeting look.

"You can all leave, except for David."

The trainees got up and left the room.

The dryness in David's throat increased. He grabbed the glass from the table and gulped the water. His heart, already pounding from adrenalin, beat faster from the fear of the unknown. The door opened and he turned sharply, watching the Chief Superintendent walk in and sit at the back.

David stood up and faced him. He peered at Fucking hard bastard and then at the Chief Superintendent. Pressure in his bladder built up and tried to burst through the dam. His head began to swim with dizziness and he could see himself falling from a hilltop and down to the jagged rocks.

"What is it? Why have you asked me to stay behind?"

His eyes followed the Chief Superintendent who walked to the front and sat next to him.

David turned to face him and then stared at Fucking hard bastard.

Sweat ran down his chest to his navel. The heat of anxiety burned the back of his neck and he swallowed hard. His legs misbehaved with a continuum of trembles and his mind conjured up stories, none of which he liked.

"I'm afraid that there's been an accident. Your girlfriend, Abbie, was hurt in a hit and run today. All I know is that a van collided with her car and drove off. She's in the National Temperance hospital and in a critical condition," said the Chief Superintendent.

"I'm really sorry to have to tell you this."

David's tie tightened around his neck. He rushed to the bin and vomited. As he opened his mouth, no words came out. His lungs fought for a drop of air. The cramps attacked his stomach and swirled his insides into sickening nausea and he vomited again.

His hands shook as his brain tried to decipher the news of Abbie laying hurt in the hospital. He didn't want to perceive any possibility of her joining Ray.

"Who did this? You must have caught them," he whispered, wiping the tears from his eyes and holding his wrist to stop the violent seizure from storming through his body.

The Chief Superintendent shook his head and tapped on the desk.

David sat in the chair and his body convulsed in frenzied shock. He turned around to Fucking hard bastard who put his arm around his shoulder.

"Someone must have seen something! You must have witnesses. Who did this? Tell me! Who did it?"

He pushed his chair and it clattered into the desk behind him. Rushing to the blackboard, he beat his fists on the board until they burned with a searing pain. Anger, hatred and fear descended on him and he choked on his tears, coughing, spluttering and falling to the ground where his lips gathered up dust from the wooden floor. The whispering thought, *they've struck right at the heart of my weakness and given me a warning to stop or I'll be next,* set off the alarm of horror in his head.

"Abbie, Abbie!"

Fucking hard bastard crouched next to him and kept his hand on David's arm. He offered him a handkerchief, whilst the Chief Superintendent remained in his chair.

Loneliness was a cold place to be and he looked at the ceiling, trembling and his mind being bombarded by, *David, they're coming, you're next.*

"Take me to her now," said David, pushing his back against the wall and rising to his feet.

"It's all been arranged. One of the constables will take you. David, I'm really sorry, but we'll catch the person who did this," said Fucking hard bastard.

David followed him through the door and into the main office, keeping his head down rather than staring at the other trainees who were milling in the corridor. Three of them patted David on the shoulder. He turned and looked at the trainees in turn, seeing the concern in their eyes that appeared to offer him a vibe that he was one of them, despite being black.

The door leading to the reception area opened and Paul Broker walked along the corridor. David raised his head and his shoulders flinched. He stood still, glued to the spot and shaking from violent pangs in his brain that compelled him to charge and spill blood. His fingers opened and closed as the message of rage spoke louder and louder.

Paul sauntered towards him and his face broke into a smile.

"Fucking nigger, stupid dumb fucking nigger," he whispered.

David's right hand veered towards his left inside jacket pocket. He turned around, watching Paul receive greetings and applause from the other trainees that turned up the heat of his hatred towards him.

His tears soaked his shirt. Love called him to the hospital and revenge was guiding his steps to strike Paul with a vicious hand.

His mind was blurred by a red stream drenching the corridor floor, and a clear vision of himself plunging the knife into Paul's body over and over again, even though he knew he was already dead.

"This way, David, Abbie needs you. You need to be with her," Fucking hard bastard said.

David's hand slipped to his side and he wiped his eyes, stimulated by murderous thoughts, but with Fucking hard bastard pushing him through the doorway. He escorted David to the waiting officer and bundled him into the blue and white Panda car, slamming the car door and staring at David.

Fucking hard bastard banged on the window and David wound it down, looking up and seeing softness in his eyes.

"For what it's worth, you've exceeded my expectations. I never thought that you would last, but you have, you're an officer of the law. I'll ensure that everything is done to find those who are guilty."

He tapped the roof of the Panda car and the constable put on the blue siren and sped along the road to the hospital.

Confusion blinded David and he couldn't work out if Fucking hard bastard was a friend or an enemy. There was no doubt in his mind that he was racist, but his comments lifted David's heart that he'd gained Fucking hard bastard's authentic respect.

But can I trust him? Will he help me, or is this just another trap?

The policeman pulled up to the entrance of the National Temperance hospital and David jumped out, running to the reception desk.

"My girlfriend, Abigail Butler, was involved in a hit and run accident, I need to see her!"

The receptionist checked the incoming patients recorded and directed him towards the Neurology ward. He ran along the corridor, skipping in and out of the patients, staff and visitors that walked towards him.

Nerves jangled in his body.

Oh my God. Abbie, please be ok, I don't want you to die.

Fear took precedence and struck him with a reminder of reality, and he could sense their presence everywhere. The organisation that he was part of, slammed into his brain a reminder of its stampede of violence and that he was deluded if he thought that a nigger seeking revenge, could bring the system down to the ground.

The beacon kept flashing in his mind and burned his brain with a fiery exemplar, *let it go or be next on the list.*

***

David entered the ward, walked towards Abbie and clutched the white bed sheet that covered her body. He gazed at her, put his hand to his mouth and let out a panicked breath.

His hands stretched towards her motionless body with a tube stuck in her mouth. A tear dripped down his face. He had no control over his legs that became gelatine, and the booming of his heart was a wail of terror that hit his mind with a crucifying thought, *she's going to die.*

"Abbie!"

David moved his lips towards her cheek, touched the white pillowcase and put his hand towards her face and then pulled it back.

“Abbie, I’m so sorry, this is my fault, please don’t die!”

He kneeled at her bedside, remembering the position of submission when he came before God to seek help for the troubles of his life. His hands shook as he buried his head into the grey plastic chair next to her bed. Tears fell from his eyes and also from his heart. He held her hand and stared with nothing in his mind that he could make any sense of.

Continuing to gaze at Abbie, he listened to the ticking machine that pumped oxygen into her lungs.

Footsteps that got closer to the bed, made him raise his head and stare at the man in a white coat.

“Hello, I’m Mr Pradeep, a Consultant Neurologist. I’m sorry about what has happened to Abbie. She’s in a critical condition. She’s suffered bleeding of the brain and has internal injuries. We’re doing all we can to help her.”

David stood up and stumbled into the bedside cabinet, torn apart from another person that he loved facing death. He placed his head into his hands, wishing for quietness from the accusation of blame that thumped his head.

“Mr Pradeep, don’t let her die. I’m begging you, don’t let, Abbie die.”

Mr Pradeep nodded and left him holding onto a wish that he knew he couldn't guarantee.

Looking at all the broken pieces of his life, he was unable to find rest from his perturbed mind.

Has all this happened because I turned my back on God and now I'm being punished by losing the people that I love the most?

He held Abbie's hand, saying silently, *wake up*.

Anger gnawed at his conscience to get back to the station and do what he'd imagined when he put the kitchen knife inside his jacket pocket.

David stared directly into the face of justice, seeing an image where the wicked man had the upper hand, because he didn't hesitate in hitting back aggressively, when his back was against the wall.

"God, where are you in all of this? Why have you done this to me? Isn't it enough that you took Ray and now you've allowed Abbie to be in a hit and run accident. If you think anything of me, then I'm begging you to let her live."

Clive and Rose came running into the ward and Rose bumped into one of the nurses.

"Abbie, Abbie!" she said.

David turned around to face them as they ran towards the bed.

"Rose, Clive, I'm sorry, I'm really sorry, it's my fault."

Clive looked up at David and said, "No, it's not your fault, you're not to blame."

David stretched his hand towards Abbie's face and kissed her head. Slinking away towards the door, he watched with heartache and pain tearing him inside.

He let go mentally, releasing Abbie into the hands of God and the consultant. Neither one of them had given him a firm commitment that they'd heard clearly and were acting to fulfil his request. He couldn't do anything more by staying at the hospital and the bell in his mind rang with an urgency to get back to the police station, and take care of the unfinished business.

***

David left the ward, hot stepping along the corridor and with murder on his mind. He tapped his fingers together. His eyes were focused and glazed. The picture of Abbie in a brutalised state made him clench his fist as the aversion turned into a red scorching heat.

Accidently, he bumped into a man as he exited the hospital. No apology left his lips. He opened the door of the police car, got in and strapped his seatbelt with a furious yank.

"Will your girlfriend be ok?"

David stared through the windscreen and played ignorant to the expressed concern. He didn't trust him. He couldn't trust anyone. He put his trust in his instinct and his plan, touching the knife in his pocket and visualising Paul's face with his eyes open and then closed.

He was itching to wipe the impudence from his face, likening him to a wild dog that he had to put down.

His emotions were rising, boiling over and blowing hot steam through his snarls and contorted expressions. Rage screamed and shouted at him to act now and not leave anything to chance.

"Abbie, Abbie, Ray," he whispered, through the incision that severed his heart like a razor blade cutting into a sheet of paper.

"Sorry, did you say something?"

David shook his head and gazed at the face of the policeman, appreciating his care, but still throbbing with a thirst for revenge.

His head dropped to his chest. His thoughts dwelled on Abbie and her never waking up or recovering, but having to live with severe brain injuries.

They'll all die. I'll kill all of them for this. Paul, you're dead. I'm coming for you and I'm going to kill you, you're dead.

Chapter Twenty-three

Sensibility was a long distance from his thoughts, and the cries of his heart were heard only by the angst that thumped his head with malicious declarations.

Fear, had no place to convince him to think of the consequences. Violence roared, creating an uncontrollable thirst for him to avenge the evil deed and make the ultimate sacrifice for Ray and Abbie.

There's no turning back from this and I can't run.

He looked at the police station; his second home where he'd intended to graduate after the training and shuddered as the front door opened. His eyes were fixed on the policemen who left the building to go on the beat.

Maybe you're good and maybe you're not, but I know one person who isn't

Inside, he visualised the reprobate riding high on the waves of the sea, because he'd nullified the threat to the dismantling of the Skins for Life. The swagger and smile on his face, compelled him to run into the building and obliterate his body until there was nothing left that was recognisable.

You bastard. No way will I let you live.

This is for Ray and Abbie.

The image of Abbie laying in the hospital bed, eyes closed, potentially brain damaged and breathing through life support, was fuel to his anger to unleash his fury that silenced the mocking tongue.

He looked up, certain that Ray was watching him from heaven and he heard a stern voice in his head that challenged him to rip the heart out of the racist. The command reverberated around his conscious mind. Lucidity had gone. Sound judgement ran away from his brain and was replaced with a compounding urge to satisfy the pain.

David reached into his jacket pocket and touched the sharp kitchen knife. He walked up the stairs, twisting his neck and flexing his shoulders. His eyes glared and the steam of revenge got hotter and intensified his will to strike without remorse.

The eyes of his colleagues turned on him as he walked through the office to the training room. Whispers of condolences and compassion fell to the ground and failed to make an impact on his change of direction.

He opened the door of the training room, looking at the one seat at the front that was empty, his seat.

As he walked to the front, his stomach rumbled with retaliation.

Fucking hard bastard dropped his piece of chalk.

"David, all of us offer our sincere best wishes for Abbie."

He nodded, but David wanted to scream and he dug his nails into his hands. A lid was on his rage and he suppressed his desire to grab Paul's neck and strangle the life out of him.

David gritted his teeth, watching Paul from the corner of his eye. Impulse in his body pressurised him to strike and blow out the candle of his existence.

"Right, back to our discussion on the Police Act," said Fucking hard bastard, walking to the back of the room.

David pushed the soles of his boots into the carpet. The knife kept calling his name. It slammed his head and revved up his brain to grab the cold-hearted racist by his hair and bash his face into the desk.

He stared at the mole on Paul's chin and his neck that contained a small nick from a razorblade. His Adam's apple moved as he gulped. David slipped his hand towards his jacket pocket, seeing the image of Paul's throat slashed open and his blood running on the wooden floor.

Paul turned to face David.

"You fucking nigger! How's the fucking white nigger bitch? Is she dead yet?" he whispered.

David turned around, watching Fucking hard bastard.

Turning back to the front, he tried to pull the knife out of his jacket pocket, but his hand froze. His body was in a paralytic state. He tried to move his feet that remained planted on the ground. He could hear the sniggers, shooting terror through his body and battering down his will to beat the enemy.

"You'll never destroy us. You're weak, just like all fucking niggers," Paul said under his breath.

The anger kept rising in David's mind, putting his head into a cauldron of burning sulphur that exploded epithelium, and challenged if he really loved Ray and Abbie. He wanted to kill Paul right there in the classroom. His mind was clear on the action, but his hands were failing to respond.

The gauntlet had been thrown down in his face, but he had nothing in his physical strength to rise above Paul and show him that he too had a streak for violence.

Fury tried to motivate him to remove the knife and cut Paul's throat, but his hand fell limply by the chair. His mind had the will, but his body was unwilling to become an accomplice to murder in the first degree.

"Ok, break now, back in twenty minutes."

The trainees left to go to the recreation area and Fucking hard bastard prevented David from joining them.

"Why did you come back? You need to be with Abbie, she's your priority."

No, you're wrong, Paul's my priority, he thought.

It's now or never, and it has to be now.

The door slammed as the last trainee exited the classroom. David stared at the door. In his mind he whispered, *stop wasting time, get outside and kill him.*

"Are we finished? Can I leave?"

David walked out of the classroom and ran to the toilet. His hands kept shaking as his brain fought with his teaching of the forbidding of committing murder. He looked at his face in the mirror, remembering his failure to be able to pull the trigger and put a bullet in the head of a skinhead, who was afraid to die.

"Not this time, this is for Ray and Abbie."

Thumping the sink, he went to the door and kicked it to stir up the emotions of hate, reaffirming that he was a killer, because the right button had been pushed and made him snap. *Thou shalt not kill is a lie*, he thought. He remembered God, killing extensively to destroy the enemies of Israel. There was a righteous judgement and he had the right to apply it.

"An eye for an eye and a tooth for a tooth."

***

David left the toilet, ran towards the recreational area and slammed the door. He stood in the yard with one thing on his mind, to annihilate his enemy. Sprinting towards Paul, he clenched his fist and as Paul turned around to his running footsteps, he punched him on his jawbone and knocked him to the floor.

"Get up, you murderer! Get up from the floor, you piece of shit," said David, kicking Paul in the stomach before he could rise to his feet.

Two of the trainees stepped forward to intervene, but they were held back by the others.

"You're crazy, I'm not a murderer," said Paul, getting up from the ground.

"You were there when Ray died. I have the evidence against you, you're a member of the Skins for Life.

David hit him in the stomach and threw him into the metal rails. Every voice in his head said, *strangle him, choke him to death, he has to die.*

"I didn't kill anybody. I've no idea what you're talking about."

David jumped on him, grabbing his throat and strangling him to close the lights out of his racist existence. All he could see was blaring red, without control of his emotions that were firing on a deadly mission. They were eating up his mind that if he didn't end this with death, he could never look at his face in the mirror again with honour.

Paul grabbed David's hands, prized them apart and chopped his windpipe that caused him to grab his neck, gasp for breath and fall to his knees. He saw Paul's foot coming towards his head and swiftly sweep kicked Paul and punched him in the side of his ribcage.

"I heard you confess to killing Ray in the building at Colney Lane. You were there with Skins for Life members and policemen. You boasted that you killed him. You slashed his throat. You were there when Ray died, because you killed him."

Paul got to his feet and advanced towards David, landing a blow on his face. He knocked him to the ground and stamped on his leg as he fell. He kicked him again and wrapped his arms around David's neck.

"You fool! You had the opportunity to leave, but you wouldn't. You think that you can destroy who we are. I saw your friend die and your girlfriend, Abbie, will also die," said Paul quietly in David's ear.

The mimicry was adrenalin to David's anger. His mind was in disarray, but floated back to clarity as his lips trembled together and the tears flowed down his face. It built up his body with power, might and an energy that forced him to react as if he had one last breath to take.

David put his arms up and with all his might, elbowed Paul in his midriff that made him loosen his grip. He jumped to his feet and hit Paul twice in the face, splattering his nose and taking a step back. The blood poured down Paul's face, and David's brain burned with revenge as he withdrew the knife from his jacket, with no hesitation in initiating a public execution.

"This is for Ray and Abbie, murderer."

David pressed the blade against Paul's neck to cut him open like a pig in the slaughterhouse.

"David! No! Don't do it," shouted Fucking hard bastard.

"He has to die. You killed Ray, didn't you?"

Pressing the knife into Paul's skin, he drew a trace of blood and gazed deeply into his eyes. He wanted his face to be the last one that Paul ever saw, before he gargled on his own blood and went to the grave.

“No, son, this isn’t the way. Don’t throw your life away. Think about Abbie and Ray, this isn’t what they want.”

His brain functioned on high tension that revenge and murder was right and he had nothing else to lose. His mind couldn’t perceive living without avenging and with a constant reminder that he let a killer go.

“No! He must die today!”

“Paul, I’m going to ask you one more time, you killed Ray, didn’t you?”

He raised the knife above his head and stared into Paul’s eyes with murderous intent and brought it swiftly down to his neck.

“No! Don’t kill me, I don’t want to die. I killed him. Matthew Johnson, made me do it!”

Paul put his hands up to his face.

“You murderer, you murderer!”

David grabbed him by the hair and pointed the knife at his eyes.

He saw a vision of Ray slumped at the lamppost and without a friend to hold him before he died. A picture of Abbie, surviving on the life support machine entered his mind. He stared down at Paul and shook his head at letting him live to carry out more hate and violence without regret. It was a thorn that stabbed into his temple, and he knew that his conscience would never give him peace, if he showed mercy.

Watching the tears running from Paul's eyes, he listened to his whimpers. Compassion had no place in his heart as he looked at a coward that was only brave when he had the protection of the mob.

An eye for an eye and a tooth for a tooth, vibrated in his brain.

"You'll never walk the streets again to kill another black man, die racist, die!"

"No, David, no!" screamed Fucking hard bastard.

David raised the knife in the air and brought it crashing down towards Paul's throat.

The knife fell from his hand onto the ground. He dropped to his knees and looked down at the immobile body of Paul. His head came up from his chest and he watched Fucking hard bastard edging towards him.

"David, let me have the knife."

David's lips quivered and his body shook. The anger simmered, but still burned. He pushed the knife towards Fucking hard bastard. Turbulence overflowed in his mind, knowing he desired more than anything else in the world to kill, but he was bemused why his hand stopped from making the fatal strike.

"You took Ray's life and if there's any justice for an innocent black man, you'll go to prison and never come out."

"Paul, you don't need to say anything, as what you say may be taken in evidence against you. I'm arresting you for the murder of Ray Williams," said Fucking hard bastard.

He placed the handcuffs on Paul's wrists and pulled him to his feet.

"David, you're also under arrest for aggravated bodily harm and threatening to use a deadly weapon. Put the handcuffs on him and take him to the cell."

David walked to the cell without any resistance. The policeman in charge unlocked the door and he walked in and sat on the thin blue plastic mattress. His handcuffs were removed and David jumped as the door shut and the lock clunked, bringing him into a reality that he'd envisaged.

He sat on his hands to stop them from shaking. His mind and body were numb. Harrowed by the thought of being locked up in prison and sealed with a number that defined what he'd become, a criminal, he lay on the bed and closed his eyes.

A cloud of darkness surrounded him and he curled his arms around his chest and thought, *what's going to happen to me now?*

Chapter Twenty-four

His eyes flickered open and he murmured in his sleep. With his wings clipped, he saw freedom as he stared at the small squares of the glass window above his head, but was unable to grasp it and walk out of the police cell.

Mind chatter troubled his heart, without an answer to bring the serenity he wanted to receive, with a clear picture of his fate that lay ahead.

Thoughts of Abbie's innocence churned through his brain. Culpability tensed his body and he clutched the mattress, dripping in failure that he wasn't the knight in shining armour that saved her from the violent storm of harm.

Admiration swelled that she'd stood by his side when she didn't have to. He reflected on the racism that she suffered from black and white, knowing that he had a rare jewel and a scare of her remaining in an unresponsive state made his toes curl and his heart lose its timely beat.

David opened his eyes with the image of her face imprinted in his mind and a picture of the tubes in her mouth to sustain her life.

"Abbie, please don't die!"

He couldn't imagine her never waking up. Her courage and bravery wrenched at his heart strings and he began to cry for the woman that he loved.

Rumbles of fear came and didn't subside with a flashing headline that there wouldn't be a next time that he saw her in the hospital, because he would be visiting her tombstone in the graveyard, to say goodbye.

The door opened and Fucking hard bastard walked into the cell. He shined a torch into David's face that caused him to shield his eyes from the effulgence. He paced across the cell floor and David watched him apprehensively as he sat up on the bed and clasped his hands, remembering that anger and the rage for revenge had landed him here when he had the choice to choose right from wrong.

"David, how are you?"

David nodded nervously.

"I just want to get out of here."

Fucking hard bastard walked towards him and sat at the end of the bed.

"David, I'm an undercover policeman and we've had an ongoing investigation into the Skins for Life, and suspected that policemen were part of this organisation. I hoped that you wouldn't quit and I'm sorry that the system failed you and Ray."

"Arrests are being made and you need to tell us all you know, so we can put an end to their violence and racism."

Fucking hard bastard smiled and extended his hand, which David clenched. His eyes opened wider and an uncontrollable judder went through his legs as the shock threw his mind into a mental convulsion. He'd always believed that Fucking hard bastard was an enemy, but discovering that he was a friend and an ally in his mission brought a light of hope into his dark space.

"David, I'll do all I can to help you in court. I'm sorry for the abuse that you suffered, but the police forces across the UK will never be the same again."

"I really hope that Abbie recovers."

Fucking hard bastard patted him on the shoulder and left the cell.

Loneliness in the eight feet by six feet room filled every space in his brain. He saw himself falling into an abyss, without anyone to grab him before he reached the bottom. He stretched out his arms towards the wall. It didn't respond to ease the turmoil that bubbled and he touched his head to make it stop.

Yet, the words of Fucking hard bastard lodged in his thoughts. He questioned, *is he telling the truth or is it undercover tactics to get information because he too is a member of Skins for Life?*

Pacing around the room, he faced the wall, trying to decide if Fucking hard bastard could be trusted. His gut instinct challenged him to take a risk and believe that he'd found a friend in a racist environment, where they had the same goal, to stop racism.

A reminder of the knife in his hands and the glare into Paul's eyes flooded his brain with jumbled chatter.

"Why couldn't I kill him? I dreamt about slicing his throat open, but I couldn't do it!"

He walked to the door to listen to the noise outside the cell. His name was mentioned, but he was unsure of the context.

A sense of guiltiness overshadowed him, that the judgement that should have been carried out on Paul, wasn't done.

This wasn't the plan that he'd imagined and he thought, *why, when I tried to stab Paul in the throat did it mysteriously stop, as if someone was holding my hand back from killing him.*

"I don't get it, Paul should be dead, I should have killed him!"

The cell door opened and the policeman in charge walked in.

"David, you have to be quiet. You're going to need a solicitor, is there someone you can call?"

His mind wandered to Abbie's parents, Clive and Rose. He had a drop of confidence that they could get him out of the cell.

I know the drill. Answer every question with no comment to avoid incriminating myself.

"Yes, I have a solicitor, who I need to speak to now. Do you have any news about Abbie, my girlfriend?"

The policeman shook his head and led David out of the cell to make the phone call.

He sat down at the desk, staring at the black dial phone and putting his fingers into the small circular holes to ring Abbie's home number. His clasp of the phone was to stop his hand from shaking.

"It's David. I'm sorry, but I'm in the station in a cell. Please can you come and get me. How's Abbie?"

The phone line went dead before he received an answer from Rose. He dropped his head on the table, shook the phone and put it to his ear. The dead tone brought a strong inclination that his worst fear had come to haunt him.

"I'm afraid that you'll have to stay here until your solicitor arrives."

David went back to the cell with his mind turning upside down. He thought about the first time he met Abbie and her feistiness that put him in his place.

She made me feel alive. She's just fearless and made me see that I could be too.

Walking over to the wall, he put his head against it, splashing the patchy paintwork with tears as he fell to the floor.

She can't die, she doesn't deserve it. What will I do if she dies?

"Please God, do a miracle, I'm begging you!"

The flashbacks of his time in the church returned with an aggressive conviction of who he really was. Whether he liked it or not and despite his rejection of God, he realised that in his helplessness, he was the only one he could call on.

Conflicting messages panged his head and reminded him that God had let Ray die needlessly and if he was all about love, then which father would let his son die such a cruel death.

A reminder came back into his head.

God let Jesus die for my sins and he was innocent.

David went back to the crucifixion of Jesus Christ, letting his mind meditate on the beating and the whipping that tore his flesh into bloody shreds. His spiritual eyes saw the crown of thorns that was rammed on his head, and he realised that the one person who really understood his pain was God.

In his mind he saw who God really was and that he knew more about life than he did.

David tried to comprehend Ray's death which seemed meaningless with his human logic. He couldn't think of one reason why Ray or Jesus deserved to be murdered.

Scraping the cold stone floor with his fingernails, he longed for a revelation.

Illumination began to open his eyes and he saw that despite the horrific pain that ripped his heart every day, there was a purpose and a meaning to Ray's death.

A light shined in his mind. It brought enlightenment that the brutal murder served as a lesson that God is always love, and he'd been used to bring down the evil in the police force and Skins for Life.

David got up from the ground, walked over to the bed and fell to his knees. His head touched the blue mattress and the spirit of grace fell on him. It softened his heart and dissolved the solid brick wall he'd erected against God.

"I've strayed so far from you. I've disgraced myself because of my hatred. Please forgive me for rejecting you, because I thought that you hated me."

He lay prostrated on the floor, crying as the pent-up hurt, frustration and pain came to the surface. His tears fell copiously and he clutched the bed leg as he recognised that God wasn't against him, but for him.

David considered, *all the times I've been in trouble, God has been there for me.*

His heart vibrated with the seeds of Christianity that had been sown into him from a young age, and no matter how far he'd strayed, the truth kept navigating him back towards the straight and narrow path.

The words of the racists who called him nigger and black bastard, attempted to bring him back onto the road of hate against his abusers.

A gentle wave of love flowed into his heart and reminded him that this wasn't who he was. He understood that God had created him in his own image and that was his brand.

The murmurs in his heart were the recognition that he'd fallen short of God's mark.

I tried to kill the Christianity inside of me, but it's part of who I am and I can't change it.

David saw the gun in his hand and God saving him from shooting the skinhead. He rubbed the dirt on the floor and his heart skipped with gratitude that Paul was still alive, and God had prevented him from becoming exactly like those that he opposed.

"I'm sorry that I forgot about you, when all you wanted to do was to help me, but I'm asking for one thing, please save Abbie, she doesn't deserve to die!"

"I promise that I won't lose my faith again, but just help me, I need your help."

Chapter Twenty-five

David twitched his head on the pillow, wondering, *where has the time gone.* He had a blurred memory of being imprisoned in the cell. The lid lifted and the daylight came into his dark room, burning his eyelids with a blaze of light. He shook his hands, no handcuffs, but he was still a captive and detained for a criminal act.

Everything is going to be ok, trust in me.

That still quiet voice he'd heard many times on his knees in the bedroom and in the church, came back to give him reassurance. The fear of the consequences no longer zoomed through his mind. Peace that he remembered, when in his darkest moments surrounded him. He laid still to recall the spiritual encounter and the reintroduction to the faith that he'd left behind, with the morning being the start of a different journey.

The key turned in the lock and he stood up. Fucking hard bastard walked in, followed by Rose and David rushed over towards her and hugged her.

"David, I'm so sorry. I wanted to come last night, but I had a call from Clive, and we had to rush to the hospital to be with Abbie."

He pushed her away gently. His heartbeats started to gallop. David looked at her face with an intense stare.

"What's happened to Abbie? She's ok, isn't she?"

David stepped towards Rose and held her arm. His heart, having rediscovered a spiritual serenity began to throb with anxiety. He walked away from Rose and stumbled into the bed. His lungs began to struggle to take in air and his breaths were released through stuttering wisps. David placed his hands on his temples that quivered from the heat and felt like they were being burned from a Bunsen burner.

As he looked at Rose, the confidence that God wouldn't put on him more than he could take, disappeared. A tear fell from his eye and he looked at Fucking hard bastard, contemplating, *how can I be so wrong when I believed that after the conversation with God we had an understanding.*

"David, the surgeon carried out another emergency operation after she developed a blood clot on her brain."

No! No! Not Abbie, not my Abbie!"

He grabbed the mattress, questioning the confidence that had made a fool out of his heart and began to believe that it was his mind playing Russian roulette with his emotions.

The weight in his legs disintegrated and his knees hit the ground with the pain sending shock into his brainwaves.

Rocking on the floor, his throat muffled the grief that was cutting every chord of his heart with stabbing incisions. He tried to speak through the mucus, the tears and the image of a bandaged and lifeless Abbie.

"Abbie, no, you can't be dead, no!"

"No, David, you didn't let me finish. I'm overwhelmed because the operation was a success. David, Abbie's fine, she's going to be absolutely fine!"

Fucking hard bastard left the cell and closed the door.

David got up and walked towards Rose, holding her hand. His tears of relief fell unashamedly. Every doubt, fear and worry inside of him made room for an emotional change to coincide with the ebb of consolation that he witnessed in the night. His heart and mind had momentarily been tortured by a revelation that she was dead, but Rose's words were confirmation that his prayer had been answered.

"Abbie, is going to be ok? Abbie isn't dead? She's alive," whispered David.

He grabbed Rose, sobbing like a lamb bleating in the cold winter storm and shedding tears of joy and respite. Now he understood that his repentance had touched the heart of God and he'd been spared any further mental slaughtering.

"God, thank you, thank you for the miracle."

"Let's get you out of here, she's been asking for you."

"There's one thing, I can't represent you, but I've spoken to an excellent barrister, Mr Andrews, and he'll take the case."

David walked to the interview room and answered, "No comment," to every question.

Abbie was his focus.

I just want to get to the hospital and tell her how much I love her.

Walking through the exit doors of the police station, he smelled the fresh air. A mixture of anticipation and trepidation fused his mind and he thought, *this fight is going to get worse, but God will finish what we've started*

***

David got into the light blue Vauxhall Victor and sat still, gripping the seat and staring at the picture of his rock, his lover and his confidant in his mind. His heart brimmed to the full with admiration that she'd stood tall in the time of trouble. He reflected on the times when he sensed her fear and how her courage inspired him to not break, despite the avalanche of the hostile pressure that he had to endure.

"Abbie, is a special woman, she's so brave."

Rose looked across at him and touched his shoulder as she started the car and drove away from the police station.

"She loves you, David. She would never risk her life for someone that she didn't love."

God, you brought her into my life, it was fate, and you knew everything that would happen to us and you know what will happen next.

Thank you for saving her.

They approached the National Temperance hospital and Rose parked the car.

As they got out, David touched Rose's hand and spoke a silent prayer.

All things will work together for good, my good and Abbie's.

He walked through the hospital doors. Rose put her arm through his and his face reflected a half smile.

Heart, stop beating so fast, Abbie's going to be alright.

David pulled away from Rose when they reached the ward and ran to Abbie's bedside, staring at her bandaged head and bruised face. He needed a moment to remember that revenge wasn't his when the thoughts in his mind took him back to bloodshed and payback. Holding her hand softly, he kissed her lips and his heart gushed with effervescent surges of love and compassion.

She opened her eyes, smiled at him and touched his face. It caused his love and affection to explode and consume him with a magnetic pull that there was and only would be Abbie.

"I know I don't look my usual self David, but I'll get there."

David gently stroked her skin, imagining that the story could have been so different and the pain that his heart would have gone through if her life had been taken. His emotions tore through the depths of his soul and he broke down. Tears fell freely and he loved her more than his mind could perceive possible, realising that regardless of black or white, they were one.

"Abbie, you don't have to say anything. Thank God it's a miracle. I'm so sorry that I didn't listen to you."

He embraced Abbie, apprehensive of tomorrow and what it might bring. His heart whispered, *God I know you'll take care of us.*

"Abbie, I really love you and I don't know what I would do without you."

"I know, David, I know, I love you too."

David turned to the footsteps and greeted Clive and Rose.

They approached Abbie, kissing and hugging her.

"David, the entire police stations across the UK are going to wake up to this breaking news story and there'll be no place for the killers or Skins for Life to hide," Clive said.

He handed David a copy of The Observer newspaper. He read the front- page headline statement. *Killers exposed and Skins for Life members running the police force.*

David turned to the pages that detailed the accounts of Ray's fatal moment and the negligence of the police to find the killer. It brought back the deep waves of sorrow of a moment that he wanted to forget. Hope arose in his heart that with the exposure and evidence, those who were culpable would be tried and convicted.

David read the article again, looking at Rose and Clive. He gazed at Abbie, wounded by her injuries, but recognising that through the peril of their circumstances, the racists had been brought out of the dark. It soothed his mind with a breath of consolation that he was on the verge of justice and judgement against the murderers.

"Thank you for everything that you've done. I understand the risks you took, and I'm so sorry that Abbie was attacked and hurt by those full of hate."

They embraced him and Abbie placed her hand on his face.

"David, we believe in fairness and justice. We witnessed the injustice of apartheid and the Sharpeville massacre in South Africa, and when we came back to England, we vowed we would fight against racism," Clive said.

David looked at the faces around him, experiencing the electric current in the atmosphere that had brought him to this juncture. He studied the colour of his skin and that of Abbie's, Clive's and Rose's, sensing the powerful force that couldn't accept that black lives were less important than white.

***

Charles and Mary appeared at the entrance of the ward. David turned around to the sound of their voices and beckoned them to enter, having no malice or hate in his heart against them.

He smiled as they walked towards him and the issues of contention that he had with their prejudiced behaviour paled away into insignificance. David grasped Mary, whilst Charles stood behind him with his hand on his shoulder.

"We came to the police station when Rose told us that you were locked in the cell, but they wouldn't let us talk to you," Charles said.

Mary went to the bed and held Abbie's hand. She touched the bruises on her face and Charles joined her and kissed Abbie's head.

"Abbie, firstly, I'm so sorry about this deliberate accident and I know that God will ensure that the culprits are found. I was so wrong about you and judged you unfairly. I realise that it's not about colour, just people and we have good and bad in all societies," Charles said.

Mary nodded and clutched David's hand.

"Abbie, I was so against David being with a white girl and I'm ashamed that even as a Christian woman who should know better, I couldn't bring myself to accept this. I'm deeply sorry for my attitude, it was so wrong."

David cast his eyes on Mary and Charles and his mind opened to a realisation that systemic racism was embedded in black people just as much as white and his parents were an example of this and he thought, *if they can change, so can others.*

He looked around the bed, watching Rose and Clive. He stared at Charles and Mary and then gazed at Abbie. No tension or blame for the events of the previous weeks was in his head. His mind was at complete rest that they were all together, united and differences put aside and the only thing that mattered to him was Abbie and her recovery.

Abbie touched Mary's face and let go of David's hand and took the hand of Charles.

"Thank you both for your apologies. I want you to know that I love David. I would never do anything to hurt him. We're just two young people who fell in love."

That was the point when David lost the control of his emotions. His mind washed over with Abbie's declaration of love, and he couldn't stop his heart from responding with warmth and a glow of reciprocated love that totally consumed him. He wrapped his arms around her, kissing her lips with his eyes closed and allowing himself to float away to a place where their hearts beat at the same time and the world that he knew, was Abbie and David.

He could hear the breaths and whimpers behind him and turned his head to see Charles wiping the tears away from his face. Never had he seen him cry and his heart felt like it split in two and came back together, as the healing medicine began to release him from the wounds and the pain of rejection, bitterness and unforgiveness.

Words came into his mind, but he didn't need to speak them. The change in mode was immersing him and he let go, opening his soul to receive a message in the silence that the family bond of two different races was anchoring and strengthening him to be free of what he'd become, and setting a direction of what he could be.

Mary shuffled on the bed and clasped David and Abbie.

"I would like all of you to come to the Congregation of God church, South London, so we can pray that this will end well and that God will give us the victory."

Abbie, Rose and Clive nodded and Mary turned to David. He kept his head down, remembering, *I made a vow to never step inside another church again.* He looked at the cross around Mary's neck, reflecting on the greatest gift ever given to mankind and his heart was no longer hardened against God.

"I asked God to heal Abbie and he heard my prayer. Ray's death hurts me, but I understand the lord sees things that we can't see."

David nodded, affirming in his mind, *when I see the church doors again, I'll enter the house of God with thanksgiving in my heart.*

"Clive and Rose, thank you for your courage to fight for David and for Ray," Charles said.

"Abbie, again we apologise, but I know you'll come out of this bed soon and we'll all be in court to see justice served," Mary said.

They embraced Clive, Rose and David, kissing Abbie before leaving.

David waved goodbye and a new confidence began to fizz inside of him. It settled his mind with certainty that it wouldn't end in despair, but in victory and the months of toil would bring its reward.

"We'd better leave and David, you need to talk to the barrister to prepare your case," Rose said.

Clive and Rose stayed sitting on Abbie's bed for a few minutes longer.

"Abbie, we love you," Clive said. "We'll be back soon to take you home."

They walked away and David stroked her head and stared into her eyes.

"I should also go so that you can rest. I love you and I'll always be there for you."

He left with Clive and Rose and waved at Abbie, blowing a kiss and putting his hand over his heart that he sealed with a promise.

***

The excitement bubbled in David's mind. Two long weeks finally were at an end and he quickly unstrapped his seatbelt and jumped out of the car, running to the hospital entrance. His fingers tingled and his face beamed in sync with the gentle pulses of his heart.

He waited for Rose and Clive at the entrance, smiling as they all walked to the ward. The dew of love fell into raindrops and he could barely contain the joy of picking Abbie up, closing his eyes and falling in love with her over again.

David's shoes clacked on the corridor floor and he held his bunch of red roses. His mind was in a place of peace, and the murmurings in his heart arose to a crescendo beat when he turned into the ward and saw Abbie sitting on the bed.

She jumped up and ran towards him.

The flowers slipped through David's fingers, his arms went around her waist and his lips melded with Abbie's. He was lost in time and shut out every other person in the ward, connecting with her mentally and physically. His soul came alight with a burning glow, and love baptised him in passion with the knowledge of the turmoil of the accident and release of elation that she was well.

"Abbie, my Abbie."

Clive and Rose walked towards her, allowing David to have his magical moment, before holding her in their arms.

"Thank God, that you're coming home," Rose said.

A member of the nursing team came into the ward, followed by Mr Pradeep.

"She's been the perfect patient, a little miracle, not moaning or complaining."

David took Abbie's brown suitcase from the side of the bed and there were so many questions in his mind that he wanted to ask her. He held her hand and followed Rose and Clive to the exit of the ward. An emotion of joy poured over his soul, as he thought, *it was you God who saved Abbie from dying and you've healed her and thank you for the doctors who helped her to recover.*

"Mr Pradeep, thank you for taking such good care of me, thank you so much."

The walk along the corridor granted David the time for reflection. His candle of affection still burned brightly, but a reaction of nervousness overshadowed the petals of love that were falling on his heart.

"I'm in court next week. I don't know how this is going to work out. The Judge might want to make an example out of me."

Apprehension disturbed his confidence of a positive outcome. He wondered, *will I get a fair hearing from the judge? What if the judge and jury are racist?*

"The barrister, Mr Andrews, that mum has chosen is excellent and I'm sure that he'll convince the Judge to show compassion."

David looked at Abbie and smiled. *I wish I had her confidence.* Anytime his mind changed to pessimism, he could count on her words of encouragement to lift him up. He put his arm around her waist and she responded by kissing him on the cheek. He remembered, *no matter what the situation is, she'll always be by my side.*

"David, you have a strong case. We know the racism that you had to suffer, and all of this will be exposed," Rose said.

Clive went to the car park to get the car and arrived at the entrance.

David got into the back with Abbie, kissing her cheek and canoodling. He squeezed her hand. Romance was on his mind, and he had a strong desire to lay next to her and never let her go out of his arms again.

"I love you," he whispered.

"I know, David, I know and I love you," she said quietly.

***

They arrived at Abbie's home and David followed Abbie to her bedroom, laying on the bed and watching her standing in front of the mirror.

"Abbie, what happened with the hit and run?"

She sat on the bed and David got up and sat next to her, putting his arm around her shoulder.

"I explained this to the police when they came to the hospital. I don't know. One minute I was driving and the next a van thudded into me and I was unconscious."

It must have been Paul, the police or members of the Skins for Life.

Paul was so smug when he walked into the police station and the comments he made about Abbie.

I wish I would have.

Grabbing the sides of his head stopped the inflamed anger and he took a breath to let his head cool down and leave the judgement in the hands of God and the law.

"I hope they get what's coming to them."

"I'd better leave and the next time I see you, it will be in court."

Chapter Twenty-six

David arrived at The Congregation of God church with Abbie, Rose, Clive, Charles and Mary.

Looking up at the blue sky on Sunday morning, he was in awe of the might of God with gratitude in his heart and he repeated the words of the Judge in his mind, *Mr Morgan, you are free to go.*

"Thank you God, that I was acquitted, thank you for your mercy, thank you."

He listened to the church bells that rang out loudly and cut through the atmosphere with a sound of harmonious chords that were a perfect blend of musicality. It reminded him of the Sundays when he attended the service with expectations of an outpouring of the Holy Spirit, and the blessings of God.

The erected blue board with its advertising of the church services caught his attention. People milled outside, the women boasting hats of flamboyant colours and the men in their best suits and carrying big black leather bibles. The howls and screams of children catching the seconds to squabble and play and then shout unfairness, brought a grin across his face.

How good it feels to come to the Congregation of God church again.

He watched the young and old walking towards the dark brown doors, being greeted by the ushers dressed in their black suits with red ties, before they took their seats in the pews. Standing at the doorway, he gazed inside, hearing the tuning of the keyboards, the beat of the drum and twanging guitars and remembered that the church wasn't supposed to see his face again, but peace filled his spirit that he was home where he belonged.

David watched the choir at the front and the choir master. His heart began to experience an eruption of joy as he reflected on the praise and worship in fellowship with his brothers and sisters in Christ.

They started to sing, "Amazing Grace," supported by the band that blended their music into a sweet melody. Members of the congregation lifted their hands, and he remembered, *when I came under the baptism of the Holy Spirit, it was electrifying.*

"Hallelujah!" shouted a woman at the front. It made David jump and his heart began to thud with anticipation and jubilation. Moments came back into his mind when the church service was so fiery that he felt like he was intoxicated, and all he could do was lay on the ground and receive the bathing of holy fire power.

His body began to move to the jangling of the tambourines and the powerful beat of the drums. The guitar strumming and the man on the saxophone lighted up his brain with a display of musical ingenuity.

The trumpeters responded with a powerful sound of brass and he pretended to play a trumpet with his fingers. They hit high and low notes and created a wonderful rhapsody of song, drawing and encouraging him to not be afraid, but to enter the house of The Lord and receive peace.

There's no one like Jesus, not the Beatles who claim to be more popular than him or any man or woman, living or dead, no one can make me feel the way he does.

"That's it, lift your hands up and give praise for what the lord has done," said Father Theo.

David received the invitation in his mind, but not his heart. He took one step into the church and then stepped back out. Panic came upon him that he as a backslider from the faith would be rejected, unless he bowed before God in front of the members and begged for forgiveness.

"Praise the lord for victory," said one of the deacons.

"Lift up the Lord, glory be to God, he's the omnipotent one," said a woman.

Yet, the church that he recalled appeared different. It welcomed him to lose the fear and embrace the warmth of acceptance, without the risk that he would be condemned.

David absorbed the spiritual essence that oozed and tingled over his body.

Back in the fold and no longer the sheep that had strayed, he opened his eyes, melting in the power of the God that he'd walked away from. The peace had a soothing effect on his heart and an assurance that no matter how blistering the furnace was that he would face, he wouldn't burn, but walk out of the fire unscathed.

Charles stepped into the church followed by Mary, Clive and Rose.

Father Theo smiled and invited them to come towards the altar. They walked down the narrow gap in the middle, greeted by smiles, handshakes and pats on the back. They sat on the front row and Charles stood up and waved, before sitting down again.

"Are you ready to go in?"

Abbie tied her hair back and closed her eyes. She put her arms around David and placed her head on his chest.

He listened to her heartbeats that beat with a similar rhythm to his, revelling in the delightful fusion of singing and shouting coming through the church doors and knowing, that it wasn't just luck that had preserved her life.

His skin gelled into the palm of her hand and he kissed her on the lips.

"I'm ready, let's go into the house of God."

***

He took her hand, pride flared up in his heart, colour insignificant and love the anchor, bonded his heart to hers. As he gazed at her face, he saw the courage that eclipsed any bravery that he'd demonstrated. He reflected on what she'd endured and his soul erupted with a tenacity that he would go to the end of the world to protect her, for he loved her more than he could have ever imagined.

"I love you," he whispered, walking to the front with Abbie and the tears welling up in his eyes.

He was back at home and in the place where he first met Jesus Christ. Looking at the members of the congregation, he smiled at the blend of multi-denominational creeds and colours that made his heart rejoice that he wasn't a special entity, or owned an exclusive of Caucasian and Black Jamaican.

David sat down and gazed at Father Theo, smiling and his heart free of bitterness and anger towards him.

He let the warm breeze that floated through the church windows blow on his face. The gossip in his mind was calmed by the gentle vibe of the music that took him into a solemn place of remembrance.

“Hello,” whispered Elaine.

David smiled and his mind juddered at the experience of a horrific memory that they shared. He looked across the pew where she sat and Angela moved forward. Gazing at her face, his heart received a shooting pain from the friendship that broke and a relationship where she could have been the one sitting in Abbie’s seat next to him.

He raised his hand to acknowledge a woman he could have been engaged to. She smiled and waved. The diamond engagement ring on her finger caught his eye and he gasped and then chuckled, elated that she too had found love.

Abbie put her arm through his and he clasped her hand. Love and emotion was one thing, but he'd gone on a journey with her, encountered violence, hatred and survived death. It took the meaning of his love to a different dimension, and he knew that all the gold in the world couldn't compare to the embattling of a mission that at times had left him broken in pieces.

Father Theo tapped on the microphone.

"We've prayed constantly for our brother Ray, murdered for being black, but let it be said that when it all seems hopeless, that is when God will intervene."

He stretched out his hands towards David and Abbie and signalled to them to come to the front. They stood up and stepped towards the pulpit, turning around to face the congregation.

"We the church have been guilty of racism. All of us, in some way have created segregation and I include myself in this, but today, there are two people standing before you. Look beyond black or white and see the power that love and purpose brings."

David put his hands in his pockets and then took them out, licking his bottom lip and shuffling his feet on the floor. He wondered through the confusion and the itching of his skin where to position his eyes.

God, I'm nervous.

Father Theo stepped down from the stage, walked around to face them, smiled at Abbie and grasped David's hand.

David maintained his eye contact with Father Theo and a mixture of emotions played ping pong in his mind. Seeds of goodness that had been sown into him resurfaced and testified to his soul. It lifted him up from his personal hell. His feet were on a pedestal of spiritual power and he experienced a resurge of the anointing that was declared over his life many years ago.

Falling into an embrace with Father Theo, the months of abandonment from the church, hit him with an awakening that he'd always been a child of God and God had never changed his opinion of who he was.

"I want everyone to raise their hands in praise and worship to God."

"Before you are the handiwork of The Lord, who he has used to bring down the strongholds of racism and police brutality against the black man."

"Thank you God, thank you," whispered Mary.

She took Charles's hand and they joined David and Abbie.

Rose and Clive followed, holding hands and bowing their heads.

Members of the congregation stood up and walked to the front, whispering prayers of protection and God's grace on Abbie and David.

David looked up from the ground. His heart was softened from the overpowering support and the acceptance from people that he didn't know, and those that he remembered.

Angela and Elaine stood in front of Abbie, and David watched as they hugged her. He blinked twice and the barriers that he'd erected fell down. Nothing was held back and he allowed a bridge to resurrect the friendship that he'd destroyed.

"You're our sister, may God richly bless you," Angela said.

They turned to David, his head began to shake and his eyelids fluttered, spilling his tears onto his shirt. His eyes stayed on the faces of Angela and Elaine and he recalled the special friendship that he never expected would be broken. He wished that he could retreat and take the steps again where through the pain of excruciating loss, he didn't walk away and treat them like they never existed.

"I'm so sorry, I'm so sorry."

The final step towards them that he took closed the gap of separation and he clutched their hands, staring through a heart of remedied terror and a mind that was no longer wrenched in an abyss of remorse.

The hardness and the rejection he extended to Elaine and Angela dissolved through his wounds being healed. Forgiveness cleansed and purified his mind from the stench of bitterness that had obliterated his faith and love of his sisters in Christ.

Angela and Elaine moved to the side to let Father Theo walk through. He put his arms around David and Abbie and the throng stepped back.

"Dear almighty God, I thank you for David and Abbie. Thank you that you have protected them and saved them for a time like this. They are your creation, your children, and there are no coincidences in Christ. You have appointed them to be the mouthpiece of justice, and as your word says, the evil man shall not prosper over the righteous!"

Father Theo stepped back and David raised his hands, barely able to say the words that were embedded in his heart. He lifted his head, looking beyond the lighting and experiencing the touch of the Holy Spirit that made his body quiver, and brought him back into a reflection of when he first received the free gift of salvation.

Tears rolled down his face as he saw that even though he'd changed, God was the same today, yesterday and forever. His heart began to thump faster and he opened his mouth, knowing that he couldn't fool God any longer when he knew the truth about the strums of his heart.

"God, I'm sorry that I turned my back on you. I hated you because you could have saved Ray. I'm still hurting, because I miss him so much. I don't fully understand any of this, but as I try to trust you, please help me."

Charles and Mary held him and Abbie put her arm around his waist. He looked to the side and saw Rose and Clive crying, his family, hurting like he was. Somehow, the travesty of his pain and a reacquaintance with Christianity was the medicine to deliver him and he prayed quietly, saying, "Thank you God, for your forgiveness and that you still and will always love me."

A wave of peace swept through the church and fell upon him, taking him beyond his natural mind to a place where he could visualise that all things were about to work for his good. He'd never met an angel, but he imagined that they'd come from heaven and were in every corner of the room, strumming harps and whispering the secret messages of God.

The congregation began to sing and David didn't want to leave. The power of change was upon him and he opened his heart to receive the blessing falling from heaven. He was willing to be spiritually transported to God's throne of grace to receive his mercy and his help.

Words that he'd spoken were a testimony of his wilderness experience and journey back into the Promised Land. He raised his hands, repenting again of his prejudiced heart and recommitted to God that he would never walk the same path again.

Father Theo went back up to the pulpit and gripped the lectern.

"I want everyone to join hands as we unify and pray for what is about to come."

David's thoughts weren't God's thoughts and neither were his ways, God's ways. He gave God full recognition that he was the superior being, creator of all and judge over every man.

God I promise that I'll never take matters into my own hands again, but will trust you to sort it out for you know best.

Faith in God and his word stirred up in his spirit and he believed more intensely that those who cursed his favourites would also be cursed. No longer did he wish to own the power to wield vengeance, and he conceded that it belonged to God and him alone.

Father Theo raised his hands.

"God, we're not in control of the outcome of the trial of Ray's killers, but you are. We all come before you, that whilst we forgive those that murdered one of our sons, we still want justice that this heinous crime will not go unpunished. You are the finisher of our faith and I pray that the wicked will not escape, but that you will intervene and rain your fire of vengeance upon them."

"Amen, amen," shouted Thelma.

"Yes Lord, bring the evil ones to their knees and let them know that you're God and you fight for your children," cried Mary.

"Let the day of victory come against those skinheads and the police force members of Skins for Life on the day of their trial. Let them see that the powers of darkness shall not win, but that the force of the living God shall demonstrate who's king," Charles said.

David's spirit responded to the loudening music that lifted him into a fever of praise and prayer.

If God is for us, then who can be against us, he thought.

David held Abbie and soaked up the formidable energy that made him feel like he was on fire. The vision in his mind entertained an ending to the suffering of the congregation, who'd waited patiently for a sign that Ray hadn't been forgotten.

"Justice for Ray, lord, bring justice, now!" screamed a man.

The timing of that promise coming true seemed like it was taking forever, but David recalled, *God makes everything beautiful in his time.*

"David, this is amazing. I've never had an experience like this before. We're not alone and neither is Ray. I know God will help Ray and he'll help us in the courtroom."

Father Theo raised his hand and the congregation quietened their voices.

"Next week Friday, the trial of Ray's killers will take place at the crown court, and I want as many of you as possible to be there to show solidarity for our son, David, and our sister, Abbie. Keep praying every day for justice and that God will finally answer our prayer."

David nodded, connecting to the allegiance with Father Theo and the collective power that was running through him like a burning fire.

Elaine and Angela approached David and Abbie.

"We'll be at the trial next week, may God give us the victory," Angela said.

Father Theo came down the steps and walked towards David.

"The entire congregation will be praying for both of you and for Ray. We'll be at the court in force. The gates of hell shall not stand against us."

Thelma and Lorna approached David, and Thelma hugged him and Abbie.

"We can't thank you enough for your bravery and courage. Thank you for fighting for Ray, thank you."

David kneeled at the front and touched the altar. *I must believe that there won't be injustice.* His mind kept swinging between faith and doubt, looking at God one moment, and gazing at the might of the police force and struggling to perceive how the walls of racism would fall.

He reflected on the instruction that God gave Joshua to walk around the walls of Jericho and on the seventh time around, the children of Israel were to shout and praise God. He smiled as he remembered, *the walls tumbled down and the enemy was destroyed.*

Thank you God. The Skins for Life and the police force will also fall, just like the walls of Jericho.

He got up and walked to the exit of the church, joining Charles, Mary, Clive, Rose and Abbie outside. Staring back through the doorway, he tried to soak up the last drop of spiritual power to maintain his confidence and ease away the streak of fear that tried to wash his mind with negativity.

"We must stay strong and keep our faith," Charles said.

His words hit the centre of David's mind. He knew that the judicial system could be cruel, and he didn't want to second guess God and state exactly what the outcome would be.

David walked away towards the car with Abbie, still in a place of serenity from the church service and with renewed force in his heart. Turning back, he looked at the cross that was perched on top of the church, seeing that Jesus was no longer hanging there, but risen from the dead and ready to fight for Ray.

Thank you Jesus that the battle is yours and not mine, thank you that our day of justice is coming.

"Next week, Abbie, next week. Ray's death will be avenged and the racist police and Skins for Life, will finally be crushed."

Chapter Twenty-seven

The following nights were mental torture for David and he woke up on Friday morning, the day of the trial at 4am with sweat dripping from his forehead. He couldn't recall sleeping and his mind was like an IBM 650 computer, pounding with thoughts of victory, but also with a fear of the outcome.

Experiences of the sting of hate were still in his heart for what Paul and Matthew represented, and he said, "I wish that the death penalty had never been abolished, so they would die."

"God, you need to turn up in a big way today, don't let them get away with murder."

Walking to the living room he switched on the light.

"You made me jump!" he said, falling onto the sofa and staring at Charles who sat on the floor.

Charles turned down the music, coming from the light brown Bermuda Dansette record player. David joined him on the floor thinking, *God, like the song, don't give up by the Gospelaires, will you now take control, because Abbie and I have persevered, even if it meant losing our lives?*

"You can't sleep, just like me."

Charles put his bible on the carpet and turned to Proverbs chapter six.

"This verse makes it clear that a calamity shall suddenly come on the wicked man, for God has seen his conspiring, mischief and evil acts."

The scripture of God's action made it seem so easy that the immoral man would be destroyed, and David kept shaking his head in tandem with his doubts that didn't see an automatic triumph, because God was involved.

"I really hope you're right Dad, I pray that you're right!"

David paced across the room, meditating on the worst outcome that his mind could hardly withstand, if the words, "Not guilty," rang out across the courtroom and the police and Skins for Life looked him in the eye and confirmed that he was nothing and without the authority to command change.

Mary walked into the room and leaned against the wall.

"Let's remember that God is in control and not man. We have to trust him. This isn't the time to doubt his word."

His heart wanted to receive her affirmation of truth and he reflected on the congregation. *We were all united in believing God for justice.* David clasped his hands, closed his eyes and tried to rekindle the exact feeling of power from The Congregation of God Church, but a niggling thought of, *what will we do if there's a verdict of not guilty,* stayed in his head.

"I'm going upstairs to pray, I need peace."

The twinkle from the stars, shining through his window had little effect on pacifying his anxiety. He picked up his bible, reading about King David whose stories of being overwhelmed by his enemies mirrored the image that he saw of himself. He looked at the picture of Martin Luther King and thought, *I wish you were in my room and sitting on the bed to tell me that the impossible dream can become my possible dream.*

As he got in bed and closed his eyes, he held onto his bible for comfort.

"God, you've saved me so many times, I'll try to trust you completely and not doubt who you are."

***

The light blinding his eyes and the gentle call from Mary woke him up from his slumber and dreams of salvation. He pulled the bed cover over his face and hid from the brightness. His dream of the earth opening and swallowing the skinheads seemed real. His desire for recompense had been granted, when he watched them having to endure torment day and night forever.

"David, you've to get dressed and it's nearly time for us to go."

Mary's instruction was clarity that his dream was only fantasy. He kicked the covers off his feet, reaffirming the image in his mind of imprisonment that drove the perpetrators to insanity and without the availability of parole. Focusing on God he whispered, "This day will be remembered and God, you won't let us down."

"David, we need to go now!" shouted Charles.

After a wash and getting fully dressed, David walked down the stairs, holding onto the banister and Charles opened the door. Mary shut it, holding her cross and taking the hands of Charles and David, whose stomach began to rumble. A yell of, *fool,* sounded an alarm in his mind for believing that a black man could overturn years of systemic racism.

"Lord, be merciful and let this day be one of glory. We put our trust in you and believe that you'll show up in a mighty way for Ray," Mary said.

She opened the door, shutting it behind her and they walked to the police car. David nodded at the policeman who was there to take them to the crown court and mused on Mary's petition.

God, will you show up for Ray in a mighty way today?

"I warn you, it's not gonna be pretty down there," the policeman said.

In the car, David held his tongue, silently confessing, *it will be ok, everything is going to be ok*, as an attempt to amass trust in God. He listened to the police radios buzzing with different instructions and juddered in the backseat, as the driver arrived at the main road and waited for a signal. David knocked his foot against the front seat, the slight tremors of his heart went into overdrive and his brain was hammered with a repeated message of, *you're finished, you'll be torn apart.*

***

He walked to the entrance of the court with Mary and Charles, surrounded by policemen. As he dragged his feet, his mind desired to turn around and walk the other way, once he saw the blue lights flashing and the blaring of the sirens clattered against his eardrums.

David looked along the road, unsure if the policemen lined up on both sides of the pavement, holding onto their truncheons were really there for his protection.

He looked at the crowd of skinheads and then the church congregation and tried to bask in the support, love and solidarity. The glares of hate bombarded his brain with a torrent of terror and killed his quiet murmurs of, "Help!"

"You fucking, black bastards. You fucking monkeys. Fucking niggers, fucking niggers!"

David kept his head down, walking faster to the steps of the courthouse as he swam in a den of attack and flight.

"Niggers, fucking niggers, black bastards, you'll all burn, you're all fucking dead, you niggers!"

The animosity was a return to Skegness and his body trembled under the assault of the racial abuse. He stayed close to the policemen, with terror ransacking his brain and crushing his courage. Staring at the skinheads, he was in a state of helplessness and wondered, *where's the fire of heaven to destroy them and burn them up?*

The skinheads kept chanting, blocked by the police line.

"Go back to your own fucking countries. Niggers don't belong in England."

David nervously watched Father Theo raising his hands.

"Be still, for the glory of the lord is shining all around. He burns with holy fire," Father Theo said.

The church members began to hum and joined hands. They shouted cries of victory and praise which washed over him, strengthening his heart that when he looked at the storm, Jesus was right in the middle.

His spiritual eyes opened to the enormity of the supernatural atmosphere that soothed his fear as he listened to his church brothers and sisters singing. It reminded him, than even if he was about to go to the deepest part of hell, God would be there and was more than able to deliver him.

His mind locked onto that belief and he defiantly raised his voice in a song of unity with the congregation to stand against the tide of hatred, being hurled by the skinheads.

"The glory of the lord is shining all around, the glory of the lord is shining all around," he said.

David raised his hands towards heaven, watching the church congregation. He sang at the top of his voice, despite the racial chants and Hitler salutes.

He reminisced on the battle, wolves on the right and sheep on the left, Satan and God fighting for supremacy, heaven competing with hell, and good competing with evil to be the dominate power. It was a showdown of love and hate, with only one to emerge as victorious and he knew wholeheartedly that Satan wasn't about to relinquish his power being demonstrated by the force of racism, without a fight.

"Praise be to God, praise be to God," said Charles, pushing David through the crown court doors.

"Don't you dare give evidence, nigger, you're fucking dead if you do. Get out of that court, nigger, you can't win!"

David fell back against the door, his veins popped and his brain wanted to explode. Defeat appeared to be sucking him into a chasm and confidence and trust in God, struggled to be his security of faith.

He was wavering at the tirade of abuse. The words *nigger and black bastard,* kept ringing in his mind. The miracle of destruction he wanted hadn't happened. He could hear the skinheads outside calling for his head and he leaned against the wall, watching his shiny black shoes that trembled on the ground.

"Don't be afraid, God is with you, don't be afraid," Charles said.

Abbie, Rose and Clive came down the hallway to meet them with the prosecutor. David ran towards Abbie and held her. Not even her touch or gentle whisper in his ear could remove the turmoil from his troubled mind.

"Remember the church service, remember the prayers. Listen to the singing outside, God won't fail you," she whispered.

He nodded, wanting to believe, but mistrust swam ferociously and fired affirmations of scepticism, showing him the police force with its decorated policemen and their power. The Skins for Life, fighting for Mathew and Paul convinced him that it was doomsday. His mind couldn't perceive how the powerful enemy out in might would be overpowered.

"You all need to come into the court room," said the prosecutor, who'd collated all the evidence with his team.

The chanting of nigger and black bastard intensified outside. David twitched his neck. The worry accelerated of being in the fire and getting incinerated. He covered his ears to drown out the sound of their intimidation. They shouted even louder, hurling abuse and the police in David's mind, seemed helpless or were quietly contented that they were all aligned to ensure their white brothers triumphed, on the day of reckoning.

"David, c'mon, we need to go in," Abbie said.

***

Walking into the courtroom was like being asked to put a pillow over his head and suffocating himself. The heat of dissent that came from Paul and Matthew's supporters, blew in his direction and David stuttered, perspiring underneath his blue suit. He was in a cage of lions and his imagination conveyed the vicious snarls, before they pounced on him and tore at his flesh, until he was sinew and blood on bones.

"Not guilty," shouted a man who glared at him.

"Be quiet, or you'll be removed from the court room," said the Judge.

David and Abbie sat down behind the row of the prosecutor, Mr Collins.

David clutched Abbie's hand, uniting his mind and heart with hers, just as he had done from the beginning. With a slight shiver, he took a deep breath and prepared himself to contest to the bitter end. A young man from the defendant's families pointed at him and ran his finger across his throat. David's mouth opened and he froze momentarily on the bench.

He held Abbie's hand tighter, muttering, "God, help!"

David pushed his back into the wood and the chanting that welcomed him, bellowed more vibrantly in his head.

He glimpsed at the man, whose premeditated act of violence caused the well of fear to overflow in his mind. Crossing his arms over his chest, faint hope dangled on a fraying thread as he waited for the battle to begin, without certainty of the way, it was going to end.

Chapter Twenty-eight

The ticking of the clock made David's eyebrows rise. Alarm of the war for justice rang in his head. He watched Mr Collins straightening his white wig and brushing his black gown pondering, *does he have the skill to convince the jury of a hate and racially motivated murder?*

God, this isn't the time for you to be asleep, they need to be convicted of murder.

"Are you ready for trial?" said the court clerk to the barristers.

Mr Collins stared at the barrister, Mr Peters who was tasked with the defence of Paul Broker and Matthew Johnson and nodded his head.

The clerk called out the names of jurors, randomly selecting them, and they took their seats after being sworn in and without any objections being raised to their suitability.

David squeezed Abbie's hand tighter as his head throbbed with giddiness and his mind failed to see how those on trial for the murder of a black man, would be convicted.

David surveyed the courtroom, looking at the trainee policemen and the mass of people sitting together to support the defendants. He mulled over Abbie's testimony and when he was called to the witness stand to give his evidence.

"We have to leave no doubt in the jury's minds that Paul Broker and Matthew Johnson are guilty," he whispered.

David looked across at Fucking hard bastard and smiled that somehow God had strategically placed him in the Croydon Police Station, and a man who he thought was his enemy, was actually his friend. His eyes wandered to the Chief Superintendents called as witnesses, and their appearance of power made him shrink into his seat and become nauseous as he realised he was in a room of pure might.

Paul Broker and Mathew Johnson, who were joined by their compatriots came into his line of vision. He studied Paul Broker and the police uniform that he wore, replaying in his mind how the jury would see him and Matthew Johnson. He was unsure if Mr Collins could expose their true colours and sow seeds in the minds of the jurors, that they were racist pigs who were murderers.

They've got to be found guilty of murder, they can't walk away free.

The weight of a congregation seeking justice, bore down on David's shoulders. He looked across at Abbie, remembering the prayers and movement of the Holy Spirit in the church. In the courtroom, he couldn't see God, just a man representing Ray and the church and he closed his eyes, hoping that he would hear the words, guilty of murder in the first degree.

***

The Judge signalled to Mr Collins to begin his account of events and state the evidence.

David leaned forward as Mr Collins stood up. His mind whizzed with reservations and then confidence that overrode his misgivings and convinced him that God was in the courtroom, by special invitation. He remembered, *everything natural is really spiritual, and this is a battle between Satan and God.*

"Today, the evidence I'll present will prove beyond a reasonable doubt that, Paul Broker and Mathew Johnson, brutally murdered Ray Williams, because he was black," Mr Collins said.

He began by going into the history of Ray and described a young man with great promise and who was loved by his community and the church. He brought to the attention of the jury, four people out on a stroll in Skegness until their lives were changed forever, when they confronted the skinheads.

He turned to face the jury.

"Can you imagine what it must have been like to hear the words, nigger, black bastards and monkey and be in fear for your life?"

The shudders went through David's legs as the moment of bathing in the racial abuse came alive in his mind. His face was a picture of grimaces and his body became rigid and tense as he watched Mr Collins turn and run his finger continuously across his throat.

"Can you imagine the terror in Ray Williams, when he looked into the eyes of Matthew Johnson and Paul Broker, and they cut his throat and murdered him in cold blood?"

David gazed at the faces of the jury for a flinch of emotion to confirm that they were in the same place as he was.

"Objection."

"The jury will disregard the last comment," said the Judge.

David watched Mr Collins walk back to the table, pick up the glass of water and take a drink. Uncertainty was in his head if Mr Collins last statement was ruminating in the minds of the jurors, and if he had the psychological advantage.

God, let them be convinced. Let them see the picture of Ray, being kicked, stabbed and slashed and then murdered.

Mr Collins called other witnesses to the stand and David listened to their testimonies. Each account stamped on his heart and he turned to stare at Paul and Matthew, knowing they were culpable, but he couldn't force the jury to come back with a verdict of guilty.

"I would like to call, Abigail Butler, to the stand."

David held her hand and watched her rise from her chair and walk to the stand. The heel of his left shoe tremored against the floor and he whispered, "God, make Abbie strong, give her the right words to speak."

Mr Collins reviewed his notes and raised his head.

"Please explain what happened on the night when you went to the Skins for Life meeting on the 11th October?"

Abbie stared at Paul, turned to face the jury and then looked back at Mr Collins.

"I heard the chants of nigger, Hitler and death to the black race. I then saw Paul Broker at the meeting throwing a Nazi salute and standing at the front of the group."

"For the record, please point to the man you are referring to."

Abbie turned to face Paul and pointed.

"That's him, right there."

"She's a fucking liar, she's a liar!" screamed a young woman, sitting behind Matthew Johnson.

She's not a liar, she's telling the truth, thought David.

David nodded as the woman was swiftly removed from the courtroom, still hearing her continued outbursts of Paul's innocence. He looked across at Paul and Matthew.

You're killers. I wish they'd bring hanging back. You both deserve to be hung like Peter Allen and Gwynne Evans.

David studied the juror's faces as Mr Collins picked up the standard camera that had been submitted as evidence and showed photographs of Paul at the meeting. He began to sense the trial turning in Ray's favour as he listened to the audience's wittering, and he hoped that the jurors were being drawn in by the case.

"What did you hear, Paul Broker say?" Mr Collins said.

Abbie dropped her head and then looked up.

"Paul said, I say death to him, meaning David, the same way his friend died on the memorable day in Skegness."

"He also said, I still remember that nigger pleading for his life when I slashed his throat, we'll never show mercy to niggers, they must all die."

The sighs from the crowd ricocheted around the courtroom and David crossed his arms and legs to stop them from shaking. He sensed that the screw had just been turned even tighter. Peering at Abbie, he willed her to remain quiet and let the tension knock on every wall, convinced that her testimony had landed a killer blow to the defence.

"No more questions."

Mr Peters jumped to his feet.

"You say that Paul Broker was at the meeting, but the photograph you took isn't a clear picture of my client."

"It is, he was there and that photograph is him."

"We only have your word with no other witnesses that my client confessed to the murder, and it's possible that you misheard and have conjured up this entire story, because you want someone to pay for the crime, even though my client is innocent?"

"Objection, objection," shouted Mr Collins.

"Overruled," said the Judge.

"We know that you had an accident and ended up in intensive care. We all sympathise with this situation. However, the nature of your accident calls into question, clarity of thought and it's possible that your memory has been affected and what we have heard from your testimony doesn't reflect the truth."

"I submit to the jury that the evidence presented is flawed and isn't conclusive that my clients are guilty of murder."

Mr Peters smiled and David dropped his head. The sudden euphoria he experienced minutes ago, was overshadowed by doubt in Abbie's credibility. He saw a picture in his mind, painted by the defending barrister of a woman prepared to bend the law for her own end and mulled over how the pendulum could swing back in Ray's direction.

Abbie came back to her seat and David gripped her hand. The expression on her face triggered nervous emotions in his mind. It brought him back to a reality that the police were too powerful and he was about to be squashed.

"Next, I would like to call, David Morgan, to the stand."

David lifted his head, looked at the jury and then stared at the Judge. He walked slowly to the witness stand and placed his hand on the bible and sat down.

God help, I'm scared.

"What happened on the night of the meeting of the Skins for Life and the police that you accessed on the 11th October?"

David stared at Mr Collins and breathed in and out twice. He placed his hands on the table and planted his feet firmly on the floor. His head turned and he gazed at Paul Broker and Matthew Johnson, intimidated by their stares. He licked the roof of his mouth to create enough spit to lubricate his throat.

"Mr Morgan, please explain what happened at the Skins for Life and police meeting, 11th October?"

David squared his shoulders and a small cough left his mouth.

"Paul Broker said, there's a nigger who wears my uniform. I say death to him, the same way his friend died on the memorable day in Skegness."

"Paul Broker also said, I still remember that nigger pleading for his life when I slashed his throat, we'll never show mercy to niggers, they must all die."

David rubbed his lips, soaking up the tenseness of the atmosphere and hoping that the jury were cogitating on his words. He stared at them and then looked at Mr Collins, getting his mind ready for the next question.

"Take me back to the fight in the courtyard at the police station?"

David looked across at Paul and he gazed back.

"We got into a fight and I had him on the ground."

David's body shook as he thought, *I wanted to stab Paul and slash his throat and tell Ray that I am my brother's keeper and I kept my promise.*

He looked up at Mr Collins, opening his mouth before silencing the words that wanted to leave his lips.

"And then what happened?"

His head turned in the direction of Paul and Matthew before looking back at Mr Collins.

"He confessed that he killed Ray, and Matthew Johnson sitting next to him made him do it. They murdered him. He didn't deserve to die and he should be alive!"

The courtroom erupted into gasps and David sat still, trying to stop the nerves from controlling his mind. His lips were glued together to let the courtroom emotion wash over the jury. He willed them with his stares for justice to look beyond colour and see the crime for what it was.

Mr Collins submitted more evidence, including the fifty pence coin that had been examined using the Fingerprint System, and confirmed Matthew Johnson had held the coin. David watched as he presented further photographs and he hoped that his testimony was enough to let Ray rest in peace, and for the trauma in his head and heart to stop.

Mr Collins said, “No more questions,” and sat down.

Mr Peters perused through his notes and glanced at Paul and Mathew. He looked at David, then at Mr Collins and stood up.

“At the time you heard Paul Broker state that Matthew Johnson made him do it, were you not holding a knife to his throat?”

“Yes, I was.”

“Were you yourself, not being driven by murder, because of what you believed about Paul Broker?”

“Did you not also believe that Paul Broker was involved in the hit and run accident that injured your girlfriend, and therefore you were motivated by revenge and murder?”

“Objection, objection,” Mr Collins said.

“The jury will ignore the question. The witness is not on trial for murder,” said the Judge.

David twitched his fingers, looking at Mr Collins for advice and forgetting what they'd rehearsed, before he took the witness stand. He sat helpless and on tenterhooks, wanting to go to his chair, rather than face the cross examination.

"Didn't you initiate the fight with Paul Broker and threaten his life and because of that he confessed under duress to a crime that he didn't commit. You forced the confession, because of your anger and your intent to kill him. He was afraid and screamed out a name, because he thought that he was going to die. Were you not on trial for attempted murder of my client?"

"Objection, objection!" Mr Collins said.

The Judge indicated to David to answer the accusation. He dropped his head and placed his hands on the arms of the chair.

I wanted to kill him and even now he's sitting there with a smug face, like he already knows that he won't be found guilty.

"It's true that I was angry at Paul Broker, because he confessed that he was there at the time Ray died. I wanted revenge and yes, I wanted him to die because he murdered my friend Ray with Matthew Johnson and the other skinheads."

"Objection, the witness is leading the jury, objection, objection."

"The jury will strike the last comment from the records. Please continue, Mr Morgan," said the Judge.

God, are you here with me? Help me, tell me what to say.

"I couldn't kill Paul, despite my opinion of him. I had the opportunity to hurt him, but I didn't. I'm just a young man who lost a friend who was murdered because he was black. Wouldn't any of you feel angry, upset and want revenge for someone that you loved who was murdered?"

His lips twittered as he surveyed the courtroom. His eyes caught Abbie's and her mutter of, "I love you," whispered to his heart that he wasn't on the witness stand alone, but she and an entire congregation were with him, giving evidence to stifle the harsh interrogation.

David studied the jury and they gave him the impression that they were mulling over his question and imagining what they would do, if someone they loved was viciously killed.

Matthew Johnson coughed and Mr Peters stared at the jury, who were all transfixed on David. He went back to his notes, looked around the courtroom and then gazed at the Judge.

"You attempted to murder my client, because of your own misgivings and inaccurate information. We all empathise with the death of Ray Williams, but you took the law into your hands and by threatening to kill, forced a confession, that wasn't true! Is that not the case?"

David breathed heavily, sensing the different direction of the breeze, seeming to be blowing in favour of the defendants. He stated the response over and over in his mind. The pressure from the words of the defending barrister that twisted his statement, made him reel and question the accuracy and validity of his evidence.

David stood up and turned to face Matthew Johnson and Paul Broker. He glanced at Mr Collins, interpreting the wave of his hand as a message to remain seated. The fear of not being able to express himself and convince those with the power to decide if Paul Broker and Matthew Johnson were guilty or not, disappeared. His mind went to a deeper place, a place where hate was overcome by love.

"Ray was my friend and I loved him. I was angry and enraged, because he was killed by racists. It's not about black or white, we are all people and if you cut us open, we're the same underneath."

No more trembles were in his legs or black clouds circling his brain. He stood as a man, making a plea not just for justice, but for change, a change that he'd dreamed about as a boy and that had driven a desire to make the world free.

Mr Collins nodded and David pressed his lips together. The storm of personal torment subsided in his heart and as he gazed at Paul Broker and Matthew Johnson, he thought, *what next, God? What do you want me to say?*

"I wanted to hurt those who killed Ray, I wanted revenge, but I was wrong."

"Paul and Mathew, I want you both to know that I forgive you for murdering Ray."

"Objection, the witness is trying to lead the jury, objection!"

The Judge signalled to the jury to confirm his agreement with the defending barrister.

David sat back down and that's when his feet began to tap dance on the floor. He looked at Mr Collins who smiled, but his smile didn't assure David that just because he spoke from his heart, the jury would now convict.

Mr Peters consulted his notes and then stared at David.

"No further questions."

David returned to his chair and grabbed Abbie's hand. Sweat ran into his eyes and the extent of what the trial represented, became more real.

"I don't know, Abbie, I don't know if we'll see justice today," he whispered.

His body twitched as the Judge tapped the table and said to the barristers, "You will now both make your closing remarks."

Mr Collins stood up and faced the jury.

Help him God, help him, this isn't just for Ray, it's for all of us.

"There's no question that the evidence presented today is overwhelming. Mathew Johnson, Paul Broker and their accomplices murdered Ray. The Fingerprint System matches Matthew Johnson's fingerprints on the fifty pence coin thrown at David Morgan, confirming he was there on the day Ray was killed. We can pinpoint, Paul Broker, at the scene. He confessed that he was there at the Skins for Life meeting, 11th of October, and he confessed that he and Matthew Johnson slashed Ray's throat and took his life and other witnesses have confirmed this confession."

"There can only be one verdict, guilty of murder in the first degree."

He took his seat and gazed at Mr Peters who eased out of his chair.

"The question is, is there reasonable doubt? Yes, there is. The key witnesses of the prosecutor lack credibility and out of desperation, they have tried to find a culprit who they can blame the murder on."

"We are all very sorrowful for the death of a young innocent man, but the evidence presented against my client was forced, given under duress and in fear, because he believed that he was going to die. Wouldn't you confess if you believed it would save your life?"

"You can only reach one verdict, not guilty of murder."

David watched him walking to his seat and his powerful voice that stated, not guilty of murder, lit up his nightmare that when the jury came back, the sorrow wouldn't be over and the pain of Ray's death would linger.

The Judge made his final notes, gazed at Mr Collins and Mr Peters and turned to face the jury.

"It's for you the jury, to go away and consider all of the evidence and reach a unanimous decision."

The foreperson got up and was swiftly followed by the eleven jurors.

David's eyes followed their movement and when the door shut, his throat swelled and his lips became dry. His mind pondered on their neutrality or if they were bigots. He sat still, looking at the witness stand, replaying his testimony and seeing the holes, but helpless to do anymore, except wait, and hope.

Chapter Twenty-nine

David's fear dived overboard, stirring up a belief that the racists weren't only outside, but also in the jury and ready to set the guilty free.

"Where are they?"

He held onto Abbie's hand and her smile was a constant irritant to his flaking confidence that this was the day that The Lord had made.

David rubbed his fingers together and wrestled with his soul to determine if the previous sins that he'd committed were now coming back to haunt him, with a blistering judgment.

Looking behind at Charles and Mary he thought, *why can't I hear their prayers telling me I've got nothing to worry about.*

Mary raised her head and looked down at David. He smiled. *Why isn't she smiling back*? It deepened his doubt of a result of exhilaration and he placed his head in his hands. He wanted to trust and believe that his heart would be dancing inside his chest, but he was combating the thought, *Paul Broker and Matthew Johnson might not be found guilty of murdering Ray.*

On studying Paul and Matthew's supporters, he sensed their air of arrogance. Reflections on Mr Peters, increased his conviction that he'd persuaded the jury with his articulating of the evidence and his manipulation of his character that made him look like he couldn't be trusted, because of his murderous intentions.

David gazed at Matthew and Paul, trying to read their muttering and conniving. He muddled through his thoughts that were like rolling a dice and he hoped that it landed on his preferred number, six. Certainty of absolute vindication of the crime deepened his worry that God had another plan and it didn't include a conviction.

***

The opening of the main doors and the jury walking into the room sent his nerves into a freefall spin. His eyes glued on them taking their seats and his heart hopped that he couldn't even breathe. He squeezed his thighs as if trying to pierce through the flesh and flicked his bottom lip against his teeth. His mind throbbed with a hammer of doom that the noise outside was about to rise, as racism claimed the day.

Oh no. What's the verdict? Are they guilty of murder?

David looked at Thelma and Lorna and then stared intently at the Judge and the foreperson. He gripped the sides of his chair, hurtling down an imaginary hill with jubilation and great sorrow exchanging places in his mind. The biting fear struck his heart and the condemning whisper in his ear of, *God hasn't heard you and the congregation,* vibrated even louder that his brain bathed in a wave of terror.

David, Paul and Matthew met in a battle of eye contact. They smiled and their nodding and swagger of the shoulders hit his brain with an ice- cold tremor and a shrill of, *who do you think you are? You're a nigger and niggers can't take on white power and win.*

Abbie leaned over and whispered in David's ear, "They must be guilty, they must be!"

He gripped her hand, holding onto a fraying strand that goodness would triumph. It weakened when the foreperson stood up to face the Judge and David closed his eyes. His neck stiffened and his heart boomed with a disposition of nervousness, that his mind turned into a raging inferno of burning stress flames.

"Have you reached a unanimous decision?"

The foreperson nodded.

“How do you find the defendants, guilty or not guilty?”

David muttered, “Guilty, they’re guilty,” with a cloud of scepticism misaligning to his words.

The foreperson looked back at the jury and then turned to face the Judge.

“We find the defendants, guilty of murder in the first degree.”

“No!” screamed Mathew’s mother.

“It’s not true, my son didn’t commit murder, he’s not a killer!” shouted Paul’s mother.

The din inside David’s head banged with a clatter of the beat of the drum and cymbals. His legs shot out and kicked the chair in front of him and he heard the wailing and the crying in the courtroom. A spinning wheel is what his mind and heart resembled, and he was unable to decide if he should be rejoicing or crying.

“David, David, they’ve been convicted of murder!” Abbie said.

He couldn't move, only shake in his chair. Tears streamed down his cheeks. His mouth opened slightly without utterance of the words, *guilty of murder, in the first degree* rebounding around his head. He tapped his head to be sure he'd heard correctly, or if it was a scam to make him believe the very thing that his heart desired.

As he studied Paul and Matthew, his heart only knew forgiveness, but a slate of malice and hate still existed. He let go of Abbie's hand and his mind became consumed with the authority of the most High God. His body trembled in awe that he'd showed up in the courtroom and demonstrated who he was.

Racial hatred has been destroyed, you did it God, thank you for remembering Ray.

Now the murderers will be locked up for life.

The Judge shuffled his papers and David knew that the verdict wasn't a misconception, but real.

"Will the defendants, please rise."

Matthew and Paul rose to their feet.

Justice, justice, thought David.

"You have been found guilty of murder in the first degree and I hereby sentence you both to life imprisonment, without parole."

He sentenced the other skinheads who were there at the scene and involved in the murder and said, “I also authorise a full investigation into the policemen belonging to the Skins for Life and an immediate review of the discrimination policies of the police forces across the country.” David clinched his hands together and said, “Justice, this is justice for Ray.”

Falling to his knees, his mind and heart throbbed with elation and he could only breathe softly. He didn’t care that he was in the courtroom or who watched him. All the rejection and hatred that he had towards God was gone.

Clasping his hands in recognition, he remembered the note that he’d torn up in anger when he believed that God had forsaken him.

I will never forsake you. I will not, I will not, I will not.

He stood up, took Abbie’s arm and joined the congregation at the exit of the courtroom, embracing them. Smiles of rapture reflected through his glazed eyes at the power of unity that met him with tenacity, and conveyed that love would always overcome the bitter vein of evil.

Months of pain, negligence from the police and the attempted murder of Abbie all poured out of him. David lifted his hands without a care for the unbelieving man, worshipping the Lord and giving thanks from a heart of humility as the victory sank deeply into his mind.

"Let's walk out of here with our heads held high, for today, God has won the battle and all of the glory goes to him," Father Theo said.

David, Abbie, Charles, Mary, Rose and Clive joined hands and walked towards the exit.

David's heart murmured at the praise and the worship from outside that became louder as he walked along the corridor of the courthouse.

The doors opened and the mighty roar of screams and shouting of adulation, made his face beam with pride that it was possible for a nation to come together and stand in solidarity against racism.

Whistles and clapping, hugs of celebration and a wave of vindication strengthened his faith. He took Abbie in his arms and kissed her with passion. Love, as his offered gift was stronger as the power of two and he couldn't imagine walking down the road of life without her by his side and in his arms.

David looked towards heaven, staring at the dark sky that had turned clear blue. Strongholds of Satan in his mind were totally destroyed. He was assured that whatever tribulation came against him as he sought to activate change, he could take comfort that God would make a way out of the wilderness and bring him and Abbie into a glorious light.

Standing on the steps, he watched the policemen and the skinheads with razor sharp eyes. Their silence strummed his heart with a chord of grace. Refreshing water ran through his soul, rather than the sting of hatred coming from their lips.

No more salutes of Hitler, no cries of nigger and black bastard hit his brain with a damaging definition of his ancestral heritage.

David bowed his head and as he lifted it and watched the police and the Skins for Life, the confirmation of an electric force blew through his mind that they were finished.

He clenched his fist and held it up in the air, staring down at bigotry that had been torn apart and humbled because of his stand with Abbie. The grief and the pain that he'd endured left its lingering fragments, but his spirit lifted up for he recognised that sorrow was for a night, but joy had come, despite the turmoil that rained the unleash of hell upon his body, mind and sanity.

His fingers curled around Abbie's hand. His heart panged for moments that guaranteed her face was the last one that he saw at night and the first that he woke up to when he stirred from his slumber, and heard the morning dew falling on the windowpanes.

"Abbie, I love you. I want to spend the rest of my life with you, will you marry me?" he whispered.

Before he could hear her response that he hoped wouldn't be a crushing no, Father Theo took his arm and led him down the steps.

David held Abbie's hand, seeing a glint in her eye that stoked up a breath of confidence that maybe she might say yes and make his happiness soar.

"These two people are heroes. God bless you both forever," Father Theo said.

David walked to the front of the court steps and lifted his hands with modesty.

Charles, Mary, Rose and Clive touched him and David gazed into Mary's eyes, absorbing the reassurance of a mother that he loved and no longer considering himself as the prodigal son.

David turned to face the Skins for Life. No fear and no terror vibrated through his body. He didn't have the motivation to gloat, but rather hope that the bridling of their mouths and the racist mantras of corruptive speech would change into words of love and recognition, that they were one with him and he was one with them.

He reminisced on the labelling that they'd given him. Musing on the racist slurs of, *nigger, black bastard, monkey, rubber lips* and every condemning name they could think of, his heart and mind brought him into a strong revelation that he wore none of those names, but carried the brand of Child of God and an ambassador of faith.

"This is truly the work of God, this is him, David!" Abbie said.

He took her hand, standing with one voice and as the catalyst of change.

His love broke down the boundaries of hate and demonstrated that colour was nothing. His kiss on her lips received rapturous applause and her whisper of, "Yes," exploded fusion, paradise and a rippling tingle all over his body that he wanted to dance and scream out with a passion to the world that Abbie had agreed to become, Mrs Abbie Morgan.

David watched the racists dispersing and ruminated on his mission to make all races see that hate is a recipe for war. He pondered on Matthew and Paul and their imprisonment for life, saying a quiet prayer, *God, when they hear the lock of the cell door, open their eyes and let them see that black people are no less than white and that we are all just the same.*

David let go of Abbie and raised his hands towards the heavens. Rays of light fell upon him and showed him the visual of a dream and vision that all men are equal in the sight of God. *I'm going back to law school to fight for the under-privileged.* This day had changed him forever, and caused him to be reborn into a man of greater principle and to do greater exploits.

Lost in a moment of time where he remembered Ray, his precious brother and friend, he put his hand over his heart. He knew that even if he would never see Ray again, he would always be with him, kicking his backside when he went astray and reminding him of his cause.

He walked down the road with Abbie in the path of the police and the remaining Skins for Life, in full acceptance that he would never be the same again. His heart was on fire and in his mind he said, *change won't be easy, but I'll never stop trying.*

David pushed open the door to his purpose to fulfil the dream that had been set in his heart from a young age.

Looking at Abbie he said softly, “We have to make the world a better place, not just for black people but for everyone.”

His eyes fell on her and a deep love consumed his heart and convicted his soul. As his arm went around her waist, he heard the clock ticking that even though he’d won a major battle, the war was still erupting through his veins and he was only on the edge of racial change.

He glanced upwards and allowed the gentle raindrops to fall on his face. A reminder of God, who’d given him assurance that he would never neglect him, came back into his mind.

“Thank you, thank you. You gave us the strength to believe and you gave us the victory, thank you.”

So with his mind set on the path ahead, the bible as his sword and Abbie by his side, he walked with confidence and might. Danger lay ahead in his quest for an egalitarian society, but he decided, "I'll never stop until injustice has been totally destroyed." The desire for change became stronger, and he was determined that his legacy would be remembered as one who fought for the deprived and created a world where love was the driving force, and not hate.

I'll make the world a better place and won't stop until all men and women who are oppressed by prejudice are free.

That is my mission, so help me God.

Dear reader,

I hope that, "A Black Saturday Afternoon" inspired you to see that we are better and stronger together and all walls of division will fall through unity and love.

As a writer I'm committed to writing stories to take you out of your world and into mine of suspense, mystery, the paranormal and fantasy where you'll meet characters you know and some you don't.

- You can follow me on Instagram: www.instagram.com/rd__valentine/
- YouTube: R.D.Valentine@r.d.valentine

I can also be found on Facebook and TikTok where I share information on my future novels and aspects of my life so you get to know who R.D. Valentine is.

On my website, www.rd-valentine.com, you can sign up to receive a short story each month in your inbox, so please sign up now to enjoy this free offer as my way of giving back to you and the publishing industry. You'll also be able to watch videos that are extracts of my books and be advised on when my new novels will be released.

My future releases include:

- A Black Saturday Afternoon
- Ambassador of God

- Faded Flower
- Bright Light in Shades of Dark
- Red Heat
- Daffodils Aren't always Yellow
- Kiss of Jezebel
- Silencing the Raging Thunder
- Cauldron of Fire
- The Church of the Cross

So go to, www.rd-valentine.com and sign up to receive information on when my new novels will be available and also to enjoy a riveting short story each month in your inbox.

Thank you so much for taking the time to read my stories. You are my inspiration to keep writing and I look forward to meeting you soon.

All my love,

R.D. Valentine.

Printed in Great Britain
by Amazon

a6d6f86e-9d2b-4aac-bf6d-c217be14ccd7R01